THE ECHO OF BROKEN DREAMS

AFTER THE RIFT, BOOK 2

C.J. ARCHER

C.J. ARCHER

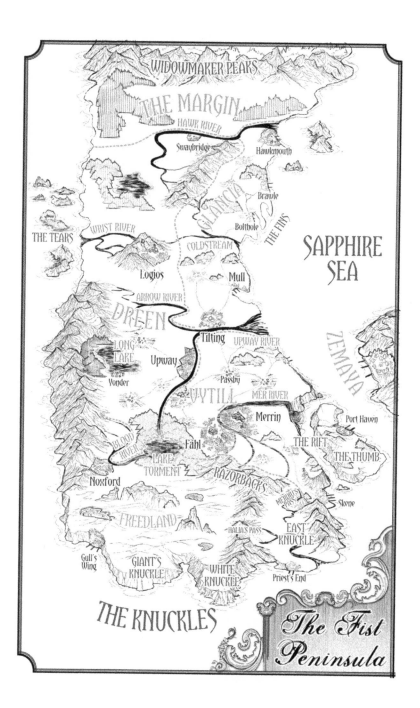

WIDOWMAKER PEAKS

THE MARGIN

HAWK RIVER

Swaybridge

Hawkmouth

GLANCIA

Brawle

Bolthole

THE FINS

WRIST RIVER

THE TEARS

COLDSTREAM

SAPPHIRE
SEA

Logios

Mull

ARROW RIVER

DREEN

Tilting

UPWAY RIVER

ZEMAYA

LONG
LAKE

Upway

Passby

Yonder

UVTILL

MER RIVER

Merrin

Port Haven

BLOOD
RIVER

Fähl

THE RIFT

THE THUMB

LAKE
TORMENT

RAZORBACKS

Noxford

METUNIS PASS

Skene

FREELAND

HALIA'S PASS

EAST
KNUCKLE

Gull's
Wing

GIANT'S
KNUCKLE

WHITE
KNUCKLE

Priest's End

THE KNUCKLES

The Fist
Peninsula

AUTHOR'S NOTE ABOUT THE MAP

To zoom in, download or print the map, go to C.J's website: www.cjarcher.com

CHAPTER 1

*T*he arrival of foreign noblemen at the palace barely caused a raised eyebrow in Mull. Few weary travelers bothered to look up from the dirt beneath their worn boots to witness the procession of polished carriages passing by, and the villagers were indifferent to the presence of esteemed personages. After all, the palace—and therefore Mull—was still overrun by Glancian nobles. The visitors and their entourages were as common as any other newcomer.

Most didn't know that King Leon hadn't invited the foreign lords. He'd invited the Vytill and Dreen princesses to court, with a view to choosing one as his bride, but their fathers, the kings of Vytill and Dreen, sent representatives to negotiate instead. Dane, the captain of the palace guards, had informed me of that much, but I hadn't seen him lately and didn't know what King Leon thought of the changed plans.

It was the only time Dane had visited me since the day he'd planted a riverwart seedling behind my father's headstone. He'd bought some hollyroot for Theodore, the king's valet, to ease a headache. I felt his absence more than I cared to admit and was disappointed that he didn't seem to miss me as much. That was until Meg pointed out that he could have sent a footman or guard to fetch the hollyroot, but he had come in person. She assured me

1

it meant he wanted to see me, and the hollyroot was simply an excuse. I liked her theory.

"Do you have any patients to call on this afternoon?" Meg asked as we walked from the graveyard together. She often accompanied me when she wasn't busy helping her mother at home. If it wasn't too hot, we walked up Lookout Hill and gazed down upon the palace in the distance, but I usually discouraged her. Seeing the palace reminded me of the times I'd been there, the people I'd met, and the amazing things I'd seen, and that was a little painful. The palace, and everything associated with it, was interesting, yet the days in Mull passed by with an unvarying monotony.

"Not today," I said. There were only two women due to give birth in Mull, and I'd checked on both recently. Despite the influx of people into the village, my workload had not increased. Most newcomers were unwed men or married ones coming ahead of their families to find work. The imbalance of the sexes caused its own set of problems, most of which I didn't see first hand as I rarely visited Tovey Harbor's dock or the taverns, but I did hear about the brawls.

"Then come and share our midday meal," Meg said. "Mama says she'd like to see you."

"She sees me often."

"You rarely stay to dine."

That was because Meg's brother was there at meal times, and he'd decided I was worth noticing, now. I wasn't sure when he'd started to actually see me, but it was unnerving. He'd always been like a brother to me, and not in a good way. He'd teased me as much as he'd teased Meg when we were children. He'd called me names, held things out of my reach, pinched me to make me cry, and told lies about me to his parents. If he thought I was going to forget it all, and allow him to court me, he needed to think again.

"Please say you'll come, Josie." She plucked a long blade of grass from a clump at the side of the road and tickled my cheek with the feathery gray-green flower plume. "Pretty please."

"I will if you stop tickling me." I scrubbed at my cheek. "But only for tea, not a meal. I don't want to be a burden."

"You're not. And besides..." She pressed her lips together and glanced left and right. We were only around the corner from where we lived, and there were few people about. Even so, she lowered her voice. "Tilly has a cough. Mama wants you to check her."

"You know I can't do any doctoring," I whispered back. "If the authorities found out—"

"No one will find out. We're friends. You're expected to visit from time to time." She hooked her arm through mine. "Besides, you know how Mama is. She wants to take care of you. She thinks you're getting too skinny."

"She wouldn't think so if she saw my hips."

Meg nudged me, and I almost walked into a bollard. I laughed, only to stop when she asked me how I was doing. "I mean *really* doing. Are you lonely?"

"Not at all," I lied. "My father wasn't much of a conversationalist anyway. Besides, I enjoy my own company."

She eyed me with sympathy. I'd never been good at keeping secrets from her. "Perhaps you should get a dog."

"I don't want a dog." Another lie. I liked animals, and a pet would be good company, but I couldn't afford to feed a dog. I could only just afford to feed myself if I lived frugally. Despite searching the entire house, twice, I'd not found my father's savings. I doubted they'd ever existed.

"This law against you practicing medicine is absurd," she said, reverting to our former topic of conversation. "You should be allowed."

"The law is there for a reason, otherwise we'd have charlatans claiming they could cure all sorts of ills. It's good that it's regulated and only trained doctors can practice."

"Then you should be allowed to go to college and become a doctor. It's not fair."

I agreed. Not that it would matter, now. I had no money to support myself if I were in college.

We turned into the street we'd both lived on our entire lives. The wooden houses wedged into tight spaces on both sides of its narrow length were as familiar to me as my own hands. I could have walked along it blindfolded and known precisely when I was passing the Grinstens' house with its upper level leaning so far to the right that it almost abutted the Meeks's. The spicy smell of Etty Bricket's cooking seemed to waft into the street all day and night, and then it was only eight paces to Meg's front door, and another eight to cross the street to mine.

We were passing Etty Bricket's house when a horse and rider approached from the opposite end. We both stopped. The sight wasn't a common one.

My heart lifted only to sink a little when I recognized the stocky form of the rider. I raised a hand and hailed Sergeant Max before he dismounted at my house. He rode over and dropped to his feet before us. Meg instinctively lifted a hand to the brim of her sunhat, pulling it lower. She always wore a broad hat, summer or winter. When she put her hand to it, she thought she hid the wine-red stain on that side of her jaw and neck. No one ever told her that her effort was in vain.

"Good day, Josie," Max said, removing his hat.

"Good day. What a pleasure to see you again." I must have sounded a little too enthusiastic because his brow creased. "Max, this is my friend, Meg."

Max's gaze lingered on Meg's face a little too long to be polite but thankfully he showed no signs of disgust. He gave her a little bow. "A pleasure to meet you, Meg."

She dipped her head lower and mumbled a response. I would have dug my elbow into her ribs to encourage her to meet his gaze, but Max was already straightening.

"Is this a social call?" I asked him. "Have you come to taste my celebrated cakes? They're as good as the palace cook's, you know." I said it as much to tease the very dour sergeant as to get Meg laughing and warning him not to believe me. I failed on both counts. Max politely refused the offer, proving he could not be teased, and Meg remained silent.

"I've come to collect you," he said. "A carriage is—" He was cut off by the arrival of a carriage pulled by two black horses. It wasn't one of the palace's finest, but it was still shinier than anything seen around Mull. "—is here to take you," he finished. "If you are free."

"Is someone ill?" I blurted out. "Not another poisoning, I hope."

Meg gasped, only to retreat even further back.

Max shook his head. "A maid has requested your services."

4

"She's with child?"

"I have not been informed of the particulars. The captain sent me, upon Balthazar's request. She asked him if she could see you and only you."

It must be for a pregnancy or she would require the services of a doctor. The only doctor in the area at present was the finance minister's medic, Doctor Clegg. Whether he would stoop to attending a maid, I couldn't be sure. Ever since my father's death, Mull had been without a doctor. I had sent a letter to the college in Logios to ask if a new graduate could be placed here. I expected someone to arrive any day, either from the college or a more experienced doctor who'd heard of Mull's growing population. It would be a lucrative practice, if carefully managed. Thankfully there'd been no dire emergencies requiring medical attention in the four weeks since Father's passing. His regular patients had come to me for medicine. Sometimes they asked me to check them in his workshop, but I'd refused. I couldn't risk it.

"The captain told me if you were to hesitate, I am to reassure you that no one else knows of your visit. Just Balthazar, me and the patient herself." Max leaned in. "He thought you might be worried about practicing medicine at the palace."

I expected Meg to chime in with a comment about me hesitating in the village too, but she remained silent. If Max had been a villager she'd known her entire life, she wouldn't have been this shy. Indeed, since I'd only ever seen her with friends and acquaintances, this shyness was new to me. I supposed it was new to her, too.

I stepped back to draw alongside her. "I'll come with you in a moment, Max, but I must check on Meg's sister first. She has a cough. I won't be a moment. Meg will keep you company while I'm gone."

I raced off before she could protest. Meg's mother let me in and glanced past me. I caught her arm before she charged out. Her lips tightened.

"He's a good man," I told her. "He's kind."

"He's from the palace," she said, as if that explained her reticence.

"They're just talking." But they weren't talking. They stood

5

exactly where I'd left them, with Max holding his horse's bridle and Meg touching her hat brim, her arm trying to cover her birthmark. "Come away," I urged her mother.

But she would not budge from the doorway.

"He won't harm her," I added.

"Perhaps not physically."

I sighed. She was over-protective of Meg to the point of being stifling. I understood that she hated the idea of Meg's feelings being hurt by someone cruel enough to laugh at her birthmark, but Meg would never learn to ignore them if she was closeted. And anyway, Max wouldn't do that.

"Come with me," I said, "or I won't see to Tilly."

That got her moving, although she did scowl all the way to the bedchamber Tilly shared with Meg.

Tilly's ailment was just a cough brought on by a tingling throat that heralded the beginnings of a summer cold. Tilly was promptly swaddled in a blanket and plied with a warm tisane that had been brewing for some time judging from the smell infusing the house. I felt sorry for poor Tilly, denied the pleasures of summer fun with her friends, but a little rest would do her good. I knew from experience that her mother would not be swayed from her smothering until Tilly was well again.

I rejoined Max and Meg and was glad to see their silence had finally broken. He was talking quietly to her and she seemed to be listening as she patted the horse's nose. She no longer had her arm up to her hat brim but had angled herself so that she presented Max with her unmarked side.

"He's so velvety, Josie," she said when I joined them. "Pat him."

"What have you two been talking about?" I asked, dutifully patting the horse.

"Horses," Max said, stroking his mount's neck. "And you."

"Me?"

"Since you are the one person we know in common, it stands to reason."

When he put it like that, it sounded like a very dull conversation.

Meg gave me a sly smile. "Apparently somebody called

6

Quentin has been asking about you. He can't wait to see you again and has been pestering the captain to be allowed to come to the village."

I laughed. "I suppose I'd better see him while I'm at the palace. To give the poor captain some peace and quiet, you understand."

"How many other admirers does Josie have there?" Meg asked.

Max counted silently with his fingers, "Five, that I know of."

"So few?" Meg said. "I expected her to have at least a dozen lords and two dozen servants pining for her."

Max blinked at her.

"Don't listen to her," I told him. "She's teasing."

He gave an uncertain smile.

Meg blushed and turned away. "I have to go," she said as she ran off to the house.

"Goodbye," Max said, but she was already inside by the time he spoke. "Is she upset that I didn't laugh at her joke?"

"She's not upset with you." I walked with him across the street to my house. "She's just shy."

"She seems relaxed with you."

"That's because we know one another very well. The mark on her face makes her self-conscious with strangers."

"May I ask what caused it?"

"She was born with it."

He waited with his horse and the carriage while I retrieved my medical pack from the house and locked the door again.

"The captain regrets that he couldn't fetch you himself," he said as he took my bag and placed it in the cabin. "He had to go hunting with the king."

"I thought the king hated hunting."

"The guests are getting restless and needed something to do."

"Can't they go hunting without him?"

"They want to be near the king," he said, assisting me into the cabin. "So he decided to go out today with the new arrivals."

"Ah, yes, I heard about the lords from Dreen and Vytill. I do hope everyone is getting along and there hasn't been much work for Captain—" I cut myself off before I said the wrong thing. Calling him Captain Hammer didn't seem right now that I knew his real name was Dane, but I couldn't call him Dane to anyone, not even to Max. I didn't necessarily agree with Dane's decision to withhold his real name from the others, but I would abide by his wishes.

Besides, it felt special to be his only confidant.

"Very little," Max said. "They've all behaved like gentlemen, so far. That may change after the meetings. That's if the meetings ever take place."

"They're avoiding them?"

"The king is." He shut the door and signaled to the coachman to move off.

I spent the journey wondering why the king was avoiding meetings with the representatives of the two most powerful nations on the Fist Peninsula. It was surely in his best interests to begin discussions immediately, both about his future marriage to one of the princesses and trade between the kingdoms. The fact he was now willing to consider marriage to one of the princesses was remarkable enough, but his reluctance to discuss it with their representatives was an indication that he might not be that keen after all. Perhaps he'd only gone this far to satisfy those of his ministers who wanted an alliance through marriage. The king had been adamant that he would wed a Glancian woman, believing that Glancian women were the fairest. It was a silly notion that I expected him to forego sooner or later. He only had to come to Mull and see the pretty women from the other nations who worked near the harbor. On the other hand, most of them were prostitutes, so it might prove his theory after all, in a way.

Thinking about the king made me wonder whether Dane had confronted him about the gemstone we'd found in the cabinet stored in his room and where that jewel was now. There were so many questions surrounding it, and why the king was so protective of it, but one thing was for certain—it was linked to the memory loss suffered by the palace staff. It had to be. It glowed when they were near and seemed to draw on their life force, but it didn't react to me.

All my questions vanished upon seeing the palace. The first glimpse of it, as the carriage turned onto the Grand Avenue, never ceased to steal my breath. Even on an overcast day, the gold edging the roofline and balconies shone. Its wings stretched north and south in a giant's welcome, the ends not yet visible, as I passed the grand coach house on one side of the avenue and the stables on the other. Each one was bigger than the temple in Mull. I'd once joked to Meg's family that the king's horses lived better than the god and goddess. Her parents hadn't found it amusing.

The guards opened the gates and the carriage deposited me on the large forecourt. Sedan chairs waited to carry lords or ladies too tired or lazy to walk from the gate to the palace entrance. It was a considerable distance, and I could understand the aged requiring a ride, but the woman dressed in deep blue silk who stepped into a sedan chair looked no older than me. A palace footman settled her voluminous skirts into the tight space around her legs, but the peacock plume shooting from her hat defeated him. He bent it then quickly closed the door and instructed the burly carriers to proceed. They set an unhurried pace in the direction of the palace ahead of Max and me.

Instead of entering through the palace's front door, we diverted to the right and followed the external wall of the northern wing almost to its end. Max was about to push open the door to the garrison when something further along caught his attention. I worried that it might be the prison next to the garrison, but then I saw the fight.

Max cursed under his breath. "Go inside, Josie," he said as he marched off.

I hesitated before following him past the prison entrance to the guards' training ground, mostly hidden from view behind a brick wall to the side of the palace. The two fighters had been visible through the arched entrance, and as we drew closer, I could see four other guards looking on. Some shouted encouragement, and one laughed, but none tried to stop them.

"Brant!" Max shouted. "Get off him!"

Brant, who sat astride his opponent, grabbed the other man's shirtfront, lifting him and shoving him back against the ground. The opponent groaned. I couldn't see either of their faces yet.

"Brant!" Max ordered. "Enough! You want to kill him?"

C.J. ARCHER

Sergeant Brant stepped back, giving me a view of the other man's face.

"Quentin!" I rushed forward and knelt by the youth's side. Blood trickled from a cut on his lip, and his dark hair was gray with dust and matted with sweat. He smiled at me, and I breathed a sigh of relief.

"Josie! What are you doing here?" He sat up only to wince and clutch his ribs.

"Let me see," I said, lifting his shirt.

Behind me, Brant snorted. "Weakling."

"I said *enough*!" Max barked.

"I was teaching him a lesson. He needs it. Pathetic."

I shot to my feet and stabbed my finger into Brant's shoulder. "Are you such a bully that you feel the need to fight a smaller, less experienced man who poses no threat to you? *You*, Sergeant, are the one with the weak, pathetic character."

My tirade was met with a silence so thick it felt smothering. I suddenly had trouble drawing a proper breath and my body felt heavy, my head light. No one moved, yet everyone seemed to tense. Brant's eyes darkened until they were as black as pitch.

I swallowed. I couldn't decide whether to move toward the safety of Max or turn away and tend to Quentin, so I simply stood there, frozen.

As if he sensed my fear, Brant's lips stretched into a hard smile. "You'd better go, Josie." He kicked Quentin's foot. "Take your pet with you." He went to walk off, but Max grabbed him by the shoulder.

"I have to report this to the captain," Max said.

Brant wrenched free. "Go ahead, run to Hammer. I don't care. The little turd hit his own lip with his sword hilt." He jerked his chin at the other guards, still standing about. "Ask any of them. They'll tell you he's hopeless."

"So why'd you fight him if he did nothing to you?" Max asked.

"I told you. To teach him a lesson. He needs to become a man. The captain ain't going to show him how, so it's up to me."

"The captain hasn't got time."

"The captain treats him like a little sister." He sneered at Quentin. "Maybe because he's as useless as a girl." He ambled off toward the two swords discarded in the dirt. "He should never have been a guard."

"I didn't have a choice!" Quentin shouted after him from the safety of Max's side.

Brant gave him a rude hand gesture. I wondered how he'd learned it, since his memory loss would have wiped such things from his mind.

I turned back to Quentin and inspected his lip. It had stopped bleeding and didn't require any stitches. "Clean it up and place a damp cloth on it," I said. "It'll sting for a few days. Now, show me your ribs."

"They're fine." He smiled but winced as it stretched the cut on his lip. "Thanks for what you said, Josie, but don't do it again. You've got to be careful with Brant. He's got a temper."

"As have I."

"Aye, but he uses his fists when he gets mad. You just use words."

"The effects can last as long, if not longer." But I conceded his point with a nod and agreed not to antagonize Brant further. "I'll do my best to stay out of his way. As should you."

"Aye," Max said, rejoining us after speaking to the other guards. They were once again sparring with swords on the far side of the training ground. "Both of you need to stay clear of Brant. Quentin, you're not to train when he's here. Understand?"

"But he's always here," Quentin whined.

"Then you wait for me or the captain, or Erik. You can't rely on them to protect you." He glanced at the other guards, sparring as if they wanted to kill one another.

"Why does he hate me?"

If Max knew the answer, he didn't say. He simply walked off toward the arched exit where he stopped and waited for me. I picked up my bag and went to join him.

"You got a patient, Josie?" Quentin asked, falling into step alongside me.

I nodded but didn't elaborate. Max had made it seem as if the matter should be kept private.

"Who? What's happened? Someone sick?"

"Leave Josie alone," Max growled. "Go clean yourself up."

"But—"

"Go!"

Quentin pouted and ambled off toward a trough of water, his shoulders slouched. I followed Max out of the training yard only to be met by Theodore striding toward us.

"There you are," he said. "The guards at the gate said you'd arrived. Max, you should have brought her straight to the garrison. I've been waiting."

"There was an incident in the training yard," Max said.

"Brant? Is that why he was puffing like an enraged bull just now?"

"Best to keep out of his way for the rest of the day."

Theodore clicked his tongue. "We shouldn't have to tiptoe around him. Hammer needs to force him into line."

"Easier said than done. Besides, Brant's just frustrated with how things are and the fact there ain't no cure for us." Max tapped his temple.

"We're all frustrated, but no one else is picking fights and acting like they're the only one who's lost their memory." Theodore took my bag. "Josie, come. Max, you should carry a lady's bag if she has one."

Max blinked then looked down at his feet. "Sorry," he mumbled. "Seems I weren't brought up with manners like Theo and Hammer."

"It's all right," I said, trying not to smile at his blush. "It's not heavy." To prove my point, I took the bag back and carried it myself.

I entered the palace with Theodore through a service door just past the garrison entrance. We climbed a set of narrow stairs, walked along corridors and trudged up another three flights. We walked what must be the entire length of the palace past an endless series of closed doors, each with a brass number nailed to it.

I peered through one of the dormer windows lining the corridor on the opposite side to the doors. It overlooked the square commons building that housed the kitchen and other service rooms. Beyond the stables and coach house, I could make out the length of the Grand Avenue slicing through the forest like a scar. The intersection with the Mull road was hidden behind dense trees, but I could see the village itself, nestled on the edge of Tovey Harbor. If it weren't for the tiny ships crowding the harbor's entrance, sea and sky would have been indistinguishable on such a dull day.

"Is this where the servants sleep?" I asked, turning back to Theodore.

"This is the southern wing," he said without pausing his brisk stride. The king's valet didn't seem weary or hot whereas my damp clothes clung to me in unmentionable places and I was a little short of breath. "The room Ruth shares with another maid is not far. The palace maids occupy the attic rooms in the southern wing. The footmen have the ones in the northern wing, while the attic rooms in the central section of the palace are currently occupied by the visiting servants. Higher nobles are housed on the first and second floors in more spacious rooms. Lower ranking nobles are accommodated in the pavilions with any visiting entertainers. Kitchen staff and some of the outdoor servants have rooms in the commons, and the remainder of the outdoor servants sleep in the stables."

"And the guards?"

"Have rooms on the ground level, near the garrison. Except for Hammer, who sleeps in a room next to the king's. I sleep in the king's room, on a truckle at the foot of his bed, and Balthazar gets a nice room all to himself not far away." He stopped in front of room two-five-one. "Do you want to know what we ate for breakfast too?"

"Oh, er, no. Sorry for prying. I find the palace fascinating."

He chuckled. "I don't mind your questions, but be careful you don't ask the wrong person." I was about to ask why but he continued. "Ruth's alone in here. If you think she needs time off from her duties, I'll inform Balthazar. I'm afraid he'll also need to know what's wrong with her, but there's no need for her to know that. Oh, and don't tell her you know about our memory loss. Don't ask her any questions that will force her to tell you. I can't stay. The king will return from his hunt soon and will probably require my services. He might want a bath," he went on, sounding distracted

13

by the notion. "Certainly a change of clothes, and I imagine hunting is thirsty work."

"If he's been gone a while, he might want something to eat."

"Good point. Thank you. He's never gone hunting before, and I'm not sure what to expect."

"I'm sure he doesn't expect you to anticipate his every need."

"Nevertheless, it's my duty." He knocked on the door and a woman invited us to enter.

She sat on the bed, her feet firmly together, her shoulders rounded, and gave me a hesitant nod. Theodore introduced us then backed out of the room and shut the door.

I set my bag down on the other bed and regarded my patient. She was young with dark brown hair and perfect skin. She was pretty but in a quiet, subtle way that required a second and third look before really appreciating just how much. She glanced up and blushed. She was nervous. No, worse than that. She was frightened. Of telling Balthazar that she was carrying a child? Of telling the father?

"Are you unwell, Ruth?" I began.

She shook her head.

"You're with child?"

Her huge brown eyes stared at me then suddenly watered. Her face crumpled and she buried her head in her hands.

I put my arm around her shoulders. "It's all right if you are," I said. "Don't be scared. I'll tell Balthazar for you, if you like."

"I don't want a baby," she said between sobs. "I don't want *his* baby."

Dread settled into my heart, a hard, bitter thing. "Whose?" I asked carefully. "Ruth, who is the father?"

Her sobs grew louder. "I don't know."

"How can you not know?"

It took several moments and quite a lot of gentle talking for her to calm down. Her crying finally abated, and she wiped her cheeks with the back of her hand. "He came up to me in the dark from behind. He forced me to the floor and lifted my skirt and…"

I folded her into my arms and caressed her hair. Her body shook uncontrollably. I rocked her and told her over and over that it would be all right, that she was safe now.

But how could she be safe? Her rapist was still somewhere in the palace. With almost a thousand staff, and hundreds of visiting nobles, each with their own servants, finding him would be a mammoth task. It could be anyone, from the lowest servant to the king himself.

CHAPTER 2

*R*uth offered to show me back to the garrison after I'd finished checking her, but I declined. I wanted the time to myself to think. It wasn't until later that I wondered if *she'd* wanted *my* company. It may be broad daylight, but some of the service corridors were poorly lit and many twisted and turned, providing ample corners to hide behind.

I'd told Ruth that I would have to inform the captain, and she was in agreement, although she asked if I could be there if he needed to question her.

I barged into the garrison without really thinking and stopped short upon seeing Brant. He sat at the table with another four guards, a tankard in one hand and a piece of dried meat in the other. He eyed me from beneath heavy, drooping lids.

"Why are you here?" he asked.

"I had to see a patient. Is the captain—"

"You ain't a doctor."

"Is the captain in?"

"He'll be back soon," said one of the guards.

Another guard offered me a cup of ale. I hesitated then accepted it when I realized it was Zeke, the guard who'd chased me into The Row when I'd been on the trail of the poison seller. He looked eager to earn my forgiveness. He pulled out a chair for me at the long table and I sat.

Brant got up and sauntered over. "I asked you a question, Josie."

"And I decided not to answer it," I said. "If the captain wants you to know, he'll inform you."

He leaned down, his face so close to mine I could smell the ale on his breath. "More fucking secrets. I reckon you're all in this together. I reckon you all know what happened to us and you ain't telling."

One of the guards mumbled something, but when Brant glared at him, the guard shut his mouth. No one else spoke and the silence stretched thin.

I was thankful when the door opened and Erik strolled in with Max. Max glared at Brant, but Erik beamed at me.

"Josie!" cried the big blond Marginer. "You are here. Brant, go away. You stink."

Brant straightened and backed away, hands in the air. He spilled some of his ale on the floor.

"Clean that up before someone slips," Max barked.

"I ain't a maid," Brant said between his teeth. "And you ain't my superior." He picked up a chair and slammed it down on the flagstones. He sat and drained his tankard.

"The captain's on his way," Max told me. "I see you've been given refreshments. May I offer you something else?" He opened the lid of a tin on the sideboard only to screw up his nose and close it again.

"It's all right," I told him. "The ale is enough."

"I can send someone to the kitchen for food."

"Merdu," Brant muttered. "I'm surrounded by pathetic fools."

Erik tore a chunk of bread off the loaf on the table and threw it at Brant. Brant caught it and shoved it in his mouth.

"I'm fine," I said again to Max. "Thank you."

Erik lowered himself onto a chair and flicked the long coils of hair over his shoulder. The dot tattoos on his forehead drew together in a frown. "It is good to see you, Josie. Why do you not visit? Are we not your friends?"

"Of course you are. It's just that, well, I suppose I was waiting for an invitation."

"Invitation?"

"To be asked," I explained.

"Why not come if you want to come?"

"Perhaps there's a different custom in the Margin," I said. "But here, we wait to be invited before we visit new friends."

He grunted. "Then how do you make friends? I could die waiting for you."

"Or you could just invite me."

He grinned. "I will."

Brant made a sound of disgust in the back of his throat. "You all make me sick. Tom, spar with me. I need to hit something."

The large man called Tom hesitated. The guard sitting next to him punched him in the arm and Tom hauled himself to his feet. "Fists only," he said to Brant as they left.

I expelled a long breath as the door shut behind them. Max finally sat. He rolled his shoulder and, with a grimace, dug his fingers into the flesh near his neck.

"You have a pain?" I asked him.

"It ain't too bad."

"Describe it to me."

He pointed to the spot and told me how it felt tight and sore with certain movements. It sounded muscular, not a bone fracture or worse.

"No heavy lifting for the next few weeks," I told him. "Is that your sword arm?"

He nodded.

"Then no sparring until it heals."

"Will you tell the captain for me?" he asked.

I laughed. He did not.

"If you wish," I said. "Regular massage will also help."

Max began to unlace his shirt.

"Not from me," I said. "It might be seen as medical assistance."

Erik grunted. "Idiot rule. You are good doctor and should be allowed. The king should make it so."

"Agreed," Max said, continuing to unlace his shirt. "No one will find out, Josie."

I glanced at the external door, expecting someone to walk in at any moment. "It's unwise."

"None of us will tell." He glared at the other men.

18

They all nodded.

"Perhaps you have a particular friend among the staff who would like to get her hands on those impressive shoulders of yours," I said.

A ferocious blush crept across Max's cheeks, earning snickers from the other guards. He sheepishly dropped his hands away from his shirt. "Sorry, Josie," he muttered.

"I suppose it won't matter this one time." I directed him to remove his shirt but stilled when I saw the scars striping his back. I'd forgotten about them. Dane had shown me his at the beach and asked me to identify what made them. I could only guess that he'd been whipped. According to Dane, he, Max, Erik, Brant and a few other guards had them, but Dane sported the most.

I pressed into the flesh at Max's shoulder. When I found the knot, I pressed harder. Max grunted then groaned, a rolling sound that rose from the depths of his barrel chest. He tipped his head forward.

The door to the internal service corridor suddenly opened. Dane stood there, unmoving, and stared at us. His lips parted but no sound came out.

"Why'd you stop, Captain?" came Quentin's voice from behind him.

"Keep going, Josie," Max murmured.

Dane entered the garrison. He removed his sword belt and hung it up on the hook by the door. "What is this?" he asked.

"Max has a sore shoulder," I said. "It required massage."

"By you?"

"By anyone."

"Is this your professional opinion?"

"Yes."

"Then stop." He plucked Max's shirt off the table and threw it at him. "You should know better, Sergeant. Josie isn't allowed. You've put her in grave danger—"

"It's not his fault," I said. "I wanted to help."

"Doctor Clegg is in the vicinity. If he'd seen you, I wouldn't put it past him to report you."

I sat down again as Max put on his shirt. "I could have claimed it wasn't medical," I said.

Dane arched his brows at me. "You're not naive, Josie. You know what rumors would be spread about you if you said that."

I crossed my arms and looked away. The captain had a way of making me feel foolish. I could have told him that I'd welcome such rumors. They'd make a change from the jokes by the village men about my frigidity, or my preference for women, or any number of rumors that had spread since I rejected Ivor Morgrain's advances a few weeks ago.

"Where's Brant?" the captain asked his men.

"Sparring with Tom," Max said.

"Keep him busy. Give him extra duties if necessary."

"Aye, sir."

"And take Quentin with you everywhere you go."

Max sighed. "Can't Erik mind him? His talking irritates me."

"And me," Erik piped up. "His voice hurts my ears."

Quentin stamped his hands on his hips. "I'm right here."

Erik shrugged. "You are like a child. Sometimes annoying, sometimes I like you. Sometimes I want to pat you on the head and say good boy."

"I think you're confusing me with a dog, but I'm happy with a pat on the head from time to time. It's better than a punch to the face." He touched his cut lip.

Max rose and clapped Quentin on the shoulder. "Don't worry, you're as ugly as ever. In fact, it's probably a slight improvement."

"This is true," Erik said. "The maids will like it. You look more like a man now and not a boy."

Quentin picked up the knife beside the bread and admired his reflection in the metal. "Do you think so?"

Max rolled his eyes. "I'd better make sure Brant isn't killing Tom."

Erik plucked a sword and belt from a hook and held it out to him. "Spar with them."

"They're sparring with fists," Max said.

Erik grinned. One side of Max's mouth lifted. He took the sword and headed outside.

Dane invited me to leave with him through the internal door. "Have you been well?" he asked me with stiff formality as we headed to Balthazar's office.

"I have, thank you," I said, equally formal. "Of course, if you visited from time to time, you'd know."

His silence made me cringe. Perhaps I shouldn't have been so caustic. "It's best if I don't visit," he finally said.

I didn't agree so changed the subject. "How is Laylana? Can I see her?"

"She won't remember you. She lost her memories again four days ago."

Poor Laylana. The maid was locked in a room for her own safety. Unlike the other servants, whose memories had been wiped only once, Laylana lost hers again and again. Every memory loss meant she had to begin her life anew in a strange place, surrounded by people she didn't know, and not knowing anything about herself except her name. It was no wonder she showed signs of madness.

"And the gem?" I whispered. "Have you discussed it with the king?"

He took such a long time to answer that I thought he would ignore me completely. "I have not," he finally said.

We'd reached Balthazar's office so I didn't have time to ask him further questions. I suspected that was the reason for his delayed response. I glared at him to let him know I knew what he was doing.

He opened the door for me and stood in the doorway so I had to get very close to him to pass. I suspected it was a deliberate attempt to distract me. It worked. The smug look he gave me as I brushed him told me he knew it too. The man was arrogant.

I glanced at him over my shoulder and winked. The smugness vanished. He swallowed.

Balthazar sat at his desk, peering at paperwork through a pair of spectacles perched on the end of his nose. "Will you ever learn to knock, Hammer?" he said without looking up.

"I've brought Josie," Dane said. "She's just seen Ruth."

Balthazar sat back and regarded me with the same scrutiny he'd just given the papers. "Sit, Josie."

I did and indicated his spectacles. "I see you did something about your eyesight."

He removed the glasses and placed them on the desk. "I had

these made by a man in Tilting. Lord Laxland's valet gave me the name. They are a great assistance." He put them back on. "For instance, I can now see why the guards are all enamored with you."

I blinked at him but quickly schooled my features. "I'm not sure whether you're flattering me or insulting me. I *hope* they like me for my character."

"If I were insulting you, you would know."

"That's enough, Balthazar," Dane chided. "Don't tease her. She's done us a service coming here today on such short notice."

"She's being paid." He opened a drawer and pulled out a purse jangling with coins.

"That's too much," I said, looking inside. "My fee is less than half this."

"Blame the captain. He insisted."

I glanced at Dane but he was too busy shooting fierce glares at Balthazar to notice.

"Tell us about Ruth," Balthazar said to me. "What ails her?"

"It's an extremely delicate matter," I said. "What I'm going to tell you cannot leave this room."

"That is our decision to make, not yours."

"It won't," Dane assured me. "Unless it becomes necessary." He leaned against the sideboard and crossed his arms and ankles. The man rarely sat.

"Is she with child?" Balthazar pressed.

"It's too soon to tell," I said. "She was raped two nights ago."

Dane swore under his breath. Balthazar rubbed a wrinkled and ink-stained hand across his mouth. When neither man asked questions, I thought it best to answer those I could anticipate.

"She didn't see her attacker. He came up behind her in one of the service corridors. All she knows is that he was male, taller than her and stronger."

"She's a slight woman," Dane said heavily.

"She has bruises which give her some discomfort but there is no pain from the act itself, however she wanted me to check her anyway. I think she wanted to talk to someone about it more than receive medical attention. She hasn't even told the maid who shares her room."

"Did you tell her she should not feel ashamed?" Balthazar asked. He looked pale and his hand shook, but I couldn't tell if it was from old age or shock.

"It's not just the shame. She feels violated." I glanced at Dane. "She no longer feels safe."

Dane pushed off from the sideboard and made to leave the room, but hesitated by the door. With his back to me, I couldn't see his face, but I knew he was angry from his clenched fists and tense shoulders.

"Captain, you must reassure her," Balthazar said. "And question her to find the man."

"Only with me present," I said. "That was her request."

Balthazar nodded and glanced at Dane. He hadn't turned around.

"There's one other thing," I said. "It's not related to this incident, but I want you to know." I wasn't even sure why I wanted them to know. It was Ruth's affair, not theirs, yet I couldn't bring myself to tell her. She'd been through enough and I didn't want to make her sadder.

My hesitation had them both focusing on me.

"She's given birth before." The small scar had been more than a year old, at a guess, and had been expertly stitched. I couldn't be positive that a midwife's hand had done the work, but I was almost certain.

"So she has a child," Balthazar said, taking up his pen. "There's nothing we can do about that."

I watched him dip the pen in the inkwell and scribble notes. That was it? He had nothing more to say?

I leaned forward but he did not look up at me. "It's evidence of a past life," I said. "Evidence that she, and therefore all of you, are real people, not magical ones conjured out of thin air."

"I never had any doubt about that. Did you, Hammer?"

Dane shifted his stance. "It's wise of you to keep it from her at this point," he said to me.

"Is it?" I shook my head. "I don't know if I had done the right thing."

"It will only make her unhappy that she cannot get back to that child."

My head agreed with him, but my heart still harbored doubts. I'd tried putting myself in Ruth's position but failed to imagine whether she'd want to know. It was why I'd chosen the cowardly option and told Dane and Balthazar instead. They knew her better than me and could decide what to do.

Balthazar finished writing. He looked over the page then held it out to Dane. "Begin your investigation with these three. One is a footman, one a gardener, the third works in the stables."

"You suspect your own staff?" I asked, rising and trying to peer at the paper.

Balthazar jerked it away. "This is for Hammer's eyes only."

Dane took the paper and looked at the names. "It's unlikely to be a palace servant."

"Why?" Balthazar asked. "It's happened before."

My breath hitched. "It has? Did you catch him?"

Dane glared at Balthazar.

"The captain did," Balthazar said. "He's no longer a threat."

Was he talking about the palace prisoners? The three men lived in cramped, windowless cells, and had not faced outside justice. I could easily imagine the feral looking Kai preying on maids. I'd not seen the other two.

"Nothing of this nature has happened since that incident," Dane said. "If a palace servant is responsible, why start now?"

Balthazar grunted a humorless laugh. "Perhaps he has only just found his courage after seeing what happened to Mal."

Mal was the name of one of the other prisoners. "What happened to him?" I asked.

"I arrested him," Dane said quickly.

"After making sure everyone saw what happens to those who attempt to harm other members of staff," Balthazar added. "If anyone was in any doubt as to how Hammer got his name, they weren't after the captain *arrested* Mal."

My blood ran cold. I'd suspected Dane had a violent streak but this was confirmation of it. The healer in me was sickened, but as a woman, I was gratified that an attempted rapist had been dealt what he deserved.

Another thought struck me. Balthazar had implied that he knew Hammer wasn't the captain's real name, that it was a nickname given to him because of that violent streak. Dane had told me he'd not corrected anyone else's use of that nickname, so Balthazar must have guessed. He watched Dane very closely for a reaction to his allusion.

Dane gave none. He calmly folded the paper and creased it between thumb and forefinger.

"I still think this latest attack could be by a member of staff," Balthazar went on. "He might have been too afraid of you to attack earlier. He's been biding his time."

"I said it's unlikely to be one of the palace servants, though it is not impossible," Dane said. "It's more likely to be one of the visiting lords or their servants, given the timing."

"You should keep an eye on the Deerhorn lordlings," I told him. "They're notorious in Mull. The village women know to stay out of their way after an incident two years ago, where the eldest forced himself on a girl. He claimed she threw herself at him but I know her, and she's not like that."

Dane nodded his thanks for the information.

"I doubt it was a lord," Balthazar said. "It's more likely to be one of their servants if it happened in a service corridor. And using your same theory, it's unlikely to be any of the visiting noblemen or their staff. They've been here over a month now, and there have been no reports of anything like this happening."

"Not on this scale," Dane agreed.

Balthazar arched his brows. "Are you telling me there have been minor incidents and I haven't been informed?"

"It was a security matter not a staff matter."

"I beg to differ. If my staff are in any danger, I must be told."

"So you can do what?"

Balthazar threw his hands in the air. "Warn them, of course."

"The matter was taken care of. There was no need to alarm anyone."

Balthazar's eyes tightened at the corners. "In what way did you take care of it, Hammer?"

"In a way that you don't need to know about." Dane put up his hand. To my surprise, Balthazar shut his mouth, although I half expected to see steam escaping from his nostrils. "I agree that based on the timing, someone associated with the Dreen and Vytill representatives attacked Ruth. They are newly arrived and are accompanied by large entourages."

Balthazar groaned. "If it is one of them, it could cause a diplomatic problem."

"It already is a problem for Ruth," Dane bit off.

Balthazar rubbed his temples and sighed. He suddenly seemed very frail. His mind might be sharp but he had the stooped shoulders, thin frame, and weary eyes of old age. "You're right. If it is one of the representatives, he must be dealt with according to Glancian law."

He had more confidence than me in bringing the rapist to justice if it turned out to be one of the Dreen or Vytill representatives. It was more likely they'd go home without so much as a smear on their name.

A servant, however, was another matter entirely. A visiting valet or footman could expect to be brought to justice. But a palace servant? Would he face Glancian justice? Or would he be beaten by Dane and thrown in the cells like Mal?

I looked up at Dane, only to see him watching me intently.

"There's something I should mention," Balthazar said. "Ruth cleans the rooms used by Lord Barborough, the Vytill representative. She shouldn't see his lordship, although it's not impossible for them to have met. She's more likely to come into contact with his valet and assistants, however."

Dane nodded. "I'll question them all, including his lordship."

"Is it too much to ask you to tread lightly, Hammer?"

The captain threw him a cool look.

Someone knocked on the door. "Enter!" Balthazar said. "See, Hammer, knocking isn't a difficult skill to master."

Theodore glanced between them. "Don't fight in front of a guest."

"I'm hardly a guest," I said. "And they're not fighting. Fights are what Brant starts. This is merely needling."

Balthazar clasped his hands on the desk. "Brant is fighting again? Hammer, why didn't you tell me?"

"Because you don't need to know," Dane said. "The guards are under my jurisdiction."

"Then control them."

Theodore cleared his throat. "Josie, if you're finished here, the king has need of you. He fell off his horse and is concerned he may have fractured ribs."

"I can't," I said. "Doctor Clegg will gladly do it."

"His Majesty asked for you."

"She told you she can't," Dane growled.

Theodore put up his hands in surrender. "*You* refuse him to his face, Hammer." To me he added, "It'll just be a quick inspection of the bruising."

"No," Dane said.

Theodore sighed. "Let me assure *both* of you," he shot a glare at Dane, "that no one will find out. We'll be discreet."

"Discreet! Gossip swarms around the palace like flies around day-old meat. She's not going."

"I'll go," I said. Perhaps it wasn't wise to let my rebellious streak rule my decision-making, but there was nothing I could do to stop it. There really wasn't. "As long as no one else finds out."

Dane muttered something under his breath and appealed to the ceiling.

"Thank you, Josie." Theodore gave me a shallow bow. "I dreaded what to tell the king if you refused. He doesn't like being told no."

"Theo, try to refrain from disparaging our king to our guests," Balthazar chided.

"She's one of us," Theodore said.

"No, she isn't."

"She might as well be. She knows our secrets."

Balthazar picked up a stack of papers and flipped through them. "If there's nothing else…"

We three filed out of his office and walked up stairs and through the maze of corridors to the king's apartments. I'd been in them before but the opulence and their sheer size still amazed me. I wouldn't want to live in such spacious rooms. There was nothing cozy or comfortable about them. Between the gilded furniture, the gold leaf on the wall panels, the crystal chandeliers and the pictures of the king framed in thick gold, I felt like I shouldn't touch anything. Only the bed looked comfortable. Indeed, the king must have found it so because he lay on it, snoring softly. He couldn't have been in too much pain.

Theodore cleared his throat and the king's eyes cracked open then flared wide.

"Josie. May I call you Josie?"

"Please do, sire." I curtseyed and found I was no better at it than last time. At least I managed to keep my balance as I rose.

The king smiled and his gaze roamed up and down my length, lingering on all the obvious places. "You're looking as pretty as I remembered."

"Thank you, sire."

"If all doctors were as pretty as you, there'd never be any healthy men to work in the fields or the docks." He chuckled. At my blank look, he added, "Because they'd fake illnesses so the pretty doctors gave them more attention."

I smiled but wasn't sure what to say. Was he flirting with me?

He stretched his hand toward me. "Come closer. You can't check my ribs from there."

I hesitated then took his hand. It was rough and callused. I hadn't expected that. I thought they'd be soft from idleness, but I supposed he hadn't been brought up as a royal. He'd lived an ordinary life before the document proving he was King Alain's grandson was found in the High Temple mere months ago. It explained why he often seemed uncertain in his role and exhibited some very un-kingly traits, like having a local midwife inspect his ribs for fractures.

"Theo, Hammer, you may leave us," the king ordered.

"No," Dane said.

The king arched his brows. "Pardon?"

"Josie has a good reputation to uphold. If it becomes known that she was in here alone with you, that reputation will be ruined. I'll remain."

The king's jaw hardened.

"As will I," Theodore said quickly. "You'll need assistance with your clothing, sire. You can't be expected to dress yourself, naturally."

"Yes. Of course. Well, come here and help me remove my shirt." The king lifted his chin and the valet knelt on the bed to undo the row of gold buttons. The king shrugged out of the shirt and puffed out his chest. I suspected that was for my benefit. He needn't have bothered. I wasn't impressed, puffed out or not. He was a slender man with a paunch that spilled over his waistband and a cluster of dark hair around his belly button and the center of his chest.

"Where does it hurt?" I asked.

"Here." He pointed to his right side. "There's a bruise."

I scrutinized the area and eventually found the bruise. It was no bigger than my thumb.

"It's very painful," he said.

"I'm sure it is." I wasn't about to tell the king that his definition of pain must be different to mine.

"My horse got scared," he said. "Something ran across its path and it reared. You saw it, didn't you, Hammer?"

"No, sire."

The king laughed. "Perhaps we need to get you some spectacles like Balthazar. Anyway, the others riding with us saw the creature. It was some kind of rat, so Lord Villers said. *His* eyes work perfectly."

"Apparently so," Dane said in a monotone.

Theodore tensed and he shook his head ever so slightly at the captain. The king didn't notice. He simply laughed.

"Hammer's mood is very grim lately, Josie," he said in a theatrical whisper. "You should ignore him as much as possible for your own peace of mind."

"He's not very easy to ignore," I said.

The king's smile vanished. "Don't you need to touch me to check for fractures?"

I gently pressed on the bruise. He sucked air between his teeth. I went to pull away but he grabbed my hand in both of his.

"You missed the area," he murmured. "Here." He pressed my palm to his ribs, over the bruise, and stroked my fingers. "And here." He moved my hand further around to his chest. My fingers touched the patch of hair and recoiled.

"There are no fractures," I said, drawing away.

He pouted. "Are you sure? I don't think you checked thoroughly enough." He went to take my hand again but I clasped his instead.

Now that I'd stopped him in his tracks, I wasn't sure what to do so I bowed over his hand as I stood. "I'll leave you something for the pain. Captain, my bag, please."

Dane had carried my bag from Balthazar's office. He set it down on the foot of the bed and I searched it for the jar of holly-root ointment. In liquid form such as a tisane, hollyroot gave all-over mild pain relief, but in ointment form, it could be applied topically. The king's bruise required nothing stronger.

I held out the jar to him but he didn't take it. He smiled. Clearly he wanted me to apply it for him.

I dropped a small amount onto my palm and gently rubbed it on the bruise. He did not lie back to make it easy for me, but leaned in so that his nose almost touched my cheek.

"You're pretty," he whispered in my ear. "Prettier than some of the ladies at court. I didn't notice at first, but now I see beyond the drab clothes to the woman."

"You're very kind, sire," I said, as I straightened, "but I'm just a simple midwife."

His hand whipped out and caught my wrist. Dane took a step toward me. "Sire," he said. "You're hurting her."

The king released me. He smiled without humor. "A midwife who aspires to be more, yes?"

"I don't understand," I said carefully.

"It came to my attention that you dressed as a noblewoman and joined in the festivities a few weeks ago."

So Lady Deerhorn had told him she'd seen me that night. I hoped she'd forgotten. "I...I'm sorry, sire," I mumbled. As uncomfortable as his attempts at flirting had been, I wished for that side of him again. I knew how to deflect a man's attentions. A king's ire was entirely different.

"That was at my request," Dane cut in. "I needed someone to walk among the female guests as one of them to detect the poisoner. You'll recall that we weren't aware who it was at the time. Josie offered to do it. If it weren't for her, I'd never have uncovered Lord Frederick."

The king's nostrils flared, and I suspected he didn't believe Dane but either couldn't say so without evidence or didn't want to.

He scooted off the bed and caught my arm. He leaned in and

THE ECHO OF BROKEN DREAMS

whispered, "If you want more, Josie, I can give it to you. You only have to ask nicely." His gaze slid to the bed. "Very nicely."

My scalp tingled and heat spread across my face.

The king chuckled. "I knew you'd like that idea."

My gaze instinctively lifted to Dane's. His hooded eyes made it impossible to read his face but his shoulders sported the stiffness of barely suppressed anger. If he barked orders at the king the way he barked orders at Brant, he could land himself in trouble. Yet I knew him well enough to know that he wasn't the sort of man to back down when his temper flared.

CHAPTER 3

"*T*hank you, sire," I said, smiling brightly at the king. "I'm grateful for the invitation, but the revels I witnessed that night are enough to satisfy me for the rest of my life. Indeed, I found them quite overwhelming. I'm the bookish type, you see, and not used to parties and late nights. I prefer curling up in front of the fire with a cup of soup and a treatise on clover spot. I'm afraid I'm quite dull company."

The king's fingers sprang apart as if he were afraid to catch clover spot from me. It was interesting that he knew the disease was contagious, considering he was supposed to have lost his memory. It was yet more proof that he had not.

Dane shoved the king's shirt into His Majesty's chest. "You'd better get dressed, sire. You wouldn't want to catch a chill."

No one mentioned how warm it was in the king's apartments.

The thud of Balthazar's walking stick announced him before he appeared in the doorway. He greeted the king with a bow of his head. "Your Majesty, the duke of Buxton has requested a meeting with you and your other advisors."

"Tell him I'm busy."

Balthazar looked to me then back at the king. "Are you badly injured?"

"I am in considerable pain, but I'll manage. I'm on my way to play cards with friends in the Sky Salon."

"The duke was insistent."

"Then he should have come to me himself, not sent you."

"He couldn't find you or Theo and happened upon me in his search. I told him I would inform you. As I said, he was very insistent. There are some matters of politics that ought to be discussed before tonight's dinner."

The king screwed up his nose. "Politics again. Will it never end?"

"Not for a king," Dane said.

His Majesty's gaze slid to Dane then back to Balthazar. "Why do I have advisors if they cannot take care of these matters themselves?"

Theodore finished fastening the last button on the king's shirt and reached for the doublet draped over a chaise. "The problem *is* your advisors. They can't agree on the matter of your marriage."

The king sighed and stretched his arms out again to allow Theodore to put on the doublet. "No doubt Buxton wants to impress upon me the benefits of marrying his niece."

"I believe a miniature of her has just arrived. He wants to show it to you."

"Why not send for the girl herself? Because she's ugly, that's why. Her miniature will be of some other, prettier girl. Perhaps the local midwife."

Balthazar arched his brows at me.

"The duke's niece isn't here because she's underage," Dane said, sounding annoyed. "Her mother doesn't want her at court for another year at least."

The king lifted his chin to allow Theodore to fluff up his lace cravat. "I suppose she is Glancian."

"Sire?" Balthazar prompted.

"She must be pretty if she's Glancian." The king's gaze lingered on me.

I looked away and busied myself with my bag. Dane took it from me before I could lift it.

His gaze lingered too, but it was different to the king's. He looked me in the eyes, not at my breasts or hips. It didn't feel as though he was trying to strip off my clothes, but rather to gauge my thoughts.

"Inform the duke that I'd like to see the miniature of his niece immediately, but informally, not in a meeting," the king said. "There's no need for the others to be present."

"Sire, you *must* meet with them before you speak to the representatives from Dreen and Vytill tonight," Balthazar said. "They were worried that you went hunting with them today, but—"

"We didn't discuss the matter of my marrying one of the princesses."

"Tonight, you might. If I may advise you, it would be to meet with your advisors this afternoon. All of them, not just the duke of Buxton. You need to hear both sides of the argument, for and against a political marriage to one of the princesses."

The king clicked his fingers. "Theo, my ruby brooch. And that new scent, the one Violette gave me."

Violette was Lady Morgrave, the daughter of Lady Deerhorn. The last time I'd been at the palace, she was trying to wedge herself into the king's good graces, despite already being married herself. I wondered if he'd bedded her yet. Perhaps the lasciviousness he displayed toward me was a result of his awakened desires. On my previous visits, he'd been gentlemanly and a little shy around women. He'd done everything right to woo the beautiful Lady Miranda Claypool but I'd not heard him mention her name once today. I knew she hadn't gone home because she'd visited me in the village and wrote to me regularly. She hadn't mentioned the king in any of her letters.

The king stood still as Theodore dabbed the scent on his throat above the cravat. "Balthazar, tell the advisors I will listen to their thoughts, but they should be warned that my preference is still for a Glancian wife. I am, after all, the king of Glancia, and my queen ought to be from this country."

"Marrying outside of the kingdom would bring many advantages," Balthazar pressed. "Not to mention peace. This early in your reign, the importance of peace cannot be overstated, hence my advice to marry the Vytill princess. It's a stronger kingdom than Dreen."

The king waved a hand. "You worry too much. Glancia is well on the way to becoming the richest kingdom on the Fist Peninsula. The Rift saw to that. An alliance with either Vytill or Dreen will soon be pointless. Anyway, why would I want to be saddled with a foreign mare for the rest of my life when I can have a Glancian beauty?" He clapped Balthazar on the shoulder. "I don't expect you to understand, Old Man. Or you, Theo. Hammer agrees, don't you?"

"No," Dane said. "From everything I've read on the history of The Fist, members of the royal families have always intermarried to ensure stability on the peninsula. Only twice did kings marry non-royalty. Both times resulted in wars that lasted years and devastated the kingdoms involved, resulting in heavy loss of life."

"And emptied their treasuries," Balthazar added. "Ignore the lessons of history at your peril, sire."

The king rolled his eyes. "Very well. I'll listen to my advisers and hear what the Vytill and Dreen representatives have to offer. I'll make my mind up when I've considered all possibilities, but I will insist on meeting any candidate, whether she's a princess or a Glancian noblewoman. I won't be marrying a horse. You can inform the foreign representatives yourself to save me the bother." He strode to the door. Theodore followed a few steps behind. "No need to accompany me, Theo," King Leon said without turning around. "Your dour face makes the ladies less inclined to have fun."

Theodore watched him go. When the king was out of earshot, he said, "I find that hard to believe. Nothing seems to stop them drinking to excess and flirting with him."

"That isn't flirting," Balthazar said, also watching. "Yesterday I saw Lady Sabine sit on his lap and shove her hand down—"

Dane's cough cut Balthazar off. Balthazar apologized to me. "I didn't think you were so sensitive, Josie, considering what you must have seen and heard when assisting your father."

"I'm not sensitive," I told him.

Balthazar smirked at Dane.

The captain picked up my bag. "I'll walk you to the gate."

Theodore and Balthazar walked ahead of us out of the king's apartments, their pace slow thanks to Balthazar's limp. Dane seemed in no hurry to pass them.

"How will we convince him to marry one of the princesses?" Theodore asked.

"One or both of them needs to be pretty," Balthazar said on a sigh that seemed to come from the depths of him. "Unfortunately, the king is shallow and can't see beyond a woman's face."

Theodore hushed him. "Don't say it too loudly."

"I'm old, Theo. He can throw me in prison for saying what I think, I don't care."

Theodore shook his head. "If you spent any time in the palace cells with the prisoners, you wouldn't say that."

Balthazar grunted. "True enough."

"The problem is," Dane said, proving he'd been contemplating the dilemma, "we don't know what the princesses look like and are unable to find out. Their fathers won't let them travel here. Both monarchs expect King Leon to make a decision for political reasons, not personal ones."

"And that means not meeting his chosen bride until the wedding day," Theodore said heavily.

"Josie, what do you advise?" Balthazar asked.

"Me?" I blurted out.

"A woman's perspective might help."

"I suppose he should do what is best for the realm, but it won't be easy convincing him of that. He hasn't always known he'd inherit the throne, so he probably assumed he'd marry for love. Anything else is alien to him." They didn't remind me that the king had lost his memory so any beliefs he held growing up accounted for nothing. It would seem they no longer believed that either. "But if you tell him he can choose a wife for political reasons and keep a mistress for pleasure, then perhaps he'll be agreeable to marrying a princess, even if she is plain."

All three men stopped and stared at me.

I shrugged. "It's common practice for royalty. King Alain had several mistresses over the years. As one aged, he'd exchange her for someone younger."

"The world never ceases to surprise me," Balthazar muttered.

"The practice is limited to kings?" Theodore asked.

"I'm sure there are other noblemen who have mistresses, but it's frowned upon for the lower orders to indulge as some of their so-called betters do. Marriage in our culture is for life, or it's supposed to be."

"So choose wisely?" Balthazar said with a chuckle. "Or don't choose at all. I wonder if I'm married."

"I don't think so," I said.

He gave me an arched look. "You think me so disagreeable that no woman could bear to be with me?"

I bit back my smile. "You don't wear a ring. Couples exchange rings on their wedding day."

Balthazar and Theodore studied their fingers. Dane didn't. I suspected he'd already read up about the custom. He didn't wear a ring and his fingers sported no tan mark as evidence of having once worn one.

"I might have removed it," Balthazar said.

"With those gnarled knuckles?" Theodore walked off. "And your disagreeable nature? I doubt you are married."

"He has a point," Dane said, a smile touching his lips.

Balthazar grunted. "I hate you both."

Outside, Theodore and Balthazar headed to the commons, while Dane and I ambled across the forecourts to the gate. Only a handful of nobles were on this side of the palace. With the formal gardens on the other side, their only reason to be on the forecourts was if they were leaving or arriving. Dane and I maintained the slow pace we'd been restricted to with Balthazar's limp. Neither of us was inclined to speed up. I knew why I wanted to spend as long as possible in Dane's company. I wondered if his reasons were the same.

"You won't have to attend to the king again," he said, focusing ahead. "His behavior with you today was inexcusable, and I'll tell him so."

"Please don't. He won't like it, and I don't want you getting into trouble. Besides, he probably won't care."

"He'll listen to me."

"If you're willing to risk such a discussion with him, why not confront him about the gem?"

Several beats passed before he answered. "Theodore, Balthazar and I decided it was best to learn what we can about it before we talk to the king."

"And what have you learned?"

"We're still looking for answers."

"How?"

"There are books in the library on the subjects of geology and gemstones, including where some of the largest gems are now located. Many found their way into crowns, necklaces, and the most valuable of all tops the Vytill royal scepter."

"Have you found anything about magic in the books?"

"Not yet."

"Perhaps you need a book on magic."

He looked at me sideways. "If you have a title, please share it. As far as I can tell, there are no books on magic."

"Not in the palace's library, but if I were going to create a palace using magic and I didn't want anyone to know, I'd hardly leave a book on the subject where a servant could stumble upon it." When he didn't speak, I added, "I do think it's wise not to confront the king without more information, just like I think it's wise not to confront him about his behavior today. He's the king, Dane, not a regular man. He can do as he pleases, and that includes throwing you in prison."

At the mention of his real name, he turned sharply to face me. A quick glance around proved that no one was near enough to have overheard.

"May I call you that when we're alone?" I asked.

He hesitated then nodded. "I want you to. It's why I told you."

I smiled. "I want to call you that too. The name suits you better."

"I don't think Hammer suits too many people, but thank you."

"Speaking of prisons," I said carefully, "tell me about the prisoners in the palace cells."

"We weren't speaking of prisons and there's nothing to tell."

"There must be or you wouldn't have avoided the issue for so long." At his arched looked, I added, "I asked you about them weeks ago and you wouldn't give an answer."

"That's because I've got nothing to say."

"Why the thoughtful look just now?"

"I'm trying to decide if telling you to stay away from the prisoners is more or less likely to encourage you to go near them."

"Very amusing," I said wryly.

He did not look amused. He set off again, his pace quicker.

That's what I got for prying—a man who wanted to be rid of me faster.

We reached the gate but instead of asking the guard to fetch a carriage for me, Dane kept walking. It would seem he was going to escort me all the way to the coach house.

"Josie?" said a voice to my right. "Is that you?"

"Miranda." I waved at the woman striding toward me. Even when she walked with purpose she moved gracefully.

She took both my hands and kissed my cheek. "I'm so pleased to see you. Are you leaving? Without coming to visit me?"

I glanced at Dane, who'd stepped away to give us privacy as if he were simply my escort, not a friend. "This isn't a social call," I said to Miranda. "I had to look in on a maid."

She eyed my medical pack in Dane's clutches. "I do hope she's all right and it's nothing serious."

"She'll be fine."

"Will you walk with me?"

"I was about to leave. The captain was taking me to the coach house."

"I'll take you." She hooked her arm through mine. "Captain, take Miss Cully's bag to the coach house and tell them to prepare a carriage for her. We'll walk slowly."

Dane acknowledged her with a curt bow.

Miranda tilted her head to the side and watched him leave. "He's very serious."

"Not always."

"He cuts a fine figure. *Very* fine."

"Does he?" I said idly.

She laughed. "Don't pretend you haven't noticed. You're not blind."

I laughed too and she hugged my arm.

"It feels wonderful to laugh," she said. "I've missed you. You must come more often."

"It's not easy. I can't come and go uninvited. You could visit me in the village again."

She sighed. "I'll try, but my parents don't think I need to go into the village. They say I have everything I need here, including suitable women to be friends with. They don't understand that most of the ladies of my age are silly creatures who wish to throw themselves at the king. The only one who has no interest in him is Kitty, the duchess of Gladstow, but her husband doesn't want us being friends. I can't think why."

I knew why, but I wasn't going to inform her that the duke of Gladstow had been slighted by Miranda's mother years ago. He'd not forgiven her. Indeed, he seemed to want to punish her. He'd gone so far as to accost her behind the hedges on the night of the revels. It wasn't my place to tell Miranda any of that, and it seemed her parents hadn't informed her either.

"Thankfully, my parents have given up on me becoming queen," Miranda went on. "I'm lucky they're not the sort of people to force me into marrying a man I don't love."

"You're no longer the king's favorite?"

The corner of her mouth lifted. "My parents and I have moved back to our old rooms. They're hot and cramped, and miles from the king's apartments, but I like my room better than the suite the king assigned to me in the ducal corridor. For one thing, the other women no longer look at me like they want to poison me, and for another, I don't feel as though I owe the king any favors. I do miss being close to Kitty's rooms. It made it easier for us to meet in secret."

"Who's his favorite now?"

She lifted a shoulder. "Lady Violette drapes herself over him at every opportunity, and he flirts outrageously with her, but I don't think it's gone further than that. He seems to want an unmarried woman."

"Has he taken any of them to his bed?"

"No, and I think that's the problem."

"What do you mean?"

She looked around. We were half way between the gate and the stables and coach house. Dane had gone on ahead but was well out of earshot. No one else was nearby. Even so, Miranda lowered her voice. "He is surrounded by beautiful women vying for his attention, some of them in very overt ways, but he hasn't bedded any. Some men might be able to manage their frustrations, but not him. He hasn't got the strength of character for it."

Her opinion agreed with mine but I didn't tell her so. I didn't want to explain why I agreed. The fewer people who knew I'd attended to him the better.

"I hope he chooses a willing participant," Miranda said wryly. "Those of us who aren't so willing but have captured his interest will thank her."

I tightened my grip on her arm. "Stay out of his way as much as you can."

"Why do you think I go on so many rides?" She nodded at the stables where several riders on horseback entered the yard through the arched entrance from the avenue. "He detests riding. I heard he fell off when he went hunting today. It happened at the start of the hunt. He pretended a scuttling creature frightened his horse, but the truth is, it didn't rear. He simply fell off."

"Did anyone laugh?"

"I doubt it. None would dare. He's not cruel or vindictive but he is a man, and men have their pride."

Our pace slowed even more. Neither of us wanted to reach the coach house and have to part. I enjoyed talking to her. She was good natured, intelligent, and had a wicked sense of humor. She was also willing to impart gossip that Dane was not.

"In a way, I feel sorry for the king," she went on. "Ruling an entire kingdom can't be easy, particularly for someone with a humble background."

"He's from Freedland, isn't he?" I tried to sound casual. I knew so little about King Leon's past, but it was time I learned more if I was going to find evidence that he was involved in the magical mystery surrounding the existence of the palace.

Miranda nodded. "The thing is, no one seems to know precisely where he was born. He evades the question when asked."

"That's odd."

She glanced around again and leaned closer. "Kitty tells me her husband sent spies into Freedland to find out more about him. She overheard him talking to some other lords who don't think Leon should be king."

"Is the duke of Buxton one of his co-conspirators?" I asked.

She shook her head. "I doubt it. Before Leon took the throne, each of the dukes were eyeing it for themselves. They wouldn't collaborate now. Neither has much support among the nobles anymore, according to my father. Most believe King Leon is the rightful heir and that's the end of it."

"But if the dukes can prove he's not the rightful heir?"

"Shhh." She looked around again. "Don't say that out loud, Josie. It's treason. Anyway, of course he's the heir. A document from the High Temple proved it, and King Alain acknowledged him before his death. If Kitty's right, the duke of Gladstow is heading down a fruitless path. Of course, she didn't know wine was made from grapes until I told her, so she could be wrong about her husband."

"Where did she think wine came from?"

"An animal, like milk."

I laughed, but it quickly faded as I thought about the duke of Gladstow sending spies into Freedland. I understood his need for information. I wanted to know more about the king's past too. It could provide a clue as to where Dane and the others had come from and how they'd lost their memories. The key point was the king *didn't* want anyone to know. Why? Why did he not want even his own advisers to know about his life before he appeared on the doorstep of King Alain's castle in Tilting?

One thing I knew for certain, the king wouldn't give an honest answer if asked directly. He had something to hide and he wasn't going to give his secrets up easily. Dane was wise not to confront him yet. But he would have to confront him one day.

We'd reached the part of the avenue that dissected the stables and coach house. Two men emerged through the entrance leading to the stable yard. One was dressed in a gentleman's doublet while the other wore plainer clothes with no embellishments, ornate collars or cravats. He spotted me and I swore under my breath. It was Doctor Clegg. The gentleman with him must be Glancia's finance minister, the doctor's employer. He certainly looked in need of constant medical attention. He couldn't have been aged more than forty, yet he was as thin as Balthazar, with hollowed out cheeks and yellow skin. We weren't close enough to see his eyes but I suspected they'd be yellow too. It was impossible to know what underlying illness ailed him without further study as the visible symptoms pointed to several.

Doctor Clegg spoke to the finance minister, drawing his attention to me.

"Why are they looking at you with such suspicion?" Miranda asked.

"Doctor Clegg thinks I'm dispensing medical advice."

"Then lets set him straight. Come along."

I held her back. "He won't believe us, and I'd rather simply avoid him." I tried steering her to the coach house on the other side of the avenue, but someone else leaving the stables had caught her attention. I groaned. It was Lady Deerhorn with her daughter, Lady Violette Morgrave, and her eldest son, Lord Xavier.

"It seems the Deerhorns have been plotting again," Miranda said.

"Plotting?"

"To get Violette into the king's bed. Whenever I see two or more of them together, that's what I imagine they're discussing. It's certainly not whom the king will marry, since there are no eligible Deerhorn ladies. Why were they invited to the palace anyway? I thought only those families with eligible daughters were invited."

"The duke and duchess of Gladstow have no children and they're here," I said.

"Yes, but he's an advisor and duke. Lord Deerhorn is just a regular count. He's not an advisor and his only daughter is married."

"Perhaps because they're the local nobility. It would have seemed odd not to invite them since they live nearby."

"And doesn't Lady Deerhorn like to crow about being the king's neighbor." Miranda rolled her eyes. "That one's a wasp, Josie. Stay out of her way or you'll get stung."

It was too late for that. "Speaking of staying away, be careful of her sons," I told her. "Xavier is the worst but the other two aren't much better."

She frowned at me. "Did he do something to you?"

"Another girl in the village. Make sure you're never alone with him."

"Thank you for the warning, but I doubt he'd attempt anything here or with me. He wouldn't dare."

She was right, to a certain extent. Lord Xavier was smart

enough not to touch a noblewoman, but he was definitely cruel enough to rape a maid.

A palace footman carrying a man's hat emerged from the stables behind the Deerhorns. He looked familiar but it wasn't until he followed Lady Deerhorn's icy gaze to me that I remembered the precise moments I'd seen him. He'd been the servant I'd met in the service corridors on my first night at the palace, and then again when he'd come to collect my father, not knowing he'd died. The way he looked at me on those occasions had been very much the same as the way the king looked at me today.

His tongue darted out and licked his lower lip. *Ugh*. Revolting.

He handed Lord Xavier the hat and said something to him. Lord Xavier glanced at me and smiled. Then he winked.

"Let's go," I said to Miranda. "My carriage must be almost ready."

I ushered her toward the coach house just as the double gates opened and a small carriage bearing the king's coat of arms rolled out. Dane led the horse by the bridle. I glanced back toward the stables, but the Deerhorns were walking in the direction of the palace, the footman having gone on ahead.

"Be careful walking alone in the palace," I told Miranda.

She frowned. "Why?"

"Just don't go into the gardens alone at night or into the service corridors."

"Josie, what's got into you? Are you worried about Xavier Deerhorn?"

"Just be careful." I kissed her cheek and left her looking dazed to join Dane, waiting for me by the open carriage door. My bag sat inside on the bench seat.

He took my hand and assisted me into the cabin. His touch lingered a little longer than necessary but was gone too soon for my liking. "Is something the matter?" he asked. "You look troubled."

"Did you see that footman? The one with the Deerhorns?"

He nodded.

"Is he one of the staff members on Balthazar's list of suspects?"

I knew from his face that I was right. "Why?" he asked darkly. "What has he done?"

"Nothing. It's just a feeling I get when he looks at me."

He stared after the footman. I put out a hand to touch the bunched muscles along his jaw but lost my nerve and lowered it again.

I also couldn't find the courage to ask him when I'd see him again. My father had taught me never to ask a question when you suspected the answer would be unwelcome.

"Goodbye, Dane," I said softly.

A smile as faint as a mirage touched his lips. "Goodbye, Josie." He shut the door and the carriage rolled away.

CHAPTER 4

$\mathcal{U}$nlike his last investigation into the poisoning, I couldn't do anything to help Dane find the guilty party this time. But I could assist with the other matter—magic. Or, more specifically, researching magic.

I spent the following morning delivering medicines to my father's regular patients. Some were a little embarrassed not to have returned to see me since his death and sheepishly purchased the medicine, ointment or salve at the discount I offered, while others eagerly invited me in for tea.

After the exchange of pleasantries, I steered the conversations toward magic and the possibility of its existence. While no one admitted to believing in it, some said the rapid and inexplicable construction of the palace had them doubting what they'd always thought to be true. Several suggested I talk to a Zemayan if I wanted to learn more about magic, but the only Zemayan I'd known, Tamworth Tao the spice merchant, was dead.

With all the medicines delivered, I went to the docks in the hope of finding a Zemayan ship in the harbor, but none of the flags flying on the distant masts bore the red and black of that nation. The crews manning the smaller vessels transporting goods from their mother ships to the piers all had the paler coloring of Fist residents. I sighed. I would have to talk to Tam's family, a task I was hoping to avoid. His death and my father's were linked in a way I didn't want to think about. I expected Mistress Tao would be equally as reluctant to see me.

I made my way back along one of the twin piers jutting into the harbor, dodging sailors, passengers and dockers. The traffic was thick and forging ahead became an exercise in patience. I was jostled and sworn at. My ankles were nipped by a dog and my thighs bumped by a cart laden with melons. The fresh smell of the sea was lost beneath the odors of sweaty laborers and the general stench of unwashed bodies. Cleanliness wasn't a priority on a long sea voyage.

I finally drew in a deep breath when I reached the concourse. It was no less busy but at least there was more space and no danger of falling into deep water.

A hand gripped my arm and jerked me to a stop. I gasped and tried to pull free, even after I saw who'd accosted me.

"Ivor, let me go this instant or I'll scream."

He did but blocked my path. He wasn't overly tall or solid, but he was bigger than me. "What are you doing here?" he asked.

"That's none of your business."

He wrinkled his nose, bunching the freckles there into a solid splotch. "I was just asking. No need to bite my head off."

I sighed. I'd known Ivor my entire life. We'd been acquaintances, rather than friends, but lately he'd been paying me more attention. The last time I'd seen him, he'd been walking toward my house, a bunch of flowers in hand. After seeing me leave with Dane on horseback, he'd thrown those flowers on the ground. I'd not seen him since. Despite his thwarted attempt at wooing, he wasn't a threat to my safety. I was simply a little jittery after learning about the palace rapist.

"Sorry," I said, more gently, "but I don't like having my way blocked."

"I ain't blocking it. I'm just standing here. *You* almost bumped into *me*." His brows arched, challenging me to refute him.

I couldn't be bothered. "It's a busy place," I said, stepping out of the way of a man pulling a cart laden with empty crates. "Is it always like this?"

"Aye, lately. Never used to be, but after The Rift, it all changed. The fishermen hate it. They've got to wait until all the

47

other ships' cargoes are loaded and unloaded before they get a berth."

"Aren't you supposed to be working now?"

He smiled and leaned closer. "Aye, but I'd rather be talking to you."

I stepped back and accidentally trod on the toes of a man carrying a canvas satchel on his shoulder.

"Watch it!" he snapped.

"You watch it!" Ivor snapped back. "She's got more right to be here than you."

The man's eyes darkened, his lips flattened. "You got a problem with me looking for honest work?"

A shadow of uncertainty passed over Ivor's pale blue eyes, but then he squared his shoulders. "I do when you take honest work from a Glancian."

The man snorted. "Seems to me you need us. Word is, the men here are just fishermen."

Two bright spots bloomed on Ivor's cheeks. "You got a problem with fishermen?"

"I do when they're trying to run an international port. Look at this place." The stranger indicated the half-finished customs house, the throng trying to pass one another on the piers, and the big ships anchored in the mouth of the harbor because the water was too shallow nearer the shore. "It's a fucking mess. There ain't no organization, no way to find out who needs to hire workers. Goods come and go through here without the proper paperwork. Your stupid authorities are missing out on taxes. New arrivals are getting charged high prices for nothing more than a shit-hole room they share with five others. Seems to me you need experienced workers from The Thumb to do your jobs for you."

"Seems to me *you* need *us* for work," Ivor shot back.

The stranger hiked the satchel higher on his shoulder and headed off, muttering to himself about The Rift.

"If you hate it here, just leave!" Ivor called after him. "Go home to The Thumb. You ain't wanted in Mull."

The problem was, the man wouldn't have work to go home to. The Rift caused the outcrop of land known as The Thumb to be cut off from the mainland. For the most important port on the Fist

Peninsula, it was a disastrous outcome as it meant it was no longer even part of the mainland. It was an island. Ships destined for The Fist bypassed it and docked in Mull instead, leaving most of Port Haven's residents without work. The Thumb's plight was magnified when the downstream section of the Mer River dried up after being cut off from its source. Without fresh water, The Thumb's farms couldn't thrive. It was a disaster for Vytill, the kingdom The Thumb belonged to. Port Haven had been a source of riches due to its customs taxes on goods and passengers passing through the port. Now, The Thumb was a burden on Vytill's treasury as the remaining residents survived on the king's charity.

Ivor gestured rudely at the stranger's back. "Arrogant prick."

"Ivor," I hissed. "He's just frustrated with the madness of this place, and he's probably worried about finding work and feeding a family back home."

He folded his arms, tucking his hands high up under his armpits. "People like him are taking jobs away from honest, hard working Glancians."

"Hard working? You haven't done a thing while you've been talking to me."

"Look at 'em all!" He indicated the men around us, some simply standing about doing nothing, others asking anyone who passed if they were in need of workers. "A year ago, I knew every single person here. Now I hardly know anyone. Mull is full of strangers."

"That's no reason to be angry at them, Ivor. It's nobody's fault that Mull is changing. It's just the way things are, and we have to adjust the best we can."

"Why are you taking their side against people you've known your entire life?"

"I'm not taking anyone's side."

He sniffed, wrinkling his nose. "Ever since going to the palace, you've been all high and mighty. You haven't got time for us no more."

"I certainly haven't got time for your hostility."

"Me? Hostile? I'll have you know, I was willing to court you, Josie, maybe even marry you."

"Willing?" I laughed. "How charitable of you."

Ivor bristled. "Aye, it was. But now I'm glad I lost interest. You ain't the girl you used to be, now you've been to parties with lords and ladies. They say you even pretended to be a lady, all dressed up in silk and jewels."

"Who says that?" Only Lady Deerhorn had recognized me but it wouldn't surprise me if she'd spread the rumor among her staff. A Deerhorn maid or footman must have taken that rumor to the village on their days off.

Ivor simply smiled.

"It was one party," I said. "As for my other visits, I've had work to do, just like the servants. Would you deny me a way to make a living?"

"If you married, you wouldn't need to make a living. Your husband would take care of you."

This conversation was going to make me angry if it went on any longer. It was best to end it if we were to remain civil. I pushed past him.

"Do you know what everyone's saying about you and the captain of the guards?" he called after me. The sneer in his voice should have warned me. I should have walked faster, or turned around and ordered him to stay quiet. "That he's your whoremonger."

Several passersby looked at us while others slowed down to listen. I knew some of them. I'd delivered their babies or attended to them with my father. None told Ivor to retract his words. It was up to me.

I marched back to him. "Nobody thinks that except you. And if you believe it, then you're pathetic and I thank the goddess that I wasn't foolish enough to encourage your advances."

The two spots of color on his cheeks brightened with each passing moment until the freckles looked as if they'd explode off his face. Before he could speak or intercept me again, I strode off through the crowd. A few snickers followed me but I wasn't sure if they were directed at me or Ivor, and I didn't care. I couldn't believe he'd say such things to me when mere weeks ago he'd wanted to give me flowers. I couldn't believe I'd never seen this side of him before. We may not have been close, but I hadn't realized he was cruel.

By the time I left the concourse and entered the main street behind the warehouses, where the permanent shops were bustling with trade, my anger had faded. Ivor's words still stung, however. I felt betrayed by one of my own.

My own what? I hardly recognized parts of my village anymore, let alone some of the people in it. Thank goodness there were still good people like Peggy in the Buy and Swap Shop who waved at me as I passed her window where she was setting out a display of tin plates.

People like the Taos, too. It was time to face them. The sooner I did, the sooner I'd feel better about buying supplies from Mika's stall again.

The door was opened by one of the younger children who informed me that Mika wasn't at home. I asked to see his mother instead and was led to the kitchen where Mistress Tao stood at the table cutting up a bunch of herbs. The tang of spices tickled my nose and the back of my throat. There were too many for me to identify individually but the combination smelled delicious.

Mistress Tao wiped her forehead on her sleeve and offered me a seat. "Tea?" she asked.

"If you'll join me," I said, sitting.

She checked a small pot hanging over the fire beside a larger one and threw in some dried leaves. "If you need supplies, Mika is at the market."

"I've got enough stock for now," I told her. "The apothecary business has been slower than usual since Father died."

She gave me a sympathetic smile. "So has the spice business."

In my case, it was because Father wasn't around to prescribe the right medicines to those in need. In Mistress Tao's case, it was the association with her husband and his crime of knowingly selling poison to the poisoner. The other spice merchant in the village was servicing more customers than ever. I made a silent promise to go to Mika's stall next time.

I glanced toward the door to make sure none of her other children were within earshot. "How have you been?"

"Fine," she said, lifting the pot off the hook. "The younger ones still cry for him. Mika doesn't say much but I know he misses Tam."

"And you?"

She stared into the pot. "I miss him too."

"If there's anything I can do to help, Mistress Tao, please come and see me."

She poured the tea into two cups and joined me at the table. We sat in awkward silence as I tried to find a suitable way to broach the topic of magic. I wished I'd known her better, but her reclusiveness had made friendship impossible.

"Do you know any other Zemayans in Mull?" I finally asked.

She shook her head. "As far as I'm aware, there aren't any living here permanently. Sailors come and go with their ships but few remain. Most Zemayans prefer to stay on their side of the Sapphire Sea."

"Do you communicate with your husband's relatives regularly?"

"Not particularly. Miss Cully, I appreciate your concern for our wellbeing, but just because my children are half Zemayan doesn't mean Zemayans should seek them out now that my husband has passed."

"That's not why I'm asking." I sipped my tea. It was warm and spicy. "I actually want to ask someone questions about magic."

"Magic?" She frowned. "Why?"

I lifted a shoulder. "Just a passing interest."

She leaned forward and whispered, "Does this have something to do with the palace?"

I stared at her then forced myself to chuckle. "Nothing like that. My father believed in magic, and I find I want to know why, now that he's gone. It's my way of remembering him."

She sat back, looking somewhat disappointed. It seemed everyone wanted to gossip about the mystery of the palace. "I can't help you. Tam believed too, of course, like most Zemayans, but we didn't speak about it." She shrugged. "It simply wasn't a topic of discussion."

"My father said he didn't believe until he traveled to Zemaya, but I don't know why he changed his opinion. I suppose he heard stories."

"There are a number that involve magic. Some are just tales to scare children into being good or to teach them right from wrong. Tam used to tell the children their teeth would be made into a necklace by the sorcerer if they didn't chew bark from the chalk tree to clean them."

"Sorcerer?"

"Zemayans believe there's a sorcerer who controls all the world's magic. He can wield it as he sees fit."

"What kind of magic?"

"Manipulating objects. Making things appear out of thin air." She watched me over the rim of her cup. "Such as a palace and all its inhabitants."

I swallowed more of the tea. It burned my throat as it went down. "And where is the sorcerer supposed to be now?" I asked, setting down the cup. "According to Zemayan beliefs?"

"I don't know. As I said, we didn't discuss magic much. It was just a belief Tam had but one I didn't share. Not then, anyway. Not until a few months ago when the palace appeared."

I met her gaze. "Why did Tam believe in magic?"

"Why did your father?"

"I don't know."

"In Tam's case, it was part of his culture. I don't think he'd seen or heard anything in particular, though. He just assumed a sorcerer existed and could use his power when he wanted. He'd just had no need to use it in centuries."

"Where did Tam think the sorcerer went in that time? Why did he have no use of his power until...?"

Another shrug. "I really can't tell you anything else."

I sighed. "I have to ask a Zemayan." That meant waiting at the harbor for the next ship from that country to arrive. After meeting Ivor there, I didn't want to be near the docks.

"There is a prominent believer based on The Fist," Mistress Tao said. "He wrote a book on magic, many years ago. Tam wanted to find a copy for me to read but I wasn't interested." She tapped her finger on the cup and frowned in thought. "What was the title?" she muttered.

"Is he originally from Zemaya?"

She shook her head. "Vytill, I think. He spent a few years in Zemaya. Even so, Tam thought it a good book for me to read to learn about magic. He thought I might appreciate it more, knowing an educated Fist lord believed so strongly." She blinked watery eyes into her cup.

I reached across the table and touched her arm. She smiled sadly. "Do you remember the lord's name?" I asked.

"Something starting with B."

I knew the name of only one lord from Vytill beginning with a B. Surely it couldn't be him. "Barborough?"

"That's it. Lord Barborough. Do you know him?"

"No. It's just a name I've heard." I stood and thanked her for the tea. "If you're near my house, please do stop in," I said. "I'd like to return the favor."

She promised but I knew it was an empty one. She was unlikely to leave the house after all this time.

Heading home, I considered how best to give the information about Lord Barborough to Dane. He should be informed, but a note might not be taken seriously. I'd have to go in person. At least, that's what I told myself.

I was about to set out the following morning when I met Meg leaving her house to go to the market.

"Want to come with me?" she asked. "I can even carry your things in my basket. I doubt I'll fill it otherwise. The prices are even higher this week than they were last week. It's outrageous. Papa says we won't be able to afford to live in Mull soon."

"Not today. I'm going to the palace."

She looked up and down the street. "Have you been summoned again?"

"I have a message to deliver. About the maid I attended yesterday," I added when she gave me an odd look. "Something about her condition."

"Oh, poor thing. I do hope her pregnancy isn't difficult."

I pressed my lips together. I hated lying to her, but I couldn't tell her Ruth's problem. I'd promised secrecy.

"Who will you speak to there?" It sounded like an idle question, but the fingernail picking at one of the broken rushes on her basket handle told a different story.

"The captain, I suppose," I said. "I might even see Sergeant Max."

The picking became more determined. "Oh? Who?"

"The handsome man who collected me yesterday."

"Is that his name? I'd forgotten."

"Liar," I said, laughing.

Her face blushed fiercely. "You're imagining something that wasn't there, Josie, and I'll thank you not to spread rumors about me being interested in him."

My smile died on my lips. "No, of course not. I'm sorry, Meg, I didn't mean to upset you."

She glanced back at her front door. "I'm not upset, I'm merely being cautious about rumor-mongering, especially when the rumor involves someone from the palace. Speaking of the palace and rumors, I heard what Ivor said to you. I can't believe he would say that about you and the captain. My brother was appalled when he heard."

"Ivor has shown his ugly side," I said. "I want nothing more to do with him."

"Nor I. And don't worry, nobody who truly knows you thinks that of you. Those who do are just jealous because you've been to the palace several times, including to a party, and they're stuck here in dull Mull."

"Mull isn't dull of late," I murmured, wondering how many besides Ivor felt the way he did.

She hooked her arm through mine and we walked to the end of the street together where we parted and went our separate ways. I decided to walk to the palace since I was in no hurry. The day promised to be warm but the sun hadn't reached full strength yet. Even so, I was hot by the time I reached the gilded gates. Despite recognizing me, the guards wouldn't let me through, but one did fetch the captain. I was allowed through only upon Dane's say so.

"You've increased security," I said to him as the guard bolted the gate behind us.

"I have."

I waited until we were out of earshot of the guards before asking, "In response to what happened to Ruth?"

"Yes."

"But if the rapist is living or staying here, how is locking the gates going to keep him out?"

"Did you come here just to ask questions about my security measures?"

"Sorry. I have something to tell you, but not here or in the garrison. Can we go somewhere more private?"

"Balthazar's office is the best place."

"Not if he's there."

He frowned. "You can trust Balthazar."

I offered no comment. I couldn't tell him my suspicions about Balthazar. Indeed, I didn't quite know what I suspected him of doing. Aside from his sharp tongue, the master of the palace seemed to be keeping something back from Dane and Theodore. Surely he knew more than he was letting on about the palace's construction. And how had he achieved such marvels on the night of the revels? I'd not seen an orchestra, yet the music came from all around us. The dancers had performed beautiful dances and the acrobats performed feats that defied death, yet no one had seen them practice. No one in the village knew where they'd come from either. They'd not been through Mull. How could someone who never left the palace and have a memory going back a mere four months even know where to find such people?

"Very well," Dane said cautiously. "We won't go to the palace. Do you feel like walking some more?"

"Where are we going?" I asked as we headed past the commons.

"As far away as necessary."

We left the southern wing of the palace behind and kept walking. Dane's purposeful strides took us down a long series of steps that turned out to be on top of one side of a U-shaped building flanking a semi-sunken garden. The building's enormous arched windows offered a view of the lush trees and shrubs inside. We continued on, past the pottage garden where several gardeners prepared a fresh bed while others picked what appeared to be lettuce. For a garden only a few months old, the plants were well advanced.

On the other side of the path was another lake bordered by lawns that in turn was bordered by trees. We finally stopped at the end of the lake. From there, we could see the top of the palace over the greenhouse with the arched windows.

"The guests prefer the flower gardens on the western side of the palace," Dane said. "And the view of the palace is better from Lake Grand. Sometimes the staff come here when they have time off, but the mornings are always their busiest. We seem to have this spot to ourselves."

He finally turned to face me, and I momentarily forgot what I wanted to say. Those clear blue eyes had a way of making me feel as though we were miles from anywhere and anyone, and that anything could happen between us.

He turned away and the magical moment vanished, leaving me wondering if it had ever been there or if I'd imagined it.

"What is it you wanted to see me about?" he asked.

"Do you mind if I sit down?"

"Please do. You've been on your feet for some time."

I was tempted to remove my shoes and dangle my feet into the water, but this was the palace, not the beach at Half Moon Cove. I sat on the lawn instead. Dane hesitated then he sat too, pushing his sword out of the way behind him.

"I made some inquiries about magic yesterday," I told him.

He looked sharply at me. "Why?"

"Why not?"

"Because it could prove dangerous."

"How?"

"If the magician who made the palace wants to keep his creation a secret."

"If he wanted that, he should have taken more time to build it. He should have made sure his magical builders were seen and heard."

His lips flattened. "You should still be careful."

"I was careful," I said snippily. "Do you want to know what I learned?"

He glanced at the nearby trees and nodded.

"I learned that the Zemayans seem to treat magic like a religion. They believe in it even though they have no real evidence that it exists."

"As you do with your god and goddess."

"Precisely. They have stories about magic and an all-powerful sorcerer, but I don't know if those stories are based on real events that occurred centuries ago or if they're made up. The Zemayans seem to believe them, though."

"Do any of the stories include a gemstone?"

"I don't know, but there may be a way we can find out."

His eyes narrowed. "We?"

"Yes, we. I plan on helping you."

"That's not wise. "

"It's very wise, since I have the time and you don't. Also, I am in possession of the information you need."

He grunted. "You're blackmailing me."

"You forced me to it."

Another grunt. "I'll consider it."

I lay back on the grass, closed my eyes, and linked my hands over my stomach. "Let me know your answer when you've made up your mind."

He took far longer than I expected. The silence stretched on, the only sound coming from a bee buzzing nearby. There wasn't even a breath of wind to rustle the leaves or ripple the water. It was one of those summer days where the heat seems to slow everything down, including time itself, and where cares melted away beneath the sun.

"Josie," Dane murmured.

"Hmmm?"

"Are you asleep?"

I sat up, smacking my forehead against his cheek. He must have been leaning over me.

"Sorry!" I winced and rubbed my forehead. "Did I hurt you? Let me see."

"It's fine," he said, laughing softly. "You were asleep."

"I was not. I'd only just closed my eyes."

"So you drool when you're awake?"

I swiped my hand across my mouth. Dry. I checked the corners. Dry. So I did what any girl would do when she likes the man teasing her. I thumped his shoulder. He held up his hands in surrender but the smile lingered, and it was delicious.

I couldn't stop staring at his mouth. Were his lips as warm and soft as they looked? I instinctively reached out but checked myself at the last moment and touched his cheek instead.

"There's a mark," I said, stupidly. "Sorry."

He cleared his throat. "It'll vanish."

I wanted to ask him why he'd been leaning over me when I was sleeping, but he got in first.

"Do you want to know my answer?" he asked.

It took me a moment to refocus on our previous discussion. I nodded.

"My answer is yes," he said. "You can help me find out more about magic, but on the condition we do it together."

I liked his condition. "I agree."

"Now tell me what you know."

"I know the name of a man who wrote a book on magic. He's a Vytillian lord and he happens to be here in the palace. It's the Vytill representative."

"Barborough?"

"Apparently he spent some years in Zemaya, where he learned about magic. He wrote a book upon his return to Vytill. We could ask him to teach us, or perhaps ask for a copy of the book."

Dane pulled up his knees and rested his forearms on them. He stared at the palace roof, with its golden capping, so striking against the black slate.

"Are you worried that he may be the rapist?" I asked, having wondered the same thing myself. Ruth had been assigned to clean Barborough's room, after all.

"Yes, but there's more. He must already suspect magic built this place and will be alert for signs of it, including strange behavior from the servants. A staff member's inquiries will only fuel his suspicions. I don't want to give him a reason to ask me questions about my past and how I got here."

"Then I'll make the inquiries. I'll say my father had an interest in magic and now I find I want to know more to bring me closer to him."

He gave a curt nod. "Very well, but I'll stay nearby. He's a suspect in the attack on Ruth. I won't leave you alone with him."

"Have you advanced far in your investigation?"

"I've inquired into the whereabouts of the three servants at the time of the attack. Only one has no witness to vouch for him—the footman. I've questioned him but he claims he's innocent."

"Of course he does." I blew out a frustrated breath. "At least he knows you're aware of his behavior. If he is the rapist, it might stop him doing it again."

"Or it might make him more careful next time."

With a palace full of maids who often walked alone through the dark maze of corridors, the horror of it happening again was very real.

"You should warn the maids," I said. "They should be told to go about their business in pairs."

"Pairing up isn't always practical. But you're right. I know Ruth wants to keep the incident private, but the maids must be warned."

"No one needs to know she was the victim."

Neither of us mentioned the likelihood of the other staff guessing. It was known that I'd visited her, and some would put the two facts together.

"At least your list is smaller with the elimination of the other two servants." I held up a finger. "There's the footman...what's his name?"

"Seb."

"There's Seb, Lord Barborough and Lord Xavier Deerhorn." I put up a second and third finger.

He arched his brows. "You seem to be under the impression that you're helping me with this investigation too."

"Of course I am. Ruth trusts me, and since I'll be talking to Barborough about magic, I can—"

"You will *not* confront him about the attack. Is that understood?"

"I'll be guided by you, Dane. Now, the fourth person on your list must be Sergeant Brant," I said before he could interrupt again. "He seems likely, if you ask me."

"Brant isn't a suspect."

"Why not?"

"He was on patrol at the time with Zeke. According to Zeke, they remained together."

"They know why you questioned them about that night?"

He shook his head. "I told them nothing."

"So that brings us back to three. That's not so many."

He held my gaze without blinking.

"There's another, isn't there?" I pressed.

He broke the gaze and turned back to the lake. "If I tell you, you must promise not to talk to him on your own."

"Is it someone I know?"

"Promise, Josie."

"I promise. Is it one of the guards?"

He shook his head. "A man from the village. I had reports at the time of a stranger wandering around the palace grounds. I didn't connect the reports to the rape until this morning, when I learned he was seen in the service corridors by one of the visiting ladies' maids. She thought he was a palace gardener or other outdoor servant at the time, but on learning the gardeners are not allowed in any part of the palace, she reported the incident to me."

"Did she describe him?"

He nodded. "I took that description to the guards who were on duty at all the gates at the time of the sighting, as well as the stables and commons. The maid's description matched a man who'd helped deliver fresh crayfish from Mull." He paused.

"Go on," I said. "Out with it."

"A change in the guards on the gates occurred after the cart arrived and before it left which explains why the cart wasn't stopped when only the driver left with it. The new guards didn't know he had an assistant." He'd given the account in a matter-of-fact tone up until the end. "Damn it," he growled. "The procedure for changing the guards isn't secure enough. It leaves us exposed."

"You weren't to know."

"I *should* have known!"

I swallowed and kept my mouth shut. I plucked at the grass and waited for his temper to cool before speaking again. "There are many strangers in Mull at the moment," I said. "Some could have a violent background and we wouldn't know it." I had to consider that perhaps not all were refugees from The Thumb looking for honest work. Some could be escapees fleeing the authorities, hiding among Mull's chaos.

"This isn't a stranger," he said darkly.

"Who is it?"

"One of the Deerhorn maids saw him arrive on the cart and was able to give me a name." He held my gaze. "It's Ivor Morgrain."

CHAPTER 5

"*N*o." I shook my head over and over. "Not Ivor. I've known him my whole life and he wouldn't rape anyone."

Dane said nothing but he watched me with that intense stare of his, the one where he seemed to be trying to read my mind.

I had to look away. "He wouldn't. He might have turned out to be a bully but he's not a danger."

"He wasn't always a bully?" he asked.

"No." I tried reconciling the man who'd argued with the stranger on the concourse yesterday with the one who'd brought me flowers as recently as a month ago. I gave up. Ivor had changed, but not as much as Dane was implying. "That's why the gates weren't opened for me. You're taking extra precautions in case Ivor returns."

"It's not just for him. Josie, did he..." He huffed out a breath and appealed to the sky. "Was there once something between you?"

"Ivor and me?" I barked a laugh. "Dear Hailia, no."

"The Deerhorn maid said you knew him. She thought perhaps that's why he was here, because he wanted to see where the woman he was courting spent some of her time."

I scoffed. "First of all, I haven't spent much time here of late. Secondly, we are certainly *not* courting and never have."

"Isn't he the man who brought you flowers that day?"

I plucked at the grass again. "He *wanted* to court me, but..." I shrugged.

"Go on."

My gaze flicked to his, only to dash away again when I noticed the intensity still there, deep in his eyes. "I'd rather spend my time reading medical books than talking to Ivor Morgrain. Does that answer your question?"

His lips twitched. "It does."

I lay down on the grass again and flung a hand over my eyes against the bright sunshine. "I cannot believe Ivor would flout security and stay on palace grounds without permission. He was a little wild a few years ago but most of the village boys were. They did stupid and dangerous things like jumping from cliffs into the sea. Sometimes I wonder how any of them survived to adulthood. But Ivor never broke the law."

"As far as you know."

I peeked at him from behind my arm. He shrugged at me. "Mull is—or was—a small village. I would have heard if he'd so much as been fined for urinating in public."

"People change, Josie."

I sighed. "People change, places change, everything changes."

"You don't like change?" He sounded concerned. Perhaps he thought he was about to have a weepy female on his hands.

"I don't like it when good things go bad. Not even Ivor, the fool." I lowered my arm and sat up again, this time making sure not to hit Dane. "You do realize it's a big leap from flouting palace security to rape, don't you?"

"I am aware, yes," he said wryly. "And I'm not saying he did it, just that he's a suspect."

"Very well. We'll include him, but I doubt he's guilty."

"Your opinion is noted. Indeed, I'm grateful for it. First hand knowledge of our suspects is valuable. If only someone can vouch for Lord Barborough's character." He leaned forward and dusted off his hands. "Don't forget your promise, Josie. You're not to question Morgrain. You're not to go anywhere near him. The main reason I gave you his name is so you can avoid him."

I bit my lip.

"I know that look," he said. "What is it?"

"I spoke to him only yesterday. He didn't mention coming here." I frowned as I tried to recall the conversation. "Although he did say he'd heard a rumor about me going to the palace revels. I assumed he'd spoken to one of the Deerhorn servants in the village, but perhaps he heard it here."

"It's likely." He stood and rested one hand on his sword hilt. "Promise you won't go near him again."

"I'll not go out of my way, but I can't help it if I bump into him again. Believe me, Dane, I am not interested in seeing Ivor."

There was that wan smile again when I said his name, the one that was like a ghost of itself, there one moment but gone the next, as if it had never existed.

He held out his hand to me. I took it and he assisted me to my feet. Neither of us let go, however. We stood toe to toe without moving, as if our feet were stuck in mud. I didn't want to move away.

I peered up at him and he down at me, giving me the full effect of his warm gaze as it searched mine. He leaned in a little and his finger brushed my wrist. It found my pulse and gently caressed. My blood quickened. My heart pounded, knowing what came next. Eager for it.

He pulled away and strode off, leaving me staring at his broad back. It took several moments before I was thinking clearly again, and by then, he'd reached the trees.

I picked up my skirts and raced after him. He did not wait but forged ahead, his long legs keeping him well in front on the path back to the palace.

"Dane..." How did a girl ask a man if she could explore the feelings she had for him, or the feelings she suspected he had for her? Every sentence in my head sounded pathetic. Besides, I'd be a fool to ask when I didn't know the answer. Going by his tense shoulders, his purposeful strides, he certainly did not want to discuss feelings.

By the time we reached the steps leading up one side of the semi-sunken garden, Dane had slowed down to keep pace with me. He still seemed tense and unwilling to meet my gaze, but I was prepared to pay that price *if* it meant he was angry with himself for having feelings for me. I wasn't entirely sure, but I now had some hope where before I had none. We had almost kissed, after all. I thought.

"Where will we find Lord Barborough now?" I asked, returning to a safer topic.

"He was in a meeting with the king when I came out to greet you. He might still be there."

We were hailed by Ruth as we walked past the commons, and I was pleased to see her smiling. On closer inspection, however, it didn't ring true, as if she'd plastered it on for our benefit.

"How are you today, Ruth?" I asked.

"Fine," she said.

"Do you need to see me?"

She glanced at Dane. He discreetly moved out of earshot. "I wanted to ask you a question." She lowered her voice. "When will I know if I'm with child?"

It was a question that most women over the age of fifteen knew the answer to. Without a memory, the lack of such basic knowledge made Ruth seem childlike, and that made the crime committed against her even more despicable. "In the coming weeks," I told her. "If your monthly courses stop, that's a sign. Send for me if that happens."

She hugged the folded linen in her arms. "Thank you, Miss Cully. I won't forget your assistance."

"You've been very brave." I squeezed her arm. "But you're going to have to be braver. We must tell the other maids so they can be more careful going about their work. We don't want this happening again."

She sucked in her lower lip and gave a small nod. "Do what you need to do. I'll be all right."

I gave her arm another squeeze and went to join Dane. Ruth followed me. "There's something I should tell you, Captain," she said.

"Do you remember something about your attacker?" he asked.

"It's not that. It's about Lord Barborough." At Dane's loaded silence, she added, "I know you think he might be the one who attacked me and that's why I've been reassigned, but I'm not sure. For one thing, his right arm doesn't work. Without it, he couldn't have done...that."

"Is there anything else?" Dane asked.

"I didn't mention this to you earlier because it was just before I was...before I was attacked and I forgot about it. But Lord Barborough questioned me over and over."

"About what?"

"About my past, where I'm from, that sort of thing. I didn't answer him. You told us not to speak about any of that, or our—" She cut herself off and glanced at me.

"You can speak freely," Dane said. "Miss Cully knows about the memory loss."

She hefted the pile of linens in her arms higher. "I heard Lord Barborough has been asking the footman who now cleans his rooms the same questions. He's been real pushy too, and getting angry when Jack didn't speak. The visiting staff used to ask lots of questions when they first came, but this is the first time a lord has asked. I thought you should know, Captain."

"Thank you, Ruth. You were right to tell me."

She bobbed a curtsy and hurried off in the direction of the palace service door, opposite the commons.

"It's confirmation that Lord Barborough still has an interest in magic," I said.

"And confirmation that he suspects magic was used here," Dane added. "And on us."

We too entered the palace through the service door and wound our way up a flight of stairs and along corridors, slipping into a richly decorated room. A lady seated at a table looked up from her hand of cards. She whispered something to her companion and both stared at me as I crossed the salon to the next chamber. I suspected their interest was a result of Lady Deerhorn telling them she'd seen me dressed in fine clothes on the night of the revels.

As with the last time I'd been in the council chambers in the main part of the palace, Theodore sat on one of the cushioned stools in the antechamber. He rose and greeted us both and pointed out Balthazar sitting in the adjoining office, both hands resting on the head of his walking stick. He signaled for us to join him.

"Forgive me for not rising to greet you, Josie, but I prefer to sit as much as possible. This old back is seizing up lately." He nodded at the doorway toward the ante-chamber. "If I sat on one of those stools, I'd never get up."

"You should have it checked by a doctor," I said. "He'll probably prescribe regular massage with a Lallak-based ointment."

"Do you stock the ointment?"

"Yes, but—"

"Then bring me some next time you come to the palace."

"But I—"

"She is coming again soon, isn't she, Hammer?" He tilted his head to the side to peer up at Dane.

"She'll be assisting me in an investigation," he said.

"Into the attack on Ruth? Is that wise, given she's a woman and therefore a potential target for the attacker?"

"Into the other, ongoing matter."

"Magic?" Theodore whispered. "Has there been a development? Do you know why we lost our memories, Josie?"

I silently groaned. I hadn't wanted to discuss magic with anyone other than Dane. In truth, it was Balthazar I didn't want knowing what we knew. It was too late now. He leaned forward, his hands tightening around the top of his walking stick.

"Not yet," Dane told them. "But Josie has made some inquiries and learned about the Zemayan beliefs."

"Only a little," I added.

"The Zemayans believe in an all-powerful sorcerer who seems to have been active centuries ago," Dane said.

"It could be merely a story," I said.

Dane went on to tell them about Lord Barborough and his interest in magic. "Is he still in there with the king?"

Theodore nodded. "They've been locked in there for an age with two of our own advisers."

"The dukes?" Dane asked.

Balthazar snorted. "Merdu, no. We wanted it to be a productive meeting, not an exercise in squabbling. The dukes have their own agenda and don't want to see Barborough succeed. The last thing they want is to make the king's position on the throne stronger by marrying him to the Vytill princess."

"They're not aware of this meeting?" I asked.

Balthazar shook his head. "They'll find out soon enough, but until then, we wanted it to take place in private."

"Hopefully it's the first meeting of many between Barborough and the king," Theodore said. "There'll be meetings with the representatives from Dreen too, to hear their proposals. Their princess is still a candidate."

I'd always thought being a princess would be glamorous and exciting, but the reality turned out to be the opposite. There was no glamor in a marriage between a princess and a king when it was discussed as coolly as if it were just another trade bargain between nations. I felt sorry for the two princesses in question. I felt even sorrier for the one King Leon chose as his bride.

"The dukes should have been included," Dane said.

Both Balthazar and Theodore looked at him in surprise. "Why?" Balthazar asked.

"Because they're the two most senior advisers and noblemen. They should be involved in the process to give it legitimacy."

"But they have a vested interest in the king not marrying either princess," Theodore said.

"It doesn't matter where their interest lies. They should have been invited and they'll be furious when they find out they weren't. It's easier to listen to their so-called advice than placate an angry pair of dukes."

"They would become just as angry when their advice is ignored," Balthazar said. "Angry now or angry later, it's all the same."

"Not unless their advice is proven to be weak and the alternative strong. In this case, no one with Glancia's best interests at heart will think marriage to a Glancian woman is a better alternative than marrying a foreign princess. They'll look greedy and selfish if they continue to push for marriage to a Glancian. Particularly Buxton, since he put forward his niece."

Theodore looked at the closed door to the council chamber. "You have a point, Hammer."

Balthazar merely tapped his finger against his walking stick. After a moment, he said, "What are you going to ask Lord Barborough?"

"Josie will ask the questions," Dane said. "It'll be less suspicious coming from her."

Theodore agreed. "We don't want him thinking *we* suspect magic is at play here."

"Josie?" Balthazar prompted. "What will you ask?"

"I hope he can give me a copy of his book so I can learn the basics of magical theory," I said. "If not, I suppose I'll ask him about a sorcerer and what he's capable of."

"What about a gemstone?" Theodore asked.

"What about it?" Dane said.

"Will you ask him why a red gemstone seemingly draws on the life force of others?"

I almost corrected him, telling him that it only pulsed in response to those who'd lost their memories, but kept my mouth shut. If Theodore was unaware of that, it meant Dane hadn't told him, and if Dane hadn't told him, he must have reasons.

I watched Balthazar very carefully to gauge his reaction but he showed no sign that he wanted to correct Theodore either. He did, however, seem very interested in my answer.

"I'll mention gemstones in a general sense," I told them.

"Speaking of the gemstone, where is it, Hammer?" Balthazar asked.

"Safe," was all Dane said.

"Why not tell us where?"

"It's safer for you if you don't know. We don't understand its power yet or its significance. If someone comes looking for it, then you can't be forced to give up its location if you don't know it."

"What about you, Hammer? Can't you be forced?"

Dane regarded him coolly. "I am less likely to succumb."

Balthazar's small smile was equally cool. "Are you sure about that? I'm an old man and have nothing to lose. Can you say the same?" He looked to me, catching me unawares. "What other questions will you have for Lord Barborough, Josie?"

It took me a moment to gather my wits. The exchange troubled me. I'd always thought Dane trusted Balthazar, but now I wasn't so sure. And if he didn't trust him, then it only firmed my own opinion.

C.J. ARCHER

"I also want to ask if it's possible for magic to make the impossible seem possible," I said.

"I see." Balthazar rubbed his palm over the walking stick head. "Like how an entire palace can appear out of thin air? How almost a thousand people can lose their memory at once?"

I smiled tightly at him. "Nothing so specific. I wouldn't want to alert him to what really happened here. I was thinking more about music and dancing."

"Music and dancing?" Balthazar's brittle chuckle ended in a dry cough.

I laughed too. "Yes, music and dancing. Like what was seen and heard at the revels."

"Ah, yes, I believe you witnessed it. So you enjoyed my little bit of theater?" He leaned forward, pressing heavily on the walking stick. "My little magic tricks?"

Theodore rolled his eyes. "Don't tease her. It wasn't magic, Josie, it was just clever machinations and well-trained acrobats."

"Machinations that no one saw and acrobats that neither arrived nor left the palace," I said.

"Good luck getting a straight answer," Dane muttered.

"No, no," Balthazar said, pushing himself to his feet. "She's right to question my methods. She's clever and inquisitive. I like that." He smiled at me. "But I'm not giving away my secrets."

"And I don't really think he used magic," I told them, smiling back. "If Balthazar could use magic, he'd have made a body for himself that worked perfectly."

Balthazar chuckled, his eyes twinkling. "Clever, inquisitive *and* witty. Add pretty into the mix and you're in possession of a diabolical combination of characteristics that will either ruin you or elevate you."

That wiped the false smile off my face.

"Don't listen to him," Dane told me. "He's just annoyed because he's old enough to be your grandfather."

"I'm annoyed because my back pains me." Balthazar dug his fingers into his lower back. "And this damned meeting has gone on too long. Theodore, shout 'fire' and let's end it."

Dane laughed softly.

"Balthazar!" Theodore threw up his hands. "I didn't think it possible, but you're even more cantankerous than usual."

Balthazar hobbled past us. "I'm going to my room. Let me know how the meeting turns out."

He got no further than the center of the ante-chamber, stopping directly beneath the domed ceiling as the dukes of Buxton and Gladstow stormed in, Buxton's cape billowing behind him.

"Stay here," Dane said to me.

I slipped behind the open door and watched through the gap.

"Are they in there?" Gladstow stabbed a finger in the direction of the council room.

Balthazar offered a shallow bow. "Yes, your grace."

Theodore stepped forward and bowed too. "His Majesty is in a meeting. If you'd like to wait—"

"I don't *wait*." Gladstow's face was always bullishly red but it seemed to glow with pent-up fury. If I were his doctor, I'd warn him against explosive fits of temper. At his age, and with his complexion indicating a diet of excess, he could damage his heart.

"Calm down," snapped another man just outside my line of sight. "There's no point getting mad at the help."

Balthazar's nostrils flared.

"You don't tell me what to do either, Buxton," Gladstow snapped back.

The duke of Buxton stepped into view. He wasn't as old as Gladstow. I pegged him to be middle-aged, going by the receding hair and soft jawline. He was shorter too and more slender with a partially hooded right eye that was most likely the result of a childhood disease known as droopy eye. I wondered if he was blind in that eye or if he was one of the lucky few who'd kept his sight. He didn't look quite as angry as Gladstow, but that could have been because the disfigurement gave him a permanently sorrowful expression.

Gladstow strode past Balthazar but Dane blocked his entry to the council room. "You can't go in," he said evenly. "You're welcome to wait." He indicated one of the many stools situated around the perimeter of the room. "Your Grace."

Gladstow drew himself up to his full height but he only came to Dane's chin. That didn't seem to concern him. He seemed quite unperturbed by Dane's superior physical presence. "Get out of my way," he growled.

"No."

Gladstow bristled. He took a moment to answer, as if he were trying to understand how someone could defy him. "I am the duke of Gladstow."

"I know," Dane said. "You're not going in."

The duke of Buxton clicked his tongue. "It's pointless, Gladstow, he's under orders."

"And I am ordering him to move!" Gladstow shouted. "I have every right to be in that meeting!"

"So do I, but I'm not making a scene and blaming the guard."

Gladstow went to charge past Dane, but Dane grabbed his arm and shoved him back. The duke looked as if he'd never been manhandled like that before. He tugged on his cuffs and thrust out his chin, causing the flesh underneath to shake.

"How dare you!" he spluttered.

Theodore shuffled forward, his hands pressed together. "Apologies, Your Grace. The captain should not have laid a hand on you."

"He should be whipped."

Balthazar went very still. Theodore swallowed heavily and stared down at his feet. Dane looked as if he hadn't heard or didn't care, but I knew better. A vein in his throat pulsed and his breathing became shallower. He was holding his temper in check, but only with considerable effort.

The door behind him suddenly jerked open and he stepped aside. "Enough!" the king snapped. "I'm in an important meeting and we can't hear ourselves over your tantrum, Gladstow."

Gladstow spluttered a protest as he bowed. "We have every right to be in there, sire. As your dukes and chief advisers—"

"You're not my *chief* advisers." The king indicated a stool. "Wait here until I summon you. Captain Hammer, you have my permission to do whatever is necessary to see that I'm not disturbed."

The king disappeared into the council room with a haughtier look on his face than when he'd emerged.

Gladstow thrust his hands on his hips and marched back and forth across the floor. "Insufferable," he muttered. "Intolerable."

The duke of Buxton swept his cape to the side and lowered

himself onto a stool with a flourish. "This isn't so bad," he said cheerfully. "The stool is comfortable enough if one doesn't lean back. Come join me, Gladstow. One gets a different perspective from down here."

Gladstow's top lip curled. I half expected him to snarl like a dog. Buxton merely chuckled at him, clearly enjoying poking the angry bear. There was certainly no love lost between these two. It was no wonder they'd plotted separately to take over the kingdom before King Leon was crowned. It amused the imp in me to see them both here, forced onto the same side yet still unable to get along. They were like two children who fought in the street yet had to team up against a bigger bully.

The door opened again and the duke of Buxton quickly rose. He aborted his bow when he saw that it wasn't the king but another man, carrying a large leather wallet tied with black ribbon.

"My lord Barborough," Dane said in a greeting that I suspected was more for my benefit.

The Vytill representative nodded at the two dukes who nodded politely if stiffly back. He was younger than I expected. I thought he'd be old, but he must have been mid-thirties at the most. He was dressed all in black, his thick brown hair swept off his forehead as if he'd been caught in a strong breeze. I found I couldn't stop staring at his right arm, trying to work out what might be wrong with it. Ruth had said it was useless and it certainly seemed that way, hanging at his side. I wondered if his fingers could move. They were neither withered nor scarred. The healer in me wanted to know the cause of its immobility.

The dukes of Buxton and Gladstow ignored Barborough and strode toward the meeting room door. Lord Barborough put out his left arm, blocking their way.

"His Majesty asked me to inform you both that he's not ready to receive you yet," Lord Barborough said with an apologetic shrug of his good shoulder.

"But the other Glancian advisers are in there," Gladstow blustered.

Lord Barborough merely shrugged again.

The duke of Buxton said nothing but any joviality he'd shown before had vanished. He looked in no mood to sit on a stool again and tease Gladstow.

Lord Barborough left the room, smirking. I emerged from behind the door, but Dane shook his head at me. It would seem he had to stay on guard. Balthazar and Theodore seemed more interested in finding out how the meeting went than questioning the Vytill representative about magic.

I stepped out from the office altogether, cast a glance at Dane and, ignoring another shake of his head, followed Lord Barborough.

"Who are you?" the duke of Buxton called after me. "Guard! Arrest that woman, she was eavesdropping!"

"Eavesdropping on what?" the duke of Gladstow sneered. "Everything important is going on behind *that* door."

"She's the daughter of the village doctor," Theodore said quickly. "She was attending Balthazar. He has a sore back."

"Where's her father?" Buxton asked. "She can't see patients on her own."

"He just stepped out," I heard Dane say.

It seemed neither duke knew that the local village doctor had died. I thanked Hailia for my good fortune and hurried after Lord Barborough. I didn't want to lose him along with the chance of finding out more about magic.

Yet even though I knew Dane could no longer see me, I felt his glare boring into my back. He had not wanted me to see Barborough alone. Not when he was a suspect in the rape of Ruth.

CHAPTER 6

$\mathcal{I}$ caught up to Lord Barborough in one of the salons where he'd stopped to talk to another gentleman. I stood demurely behind him and cleared my throat at a suitable lull in the conversation. Both men finally took notice of me, albeit cursorily.

"Yes?" Lord Barborough asked, sounding annoyed. "What is it?"

I bobbed a curtsy. "I heard you wrote a book, my lord. It's on a topic that interests me, and I'd like to discuss it with you, if you have the time."

His heavy lids lifted and he regarded me more thoroughly. "Accompany me into the garden." He gave his bemused companion a nod then led the way out.

We passed through room after room of opulence where lords and ladies conversed in small groups or played cards and games. Few looked up but those who did, frowned and nudged their companion.

"I think this is the way," Lord Barborough said to me as he we headed down a set of marble stairs. "The palace is so large. I lose my way all the time. I'm sure you're used to it, Miss…?"

"Cully. Josie Cully, my lord. No, I'm not used to it. I rarely see this side of it."

He smiled. "I'm sure. What are the service corridors like?"

"Quite dull by comparison. There's a considerable lack of gold."

He laughed softly. He wasn't nearly as stern as I first thought.

Perhaps it had been a façade, put on for the benefit of the other gentleman. Or perhaps he was eager to talk about magic.

We headed outside into the sunshine. Lord Barborough paused on the top step and used the height advantage to survey the gardens. Ladies and gentlemen strolled around each of the sections closest to the palace, some stopping to admire the flowers. From where we stood, they looked like exotic dragonflies in their colorful clothes and hats.

"Over there seems the least populated," Lord Barborough said. "We may have to go a fair way from the palace to be alone. You do want to be alone, don't you, Miss Cully?"

"I, er, perhaps if there's a garden where we won't be overheard but we can be seen."

We strode between the twin ponds then turned right. We passed more ponds, gardens and fountains to an avenue that led us further away from the palace. Instead of following it, we detoured onto yet another avenue that dissected a large lawn and led to a gate. I recognized the two guards manning it.

We followed another avenue running alongside the estate's wall until we reached yet more formal gardens partitioned into sections by gravel paths and bordered by chest-high hedges. Lord Barborough indicated I should walk ahead of him through a gap in one of the hedges to the garden beyond. A fountain sprinkled musically in the center, the water reflecting the sunlight in a rainbow of colors. Where many of the gardens closer to the palace displayed flowers, this one was all green. Lord Barborough invited me to sit on the stone bench seat nestled into one of the hedges.

I realized it was a mistake when I sat. I could no longer be seen from the avenue. I went to stand again, but Lord Baroborough sat down too. His smile was kind yet I didn't quite trust it.

"Tell me, Miss Cully," he began. "How did you hear about my book?"

"A woman in the village told me."

He frowned. "How did you know to ask her?"

"She's the widow of a Zemayan, so I hoped she'd know a little about magic from him."

His frown deepened. "Did someone direct you to her?"

"No."

"I'm a little confused. For one thing, I didn't think you were allowed in the village."

"You are confused, my lord. I'm from the village. I live there."

Silence, then, "I thought you were an off-duty palace maid." He looked longingly back toward the palace, as if he wished he'd never walked all this way with me.

"My father believed in magic," I said. "He tried to convince me, but I was skeptical. Until the palace was built, that is."

He set his leather document wallet on his lap then used his left hand to pull his right arm over the wallet to rest there instead of hanging by his side. After he let go, the right arm shifted a little, so he must have some movement in it. I wanted to ask him what had happened but didn't dare.

"If you're not a maid, why are you here?" he said.

"I'm a midwife. One of the maids needed my services."

"You have no bag."

"I left it in her bedchamber while I sought you out." I hadn't thought I'd be so good at lying, particularly to a lord. I even managed to meet his gaze.

He seemed to believe me. "You say you were skeptical about magic before the palace was built, Miss Cully. Does that mean everyone in the village thinks as you do, that magic is involved in its creation?"

"Some do."

"I heard that it appeared quite suddenly and was completed in mere weeks. Is it true that no builders were seen coming or going?"

"It's true. They didn't come through the village. Nor did the building materials."

He nodded slowly. "It certainly seems as though magic had a hand in it, yet it all seems very real to me." He knocked on the bench between us. "Solid stone. The buildings are real and the gardens are growing as gardens ought. The servants are fully functioning humans whose actions would imply they have independent thoughts."

"Is the sorcerer powerful enough to make an illusion look real?"

His lips twitched. "You seem to be under the impression I know the sorcerer personally."

I bit down on my snide retort. "You are an expert, my lord."

"I merely wrote a book on the things I heard in Zemaya. I never saw magic performed, I never met the sorcerer, although it wasn't for lack of searching. It's fifteen years since I was there. I was young at the time, only twenty, although I thought I knew everything there was to know about the world." He leaned closer to me and his gaze, shining with humor, darted across my face before finally settling on my mouth. "Except for magic."

"My lord," I said sharply. He glanced up and fidgeted with the ends of the ribbon tied around the wallet. "What if the events the Zemayans attribute to magic are just stories?"

"Perhaps they are. But is the strangeness surrounding the palace's existence just a story? *You* don't think so, Miss Cully, or you wouldn't be here. I don't think so either." He smiled. "So we have something in common."

I couldn't bring myself to return the smile. He had not leaned back but had actually shifted a little closer. I shuffled along the seat, away from him. "Then what is your expert opinion on the palace's existence, my lord? Did the sorcerer create it?"

"It certainly seems that way. I can't think of another explanation, can you?"

"Tell me about him."

"First of all, I think calling it a 'he' doesn't do it a service. According to the Zemayans, it transcends gender, just as it transcends nationality and race. It can take on any form—"

"Human form?"

"Of course. It's the favorite disguise." He winked. "How is it able to choose where and how to perform magic unless it walks among the people?"

"Why would it have chosen to create this palace for King Leon?"

"Ah. That is a very good question, Miss Cully, and I don't have the answer yet."

Yet. "Is that why you're here? To find out?"

"I'm here to make arrangements for His Majesty King Leon to marry the Princess Illiriya of Vytill," he said, his tone condescending, as if I were stupid not to know.

"Yes, but your king could have sent anyone. Why did he send you?"

His gaze narrowed. His mouth curved into a slow, wicked smile. "I see you're not just a pretty face. You're right, he wanted to send someone else but I put forward my case to represent his interests here. He chose me and here I am in this remarkable place." He stretched out his good arm to indicate the entire garden. "So far, I have not seen or felt any signs of magic."

"What signs?"

"I won't know what they are until I see them, but I know I would recognize them as signs when I do. Have you seen anything, Miss Cully?"

I blinked innocently back. "Nothing. No shimmering walls or moving doorways, if that's the sort of thing you mean."

"Precisely. You have caught on quickly."

"Perhaps the sorcerer hasn't left any signs."

"That's a possibility. That's why I also need to speak to the servants. They alone can shed some light on this mystery. Nobody seems to know where they came from before the palace was built. Unfortunately, the ones I've questioned have all been reluctant to speak to me." He regarded me again, taking in my face then going lower, lingering on my throat and breasts.

"My lord," I bit off.

He looked up and smiled wolfishly. "Yes?"

"Do you think the sorcerer can manipulate more than physical things?"

"What do you mean?"

"Can he manipulate someone's mind?"

He frowned. "I don't follow."

"Can the sorcerer make a person do something they don't wish to do? Or stop them from doing something?" It was the closest scenario to memory loss I could think of without alerting him to the servants' precise predicament.

"I suppose so. It's a sorcerer, after all."

It was hardly the definitive answer I wanted. I decided to change tactic, and bring the gemstone into the conversation. "Does the sorcerer work with a device?"

"Device?"

"An object that helps it work its magic."

"You mean a talisman. No, nothing like that. There are more to the stories, however."

"Tell me."

He smiled and tapped the side of his nose. "I'll tell you when you've done something for me." He chuckled at my disappointment. "Come now, Miss Cully, it's only fair that you help me when I've been very generous with my knowledge." He shifted closer. I was already on the edge of the seat with no more room to move. He stopped only when his thigh bumped mine.

"Please, my lord," I said loudly. "What do you want?"

"Shhh." He glanced around and leaned in. "Keep your voice down, Miss Cully. Do you want passersby to overhear us? This is dangerous talk."

"Dangerous!"

"Shhh," he said again. "Think on it. If the palace was built by magic, it must be at the behest of the king. If the two dukes find out the king uses magic, will they still want him as their king? Will they be able to trust him?"

"They won't be able to do anything about it if the king has the sorcerer in his pocket."

"They could kill him and take the sorcerer's power for themselves."

Now I understood the danger. I glanced around too, suddenly wondering if I'd made a mistake having this conversation with Lord Barborough. What if someone listened in? What if he reported me?

He licked his lips. "It's even more dangerous for me, of course, being a foreigner. But I'm willing to risk it to learn more. This opportunity may never come my way again, and I have to grasp it before I return home." His good hand reached out and snatched at the air in front of my face, making me blink. His right arm jerked but did not rise from his lap. He seemed to realize it and self-consciously pulled it into his body.

"If I can find the sorcerer," he went on, "I can learn more about it. This is a great opportunity for me, but I need your help."

"Pardon?"

"I need you to gather information. I want you to question the servants."

"I—I can't."

"Of course you can. You're a commoner too; they'll relate to you more than they do me. You're friendly and pretty." He winked. "The footmen will give up all their secrets if you ask nicely."

Ugh. If he was suggesting what I thought he was suggesting, then he didn't deserve my help. On the other hand, he wouldn't answer any more questions for me unless I agreed. That's why he'd been so willing to answer my earlier questions; he needed me. Now, we needed each other.

"Start with the maid you saw on your midwifery rounds," he said. "You have to go back to her room to get your bag, so why not ask her some questions while you're there. And if she's out, then look around her room."

"I can't do that."

He closed his hand over mine, trapping it on my lap. "Of course you can." He smiled. "If you don't steal anything, she can't accuse you of theft. Look for anything that tells you where she came from, what she was doing before the palace was built, that sort of thing. I feel as though the servants are key to this mystery."

It was the same theory Dane and I had, in a way.

"They're hiding something," Lord Barborough went on. "They must be, otherwise why not just answer my questions?"

I pulled my hand free. "Perhaps you frighten them."

He glanced at his limp arm, lying awkwardly on his lap. "Perhaps I do."

I could have told him that his infirmity didn't scare anyone, that it was his character that unnerved me, but decided against it. I wanted to get away as quickly as possible. "I'd best go now," I said, rising. "Ruth will be wondering why I haven't collected my bag."

He showed no flicker of recognition at her name. I wasn't sure if that meant much, however. Few lords would know the names of the maids who cleaned their rooms. Even if he'd attacked her, that didn't necessarily mean he knew her name.

I went to leave but he caught my wrist. His grip tightened, pinning me. "Don't back out of our agreement, Miss Cully," he said darkly. "You wouldn't want this conversation to reach the king's ear."

"You would also bring trouble on yourself," I pointed out.

"I have a reason to be wandering around the palace and gardens. *You* do not."

I swallowed heavily even though I wasn't convinced he would follow through on his threat. It could just be his way of making me do his bidding. "If I do this for you, I expect you to give me more answers about magic in return," I said.

He let me go and smiled. "We have an agreement."

I hurried off. It wasn't until I'd left the garden well behind and checked to see that he wasn't following before I rubbed my sore wrist. He might not have the use of one arm, but the arm that did work was very strong. Perhaps strong enough to overpower Ruth.

I saw Dane before he saw me. He stood on the top step outside the palace, his gaze scanning the vast patchwork of gardens spread before him. When he finally spotted me, he trotted down the steps and took my elbow. He continued to glance around, checking the faces of the nobles nearby as he steered me to the shadows near the palace.

"I've been looking everywhere for you," he said.

"Am I under arrest?" I asked as we walked close to the palace wall.

"No. Why?"

I glanced pointedly at his hand on my elbow. He let go. "My apologies. Where were you?"

"In one of the gardens." I nodded toward the avenue where I'd walked with Lord Barborough.

"Hardly anyone goes up there," he said.

"I noticed."

"I seem to recall asking you not to be alone with him. You should have made an excuse not to go that way."

"If I had, I wouldn't have learned as much as I did from him."

"Even so, I asked you."

"I don't recall agreeing. And anyway, he couldn't have harmed me. His right arm is useless, just as Ruth said." I did not tell him about Lord Barborough's strength. If I did, he'd never want me to be alone with him again, and the only way I could see us gathering more information about the sorcerer was to do just that.

"He's still a suspect," Dane said. "I have reason to believe his arm works perfectly."

"What reason?"

"The king claims he saw it move during their meeting."

"It seems to have some slight movement, but not much. Did he say to what degree it moved?"

"Just that it was a twitch here and there. Is it possible for a limb to have limited movement like that?"

"Yes, although I've never witnessed it myself."

After a moment, he said, "I'm still keeping him on my list of suspects. There's something about him I don't trust."

"With good reason."

He suddenly stopped and grabbed my hand. We were outside the theater built into the northern wing. Six giggling women emerged wearing wings attached to the shoulders of their gowns. Their eyelashes and lips were painted in shining silver and their hair was streaked with the same shimmering paint. Dane steered me further away, heading ever closer to the northern end of the palace.

"What did he do?" he growled.

"It was more what he threatened to do. I can't tell you here. We have to speak privately."

"Can you stay longer or do you need to get back?"

"I can stay. There's so little to do in the village, I welcome being here. I'd be bored otherwise."

"I thought you had babies to bring into the world and medicines to sell."

"I'm used to being busier."

We walked several more steps before he said, "If you need money—"

"I don't," I snipped off. "And don't insult me, please."

He paused in front of a door, regarded me closely through lowered lashes, then pushed it open. I entered and found myself in one of the palace's service corridors. I was beginning to think they all looked the same, with stone walls and floor, and flickering torches valiantly beating back the darkness.

"Where are we going?" I asked.

"The garrison. I thought you might need refreshments before returning home. You can wait there while I round up Balthazar and Theo. Brant is on duty."

"Do you have to inform Balthazar and Theodore? I'd rather have the conversation privately with you."

His pace slowed. "You can trust them, Josie."

"You used to say that about the king."

He stopped and rounded on me. The tip of his sword sheath scraped against the wall. The only other sound came from my sharp intake of breath.

"I never trusted him," he said. "I couldn't admit it to you at first. But Balthazar and Theodore I do trust." The torchlight flickered in his eyes, giving him a sinister air. "Everything you tell me in private will be told to them anyway, so they may as well join us."

I folded my arms against the chill sliding through my veins. I wanted to diffuse the tension but I could think of only one way. "Everything?" I asked breathily.

Dane set off again, his strides long. "Almost everything," he muttered.

I smiled at his back.

CHAPTER 7

*O*ur entry into the garrison caused a flurry of activity. A guard with his feet resting on the table withdrew them and sat up straight. Max stood and greeted me civilly. Quentin drew me into a hug. I laughed and hugged him back.

"Quentin!" Max barked. "That is not the way a palace guard behaves toward a guest."

"She's not a guest. She's a friend." Quentin pulled away but his bright smile didn't fade. "Can I pour you some ale, Josie? There's some bread and cheese too." He eyed the crumbs on the table. "Or there was."

One of the guards mumbled around a mouthful of food and patted his bulging stomach.

Quentin shook his head. "The pigs eat less than they do."

Dane slipped out again after exchanging a few quiet words with Max and Max pulled out a chair for me.

"Your lip is healing nicely," I said to Quentin as he handed me a cup of ale.

"Aye," he said, shooting a glare toward Max.

"And how is your shoulder?" I asked the sergeant.

"Fine," Max said and rolled it to prove it. His small wince of pain wasn't lost on me, however.

"What's going on? Why are you both acting oddly?"

C.J. ARCHER

"No reason," Quentin said quickly. "So why are you at the palace this time?"

"Quentin!" Max growled. "She's not here to exchange idle gossip with the likes of you."

"I was just asking." Quentin slumped in his chair with a pout. "How am I supposed to learn if I don't ask her questions?"

"Learn what?" I asked.

"Doctoring."

"You want to become a doctor? That's wonderful."

"Aye, but I can't go to college." He kicked the empty chair opposite.

"There will be a way around the entrance rules. Perhaps the captain can give you a reference instead of a local sheriff or nobleman. Surely a reference from one of the king's closest servants will suffice."

"It ain't that. We can't leave here. Not until we have our memories back. Captain's orders."

"He does have a point," I said gently. "You must stay together until you find out what happened to you."

"What if we never find out?" asked one of the other guards. "What if we never get our memories back? Will we have to stay here forever?"

He wasn't the only one thinking it, going by the nods and sighs. Even Quentin's doubts were written all over his spotty face.

"I don't want to be a guard forever, Josie," he mumbled. "I hate it. I ain't very good at it."

"Aye," several voices chimed in.

"You've got to stop listening to Brant," Max said to the men. "He's stirring up trouble, asking a lot of questions," he told me.

"He's only asking the questions we all want answers to," one of the guards said.

"We have to trust the captain. He, Theodore and Balthazar are getting closer to learning more about us."

"I trust Hammer," the guard said. "But I wish he'd tell us what he knows. I don't like being left out."

The others agreed.

I couldn't argue the point with them. I would feel the same way. If they knew Dane confided in me more than he did them, they would be even more disappointed. "Have patience," was all I said. "For now, stay together. It's safer. Quentin, you understand, don't you?"

"Aye," he mumbled into his chest.

"And when the mystery of your memory loss is solved, you can go to Logios knowing who you are. In the meantime, perhaps you can pick up some medical knowledge to give you a head start over the other students."

His face lifted. "Will you teach me?"

"She will *not*," Max snapped. "You know she ain't allowed, so don't ask her."

Quentin resumed his pouting.

Erik entered the garrison and hung up his sword and belt by the door. "Josie! Welcome." He embraced me in big, sweaty hug then clapped my shoulders. "Why you in here with these stinky men?"

"It didn't smell until you came in," Quentin mumbled.

Erik lifted his arm and smelled his pit. "I smell good." He shoved his armpit into Quentin's face. "See?"

Quentin pulled back, choking and spluttering. "I hate you."

Erik laughed. "You love me. Everyone loves Erik. Especially the maids." He winked at me. I couldn't help smiling. The Marginer was nothing like how I expected one of his kind to be. He was friendly and breezy, not backward and prone to squabbling.

"The maids just like you because you tell them they're the prettiest," Max said. "Problem is, you tell *all* of them they're the prettiest."

Erik saluted him with a tankard of ale. "They are all pretty to me. But that is not why they like me." He drank the ale and we waited in hushed silence for his explanation. When he finished, he wiped his mouth with the back of his hand and pronounced, "They like me because my little friend is big and strong."

"Little friend?" I asked.

"Don't say it!" Max cried.

Erik grinned and winked at me again.

I groaned. I should have guessed.

The other men chuckled into their cups. Quentin laughed but

turned bright red. I felt my own face heat, but fortunately no one looked at me. Except for Erik.

"Talking of my little friend," he said. "I will show you something, Josie." He set his tankard on the table and fumbled for the fastening on his breeches.

"No!" Max leaped out of the chair and tackled Erik to the floor. "Keep your breeches on unless you want the captain to kill you."

Max got off and Erik sat up. "Aye, I forgot," Erik said to me. "Hammer says you will go to jail if we ask you healing questions."

Max put out a hand to help Erik to his feet. "That isn't the only reason he'll kill you."

"What if Josie wants to see it? Josie, you ask me if you do, eh? I will show it to you."

Max sighed. "We've told you before, Erik, you can't say that to women. "

"Don't say it to men either," Quentin added. "I don't want to see your *little* friend."

"I only show maids who *want* to see it," Erik said. "I want to show Josie because she is healer and my little friend has grown a lump."

Max and the other guards pulled faces. One of them threw the wedge of cheese he'd been nibbling onto the table. Quentin asked Erik to describe the lump. After he did so, I told him I'd bring an ointment next time I visited. Erik looked pleased. Max looked relieved the conversation was over.

"If the captain overheard this, he wouldn't be happy," he said.

The door opened and the captain paused on the threshold. He eyed each of us in turn, his frown deepening when he got to me. "Why are you all looking at me strangely? What happened?"

"Nothing," Max said, pouring ale into a cup. "Nothing, Captain. Everything's fine." He handed the cup to Dane.

"Josie?"

I wasn't going to get away with repeating Max's words. Dane wouldn't be satisfied unless I gave him an answer. "Erik tried to show me his little friend but was reminded that I'm not allowed to perform medical tasks."

Dane's brows rose higher and higher with each word.

"And she didn't want to see it for fun either," Quentin added with a snicker.

"She might," Erik said, sounding put out.

"Not until the lump heals," Quentin muttered into his cup.

Dane regarded each of his men with a measure of bemusement. "Does 'little friend' mean what I think it means?"

"Aye." Erik sniffed. "That is the best translation I know for it. Why?"

"It's ridiculous," Quentin told him.

"Then I give it a name. I call it Quentin."

The other guards burst out laughing. Erik grinned while Quentin flushed again. Max groaned and shooed me out of the room.

"Take her away before these fools embarrass us further," he said to Dane.

Dane looked like he was trying not to laugh as we walked along the corridor toward Balthazar's office. "I apologize for their behavior," he said. "It was immature and unnecessary."

"True on both counts, but it's all right. I imagine that's what it's like to have brothers."

He didn't respond, and I suddenly felt awful. My thoughtless quip might make him long to learn about his forgotten family. A sideways glance in his direction proved he was still smiling, however.

He pushed open Balthazar's door without knocking. Balthazar sighed but did not mention the impoliteness. He merely indicated I should sit in the spare chair beside Theodore. With no other chairs, Dane had to stand.

Balthazar clasped his knotty hands on the desk in front of him and regarded me. "Tell us how your conversation with Lord Barborough went."

I told them about the sorcerer and how Zemayans believe it disguises itself in human form, and how it can manipulate people's thoughts. "It might explain why you have no memories," I said, watching Balthazar closely. "The sorcerer removed them."

"But why?" Theodore asked to no one in particular.

"Go on, Josie," Balthazar said.

I spoke directly to him so I could gauge his reactions. "He

thought I was a servant at first, which explained why he readily agreed to meet with me. After I informed him I wasn't, he wanted to know what the villagers thought about the palace. I told him some believed in magic and some were skeptical. He also admitted to petitioning his king to send him here instead of the original adviser so he could study the palace. He believes the staff are key to solving the mystery of the palace's existence."

"Did you tell him about the memory loss?" Balthazar asked.

"Balthazar!" Theodore protested.

"You know she wouldn't," Dane added.

Balthazar unclasped his hands and shrugged. "I had to ask."

"No, you did not. Go on, Josie," Dane said. "What else?"

"I did not tell him about the memory loss," I said with a pointed glare at Balthazar. "I also didn't mention the gemstone, but I did ask if the sorcerer uses a device when he performs magic. He called it a talisman." Balthazar nodded knowingly. "Barborough claimed the sorcerer doesn't, but his answer was rather ambiguous."

"Ambiguous?" Theodore asked.

"He said there are more to the stories, but that's all he would tell me. If I want to know anything else, I have to help him."

"Help him?" Dane prompted.

"He wants me to spy on the staff for him. He thinks I'll gain their trust easier than he can."

"What things are you supposed to report back?" Balthazar asked.

"Anything suspicious that points to the use of magic. He suspects the staff are the key to solving the mystery. I'm sure he'd be very interested in hearing about your memory loss."

"Very," Balthazar bit off.

"What if we told him?" Theodore asked on a rush of breath. "He seems knowledgeable on the subject of magic. What if he can help us?"

"No," Dane said, at the same time Balthazar said, "We can't trust him."

"But—"

"No!" Dane shook his head. "Not yet, Theo. Not until we know more about him. He could use the knowledge against Glancia and against Leon."

Theodore sighed.

Balthazar tapped his steepled fingertips together and regarded me. "So you must help him in order to get more information. Hmmm."

"What would you like me to tell him?" I asked. "What *can* I tell him?"

"Inform him that you tried to extract information from us but we wouldn't tell you anything about our pasts."

"He'll just tell me to try again until I do get answers. He has already asked me to look through Ruth's things."

Balthazar continued to drum his fingertips together in thought until he suddenly stopped. "Tell him nothing. We don't need him. All the answers are supposed to be in the book he wrote. We'll simply find a copy. Someone will have it. Hammer, Theo, make inquiries." He picked up a letter on his desk and began to read it.

"I can't tell him that," I said.

He peered at me over the paper. "Why not?"

"Because he threatened to tell the king that I suspect magic is involved in his ascension to the throne. Since I was seen leaving the palace to talk to Lord Barborough in private, it will be difficult to refute his claim."

Dane swore. "I knew I should have gone with you."

"The king won't like it," Theodore said simply. "He won't like her prying."

"Thank you for stating the obvious." Balthazar set down the paper very deliberately and clasped his hands again. "We'll think of something for you to pass on to Lord Barborough, Josie, a false piece of information that only one of us could have told you. In the meantime, you should be seen talking to various staff members. You may start with Hammer while he escorts you to the coach house. Perhaps you can begin by asking him where he has hidden the gemstone." He shot a pointed glare in Dane's direction.

Dane pushed off from the sideboard. "We've been through this. It's for your own safety."

Or was it because he didn't completely trust them, just like he hadn't trusted the king all along?

"We should be told, Hammer," Balthazar went on. "What if something happens to you? Who will know its location?"

Dane opened the door for me. "My ghost will tell you."

"This isn't a joke."

"I'm not telling you, Balthazar. That's final."

Balathazar picked up the paper again, muttering under his breath.

I followed Dane out, leaving Theodore behind with the crotchety master of the palace. "Has Brant asked about the cabinet?" I asked Dane. "He touched it in Laylana's room and felt the pull of the gem so he must suspect there's something odd about it."

"He has asked," Dane said. "He was informed it was a personal belonging of the king's and none of his business."

"That will guarantee he doesn't ask more questions," I said wryly.

"What would you have said?"

I shrugged. "I would have told him he must have been mistaken, that he felt nothing since it was simply a cabinet filled with valuables the king wanted to keep safe."

"That's more or less what I said."

"I do think it's rather more, but let's not argue over it."

He grunted a laugh. At least, I thought it was a laugh. "I don't want you left alone with Barborough again," he said.

"I don't plan to be."

"As to Balthazar's idea that you'll pretend to spy for Barborough, I don't want you doing that, either. Barborough could follow through on his threat if he discovers you're feeding him false information."

I'd worried the same thing but had been prepared to go through with it in exchange for answers about the sorcerer. "Why didn't you say that to Balthazar?" I asked.

"If you're thinking it's because I don't trust him, you're wrong."

"Then answer my question. Why didn't you tell him?"

His strides lengthened. "It's easier to ignore his suggestions than argue with him. I learned that the hard way."

I didn't press him further. He'd made it clear that if he didn't trust either Balthazar or Theodore, he wasn't going to tell me.

We left the palace through the service entrance opposite the square commons building. Visiting footmen and maids greeted Dane by name as they passed, whereas it used to be just the palace staff that did so. He'd become a well-known figure in recent weeks.

"Do you think Barborough did it?" he asked quietly, with a nod at Ruth chatting to another maid as they carried linens into the commons. "Do you think him capable?"

"Physically? It's difficult to tell if his arm works or not. I'm inclined to think it doesn't, that it merely twitches from time to time yet isn't functional. If he had two functioning arms, however, he'd certainly be high on my list. There's something about him. Something I find disturbing."

I felt his sharp gaze on me. "What did he do?"

"It was more in the way he looked at me and how he threatened me. I'll gladly avoid him in future."

"I'll keep an eye on him."

"You'll need a lot of eyes to watch all of the people you're supposed to be watching—Brant, Barborough and the other suspects."

"I'll have help." He pointed a finger at me. "But not from you."

I held up my hands in surrender. "I assured you I would stay out of Barborough's way."

"And Ivor Morgrain's."

I saluted him.

He merely grunted. This time it definitely *wasn't* a laugh.

"Captain!" one of the guards called as he jogged up to Dane. "Captain, the king requires your attendance."

"Why?"

"He didn't say, sir."

Dane hesitated.

"Go," I told him. "I can organize a carriage home."

Dane looked as if he wanted to say something but thought better of it. He left with the guard. It wasn't until he was out of view that I realized we hadn't arranged to meet again. There was no *need* for us to meet again.

Unless I devised a reason.

For half the distance to the coach house, I thought of scenarios that would bring me to the palace again. For the other half, I wondered if Dane didn't want to see me. He had not asked to do so, after all. He hadn't even looked back after walking away.

I was entirely lost in my own thoughts and didn't see Lord Xavier Deerhorn until it was too late. He stepped into my path, and I didn't stop quickly enough. I trod on his toes.

"Watch it!" he snapped.

"Sorry," I said, adding a curtsy for good measure. "I didn't see you."

"You did it deliberately."

"No, my lord, I did not." I met his gaze then wished I hadn't. His eyes were so pale they were almost colorless. Looking at them was like looking through a veil of ice to barrenness beyond.

He caught my elbow and squeezed, hard. "You did. Admit it."

"I did not, sir. Let me go or I'll shout until the guards come."

His grip weakened but not enough for me to withdraw. I struggled and received another bone-crunching squeeze for my efforts. "Go ahead. I'll tell them I caught you sneaking around *again*."

"I am not sneaking. The captain of the guards knows I'm here."

"It's true," Lady Deerhorn said, approaching. Both dressed in riding capes and high black boots, mother and son looked remarkably similar. They were both tall and fair with an arrogant lift of the chin and a high arch of the brow. "She's fucking him," she added.

I opened my mouth to protest but shut it again. It might make it easier to get away if they thought it true. Indeed, Lord Xavier released me. Perhaps he was scared of incurring Dane's wrath.

He looked at me anew, however, and I shivered. It was the same way some men look at another man's possession—with calculated envy as he plots a way to win it at cards.

I rubbed my elbow and went to push past them but Lady Deerhorn stepped in my way. She didn't grab me as her son had, but she made it very clear she wasn't going to let me pass until she'd said her piece. Her chin lifted even higher as she regarded me down her nose.

"The king was very interested to hear that you'd tricked your way into the revels," she said. "He was most upset with your duplicity. I'm sure he'll be even more upset when he hears how you're distracting his staff from their duties."

I bit down on my retort. I couldn't tell her about Ruth, Lord Barborough, magic or any of the reasons why I was at the palace. If she chose to speak to the king, then hopefully he would ask Dane or Theodore for an explanation. He was sensible enough to do that instead of listen to the nastiness spread by Lady Deerhorn. I hoped.

I tried to maneuver around her but she stepped in my way again. She smiled at my growing frustration. Her son chuckled.

"Kindly allow me to pass," I said, doing my best to keep that frustration from spilling into my tone. "I have important medicines to make at home. I cannot tell you what it's for, but do feel free to mention my visits here to the king. Don't be too put out when he doesn't look surprised."

Her mouth flattened and a forest of tiny lines formed across her top lip.

"Miss Cully?" asked a woman behind me. "Miss Cully, is that you? Look, Miranda, it *is* her. How delightful."

I turned to see Lady Miranda Claypool and Kitty, the duchess of Gladstow, walking toward us along the avenue from the palace. Miranda let go of the duchess's arm and hurried toward me.

"Is everything all right?" she asked.

"Of course," Lord Xavier said cheerfully. He bowed deeply. "You look as radiant as the sun, Miranda."

"Josie?" she prompted.

Lord Xavier's smile faltered at her snub.

"Everything's fine," I assured her. "I was just leaving."

She didn't look convinced. "We'll wait with you. Have you organized a carriage?"

"Not yet."

"Then we shall have to correct that." A wicked gleam lit up her eyes. "Lord Xavier, would you be so kind as to ask a groom to see that a carriage is made ready to take Miss Cully to the village."

He blinked slowly, and I could almost hear his mind searching for an appropriate response. He clearly wanted the attention of the very beautiful Miranda, yet running errands for me was beneath him.

Like many weak men who can't make up their minds, it was

his mother who stepped in. "My son has better things to do," Lady Deerhorn said crisply.

"Oh? He seemed to be just standing about, conversing with Miss Cully. I thought he might like to do something for her since he seems so interested in her."

"Interested!" he blurted out. "In the village girl!" He snorted. "My dear, Miranda, you are misinformed. She's nothing to me. I hardly know her. I don't even *wish* to know her. If she hadn't trodden on my toes, I wouldn't have stopped at all."

"Very well, I shall see that a carriage is organized for my dear friend myself. Good day."

"Wait! Don't go!"

"But I must. My friend needs my assistance."

"I'm sure she can do it herself. These village girls are very capable, you know. I once saw one carrying a crate filled with dead, stinking fish all by herself." He wrinkled his nose as if he could still smell them. "Would you do me the honor of walking back to the palace with me, Miranda? Both of you," he added for the duchess's benefit.

"Kitty and I are going riding," Miranda said.

"I love riding. I'd be happy to keep you company."

His mother rolled her eyes skyward.

"We don't require any company but our own," the duchess of Gladstow said.

Lord Xavier ignored her and addressed himself to Miranda. "There may be undesirables in the woods. You should have a man to protect you."

"Yes, you're right," Miranda said with utter seriousness. "We'll take a groom with us. Thank you for the suggestion."

Lord Xavier stiffened, finally feeling the barbs she'd been flinging at him.

"For Merdu's sake, Xavier," Lady Deerhorn hissed. She steered him away and bent her head to his. Perhaps she thought we could no longer hear her. It was the only explanation for what she said next. "She may be pretty but she's no longer the king's favorite and she's debasing herself by associating with that village girl. There are more important conquests to be had elsewhere."

Miranda remained remarkably calm and did not say a word, but my blood boiled. It was the duchess who spoke, however.

"Yes, run along, both of you."

Lady Deerhorn's step faltered. "Your Grace?"

"Be warned, madam, insult me again and my husband *will* hear about it." I had never heard her sound so imperial. The silly girl-ishness was replaced with ice. She even looked more commanding. She regarded Lady Deerhorn down her nose the way that lady had regarded me.

Lady Deerhorn stood quite still, her unblinking gaze on the duchess, perhaps wondering where the silly girl had gone.

"B—but my mother didn't insult *you*," Lord Xavier spluttered.

"An insult to either of my two friends is an insult to me," the duchess bit off. "Good day, sir, madam."

Lady Deerhorn dipped into a deep curtsey, keeping her head demurely bowed. "Forgive us, Your Grace. We've lived so long out here, away from the civilized world of Tilting and the old king's court, we've forgotten how to behave in fine company." She rose, grabbed her son's elbow, and pulled him away from us.

We watched them hurry off without waiting for a sedan chair to collect them.

"Well then, that's that," the duchess said with a toss of her head that set her blonde curls into a bouncing frenzy. "Being a duchess has its uses after all."

"It certainly does," I said, no longer sure if I'd been treating her with enough deference. I decided to curtsy too. If Lady Deerhorn thought it necessary, then it must be the done thing. "Thank you for intervening, Your Grace."

"Oh, don't curtsy for me, you lovely thing. Leave that for the sycophants like the Deerhorns." She hooked her arm through mine and we set off for the coach house.

Behind us, Miranda broke into giggles.

"I don't know what you find so amusing," the duchess said over her shoulder. "You've got Lord Xavier to contend with now. He seems to have taken a liking to you."

"Ugh," Miranda said, joining us. "I wish the king would banish him from court so we didn't have to put up with him."

"I know a way to stop his attentions," the duchess said lightly. "It's the reason he shows no interest in me."

"Go on," Miranda said.

"Get married."

Miranda pulled a face. The duchess and I laughed.

* * *

I WAS STILL SMILING when the carriage deposited me outside my house at dusk. I thanked the coachman and considered heading across the street to see Meg but decided against it. It had been a long day, and I ought to do the housework I'd been putting off.

The house felt strange without my father. I doubted I'd ever get used to it. I paused outside his workroom and regretted tidying it up after his death. He liked clutter and disorder, with his books only an arm's-length away. Now the desk was bare except for the thin layer of dust covering it. I rarely went in. I didn't like the emptiness of it.

I sighed but my breath caught. My heart leapt. I was not alone. I don't know what alerted me—a footstep or a creaking board? Whatever the sound, it had been small and fleeting, and it came too late to warn me.

I had no time to react before a hand clamped over my mouth and an arm wrapped around my waist from behind, pinning my arms to my sides. I was pulled back hard against a man's body. Hot breath ruffled my hair and a rapid heartbeat hammered against my shoulder blades. I struggled but he was too strong. I screamed but it came out muffled.

He found that amusing. His chuckle chilled me to the bone.

"It's about time you showed up," Brant said. "I'm glad you're alone, Josie. Very glad."

CHAPTER 8

did not struggle. Brant would like that. He wanted me to fight against him and perhaps expected it. So I simply stood there and waited for him to make the next move. When he let me go, I'd do whatever I could to escape. If he wanted me for his next victim, he was going to have to render me unconscious or kill me first.

"You're shaking," he said and chuckled again. "You ain't so brave now that you're at my mercy." He rubbed his nose along the back of my ear and breathed deeply. The arm wrapped around my waist momentarily tightened before relaxing. Not enough for me to free myself, however. "I know what you're thinking, Josie, but that ain't why I'm here. I don't want that prick's used goods. I want to talk to you, that's all. Can I let you go and we talk without you screaming? Or do we have to stay like this? Either way, it don't matter to me. So can I?"

I had a better chance of escape if he let me go so I nodded. He slowly released me only to push me in the back.

"Kitchen," he ordered. "You're going to be a good girl and feed me."

I folded my arms across my stomach. "I don't have much in the larder."

"You got ale and bread. I already checked." He shoved me again and I led the way to the kitchen.

He stood by the door, his hand resting on his sword hilt, and watched as I poured ale into a cup and set out the bread on a board. "And one for yourself," he said, taking the cup.

I poured myself a small amount of ale. He waited until I sipped before he drank too. I don't know why he thought I'd poison my own ale.

"What do you want?" I asked.

He pulled out a chair from the table and indicated the other. "Sit. Let's have a discussion like civilized people."

"You're not a civilized person, Brant."

He smirked. "Careful. That tongue of yours will get you into trouble. There's only so much I'll put up with from you."

I bit the inside of my cheek.

"Now, sit down. Please."

I sat but not too close to the table. He finally sat too. He slowly sipped his ale, watching me over the rim of the cup, until he finished it all and set the cup down. He broke off a corner of cheese and ate it without taking his gaze off me. The silence stretched to snapping point. I dug my nails into my palms and waited.

"This is pleasant," he said. "Two people sitting over food and drink, talking."

"What do you want, Brant?"

"I want to know why you were at the palace today."

I held his gaze steady. "To visit my friends."

He snorted. "You think Hammer is you friend? He doesn't have friends. He's using you. You're his link to the outside world, the world beyond the palace. He needs you to do his dirty work in the village."

"A nice theory except he hasn't asked me to do anything for him. No spying, no searching for evidence, nothing. There's nothing more to our relationship than simple friendship. But it's not only him I went to the palace to see. I wanted to see Max and Quentin, Theodore, and Lady Miranda too."

He checked his cup. Seeing it empty, he rapped it on the table as if it were a tavern and I the serving wench.

"Would you like some more?" I asked.

He grunted.

"I'll take that as a yes." I filled his cup and gave it back.

Instead of drinking, he cradled the cup in his hands. "I know Hammer confides in you."

"He told me about the memory loss, but you already knew that. So?"

"So what else has he told you?"

"Nothing. Is there more to tell?"

"You know there is," he spat. "Don't pretend. You know about the cabinet."

"Cabinet?"

"I said, don't pretend!" His nostrils flared and the knuckles around the cup whitened. "The cabinet in Laylana's room. There was something in it. What was it?"

"I don't know. He didn't tell me."

He thumped his fist on the table. "He must have!"

I swallowed and dared shake my head. "No, he didn't. Not specifically, anyway. He just said it contained something valuable belonging to the king. I assumed jewelry or gold."

He scoffed. "You're not this stupid, Josie. You ain't no fool. There was something in that cabinet. Something...alive."

I frowned. "Alive?"

He nodded, all the anger dissolved. He looked unsure, confused, exactly how I expected a man without a memory to look. A small part of me felt sorry for him. The rest of me was revolted.

"Like it had a heartbeat," he went on.

"Go on," I urged.

He shrugged. "I felt it when I held that cabinet. When I let it go, I couldn't feel it no more."

"I didn't hold it," I told him. "And the captain didn't mention a heartbeat to me, or feeling anything odd about the cabinet."

"He wouldn't, would he?" he said, his voice rising again. "He doesn't want anyone else to know about it. That's what I'm trying to tell you. He's keeping secrets."

I put up my hands to calm him down again. "That may be, but I can assure you, he's not confiding those secrets in me. To him, I am an outsider," I said, studying the table surface. "If he has something to hide, I'm the last person he'll confide in." I looked up again. "But I don't think he's hiding anything. Not from any of you, that is. You're all in this predicament together, and I do know him well enough to know he's not so cruel as to keep important information about your memories from you."

"You think that, eh?" He slouched into the chair, taking his cup with him. He cradled it against his chest between both hands. "I think he's lying. I think he knows the reason we lost our memories. I think he and the king both know and they're in it together."

"That's absurd. Why would you say that?"

"Because everyone from the village says magic was used to build the palace, and now the servants do too. The palace must be linked with our memory loss. It *must* be. And who benefits from this magic? The king, that's who."

"If you're blaming the king, then why include the captain?"

"Because he's close to the king. Maybe Theo and Balthazar are involved too." He suddenly leaned forward and stabbed his finger at me. "Don't say a word of this to anyone."

"I won't, but you should be careful. Don't spread those rumors or the wrong person might overhear you. If you're suggesting the king gained the palace and throne through magic, that's treason."

"I didn't say the throne. *You* did." He sniffed and drank down his second cup of ale. With a belch, he set the cup down. "I will find that cabinet. I've searched part of the palace already, so seems I'll just keep going, room by room."

When did he find the time to search the palace? He was either on duty with a partner or in the garrison or training yard. I doubted he snuck around at night. Sleeping servants would wake if he went into their rooms, and he was at risk of being caught by the guards on night duty if he entered the salons. He must do it during the day, and the best time for him to do that without Dane or Max noticing him gone was when he was supposed to be on duty. His partner must be lying for him.

And if his partner was lying, that meant Brant's whereabouts at the time of Ruth's rape could not be reliably accounted for.

I swallowed the bile burning up my throat and covered my mouth with my hand.

"You see it now, don't you?" he sneered. "You see how Hammer is in on it."

"Pardon?" I managed.

"Hammer, and maybe Theo and Bal. Definitely the king. You

can't trust the captain, Josie. You understand me? He's been lying to you, just like he's been lying to the rest of us."

I shook my head. "I—I don't think he has answers about your memory loss, Brant."

He slammed his fist on the table, making me jump. "Are you blind? You think because he's handsome and charming that he cares about you? You stupid women are all the same. You think the ugly men are the ones you got to be careful of. Well sometimes the handsome ones are just as mean, maybe meaner. Hammer ain't always the fine fellow he pretends to be with you. I've seen him almost kill someone with his bare hands."

"The prisoner in the cells?"

"Does it matter who? The point is, he can be all nice one minute and violent the next. He can turn like that." He snapped his fingers. My nerves jangled. "You be careful, Josie. Girls like you fall easy for men like him, then it's too late when their true nature comes out."

"And men like you are innocent and sweet?"

"I never claimed to be innocent. I never tried to be your friend or be something I ain't. I'm just passing on some advice from someone who knows Hammer better than you. Choose your friends carefully." He stood slowly, picked up the cup then slammed it down on the table. I could only guess that it was done to highlight his point. "Thanks for the ale."

I followed him to the door and locked it behind him when he left. I slumped against it. My nerves still felt fragile, and my hands shook. No matter what Brant said, I would never trust him over Dane.

It wasn't until I returned to the kitchen and tidied up that I wondered how he'd got in. I'd *unlocked* the front door when I arrived home, and the back door was still locked firmly. Somehow he'd got in and re-locked one of them. No kind-hearted soul worried about my welfare would do that.

* * *

I SLEPT FITFULLY. The smallest sound woke me, from the drunken singing in the distance to the creak of the rafters settling after a warm day. My sleeplessness meant I was awake at dawn when someone knocked. Compared to the other sounds, it was loud.

I threw a shawl around my shoulders and called out through the door. "Who is it?"

"Gill Swinson. Josie, you have to come with me. Something's happened."

I unlocked the door and invited Gill in but he shook his head. He clutched his hat, screwing it tightly in his fists. He looked pale in the early morning sunlight. Too pale.

"What's happened?" I asked.

"It's Ingrid. She...she needs you."

I'd known the fisherman and his family my entire life, although I'd never been particularly close with Ingrid, his daughter, four years my senior. I hoped he would understand. "I can't," I told him. "I'm not allowed to—"

"I don't care!" He thumped his fist into the wall then spread his fingers wide, as if reaching for some patience. "I'm sorry, Josie, but you have to come. There's no one else. It's women's business anyway."

"Pregnancy?"

He leveled his gaze with mine. I'd never seen such worry in this jovial man before, or such anger. "Just come. Please."

"I'll fetch my bag." I dressed quickly and grabbed my pack from the kitchen larder, making sure it contained enough mother's milk, hollyroot and mildwood. I didn't know which one I'd need, or whether all three would be necessary.

I locked the house and trotted alongside Gill, struggling to keep up with his swift pace. We didn't speak. We didn't have to. I was quite sure I knew what was wrong with Ingrid. It was the only explanation for Gill's anger and worry.

The Swinsons lived close to the dock, not far from the bustling hive of activity that had already begun in earnest. Dockers, sailors, crane operators, and customs officers passed the Swinson house on their way to work, while many fishermen were probably already on their boats. Not Gill, however.

His son wasn't at home, so perhaps he'd gone out alone today. Gill's wife, Faye, looked exhausted. Her eyes were swollen and her hair hung loosely around her shoulders. She still wore her nightgown.

"In there," she said, nodding at a closed door. She touched my arm as I passed her and whispered, "She's been...forced."

I let myself into the room. I'd expected Ingrid to be lying on the bed, not pacing. She looked like a caged animal with her blonde hair rippling with each purposeful stride. Unlike her mother, her eyes were not swollen. She looked tired but not upset.

"So he did fetch you," she said, finally stopping. "I told him not to."

"Your parents are concerned about you."

"There's nothing for you to do here, Josie."

"You don't want me to take a look at you? Give you something?"

"I'm not in any pain." She grunted. "His dick wouldn't leave a shadow at full mast. I've got a few bruises on my thighs and hips, but that's all." I must have looked mystified because she added, "I'm fine, Josie. I have experience with men." Ingrid had been married for five years and widowed for one. She'd moved back with her parents after her husband's death and helped Faye sell the fish caught by Gill and their son. Ingrid had a powerful voice, perfect for a fishwife. Her character was just as strong, but even so, I'd not expected this defiance.

"I know, but..." I wasn't sure what to say. I felt woefully inadequate for such a task. Ruth had not been physically hurt either, but she had cried in my arms and I think that had helped us both. Ingrid didn't look like she wanted to cry. She looked like she wanted to hack off her attacker's genitals with a blunt axe.

"Sometimes it's not about the physical hurt, it's about the violation," I said. It had been something I'd noticed with Ruth, and it made sense that Ingrid might feel the same way.

"Violated." She began pacing again. "That's exactly it. I feel violated, like he took something from me without asking first. He made me feel weak, and I am *not* weak."

"You certainly aren't. You're one of the strongest women I know, Ingrid. What happened to you last night doesn't change that."

She gave a curt nod of thanks. "When I get my hands on him,

I'm going to make him regret touching me. I'm going to make him feel like I feel now."

"Did you see him?"

"No. He came at me from behind."

Behind? Hailia. I felt sick. "Is there anything else you can tell me about him?"

"He wasn't a big man. I was taller than him, but he was stronger than me. Damn it." She turned away and stared at the wall. I thought I heard her sniff but I didn't offer sympathy. She didn't seem like she wanted it. "He smelled clean."

"Clean?"

"Not sweaty or like fish. Like he'd just washed but not with scented water."

"Where did it happen?"

"Just around the corner from here. It was early evening last night, just gone dark. I think he'd been following me for some time, but I can't be sure." She slammed her fist into the wall, just as her father had done outside my house.

Her mother opened the door. "Ingrid?"

"It's all right, Mama," Ingrid bit off. "I'm fine. Stop fussing."

I nodded at Faye and she closed the door again.

"She's going to worry about me all the time now," Ingrid said.

I could have told her she was lucky to have someone worry about her, but I did not. No matter how brave Ingrid appeared, she wasn't all right. She was angry at her attacker and she was suffering, in her own way. She just had a different way of expressing that suffering to Ruth.

"If you need a woman other than your mother to talk to, come and see me," I told her. "Also, if you become pregnant, you must definitely come to see me."

"Damn it," she muttered. "Damn that fucking little weasel's prick. If I ever find out who he is..." She made a wringing motion with her hands.

I left the room and handed Faye a bag of mildwood leaves. "Steep this in some tea," I told her. "It might calm her a little." I wasn't sure mildwood would be enough to dampen Ingrid's rage, however—or her father's. Gill looked like he wanted to snap someone's head off too.

"It's one of them newcomers," he growled. "It's got to be."

"You don't know that," Faye said.

"I do know it! It wouldn't be a Mullian. We've known this whole village all our lives. Our friends wouldn't do…that." He began pacing the floor, just as his daughter had. "They shouldn't be allowed to come here. There's too many of them, and when they don't follow our rules, *we* suffer. They think they can take our jobs, our livelihoods, and our women. It ain't right."

"You can't judge them all by one bad apple, Gill," Faye said.

"One is one too many!"

I let myself out. I hadn't been paid but I didn't expect it for doing nothing. I clutched my bag tighter and didn't stop on the way home. The sky was lighter now, the sun having chased away dawn's shadows, yet Mull felt different. The stone buildings didn't seem as warm, the gutters not as clean, the air not as fresh. Perhaps it was just my own perception, knowing what had happened last night.

The faces of the people I passed belonged mostly to strangers. Many of them looked desperate, hungry. They would be hoping to find work today after finding none the day before, or the day before that. Desperation to find honest work didn't make a man a rapist. If Ingrid's attacker was the same as Ruth's, then none of the suspects were newcomers to the village. At least we had more to go on with now. Dane only needed to learn which of the suspects had been in the village last night.

I stopped mid-stride. Brant had been in the village in the early evening. He may not have immediately returned to the palace after leaving my house.

I adjusted my grip on my pack and hurried home. I got as far as the end of my street before stopping again. Ivor Morgrain walked toward me, head bowed against the breeze. Like an animal scenting its prey on the wind, he suddenly looked up. He seemed as unhappy to see me as I was to see him. Not his prey then, but perhaps his tormentor. Or his conscience.

Unless one of us turned around, we had to pass each another. I hesitated. It might be daytime, but the street was empty except for the two of us and I no longer trusted Ivor. I couldn't rely on even the nosiest neighbor looking out their window this early in the morning.

Mistress Grinsten emerged from her house, however, a basket over her arm, her two children dawdling behind. She waved at me and I waved back. One of the children tripped over his shoelace and burst into tears. His mother bent to pick him up and her delay gave me some courage.

"Ivor," I said, approaching him. "I wish to ask you a question."

He smiled tentatively. Where before he looked like he wanted to pass me by without so much as a greeting, now he looked keen to talk. "I've always got time for you, Josie. The other day...forget that. I was having a bad day." He drew closer and the smile became more confident. "Want to go somewhere quieter?"

"This is quiet enough. Where were you last night in the early evening?"

The smiled slipped. "Why?"

"I, er, heard you were...you know." Merdu, I wasn't very good at thinking on the spot.

"With Tammara?" His lips curved into a sleek smile. "Aye, I was."

"Tammara Lowe?"

"We've been getting along lately. She heard that you and me weren't together no more—"

"We were never together. What have you been telling people about us?"

He crossed his arms. "If we weren't together, then you got to learn not to tease a man. All your flirting meant something, Josie. At least to me," he finished in a mutter.

"I'm sorry if that's what you thought I was doing. I wasn't flirting, I was just..." I shrugged. "...being myself."

He scoffed. "I was with Tammara last night. Ask her if you don't believe me. Why do you want to know anyway?"

"I was curious about what you get up to these days." I pushed past him and hurried home. For a long time, I could feel his gaze boring into my back but I did not turn around. He would have to stay confused about my question because I had no intention of telling him the truth. I had no intention of speaking to him ever again.

I deposited my pack on my father's desk and left the house again immediately. I wanted to catch Tammara before she went out. Like most unwed girls our age, she did the marketing for her mother and helped around the family home. Very few had jobs outside the home, and if they did, it was usually working in their fathers' shops or workshops. Tammara's father was a boat builder and her brothers assisted him. She would be at home with her mother now or heading out to the market.

She lived not far away and I intercepted her as she left her house, a basket over her arm. I expected her to be annoyed if she considered me a rival for Ivor's affections, but she simply looked bemused by my visit.

"I haven't seen you in some time, Josie," she said. "I'm sorry about your father."

"Thanks."

"Are you just passing?"

"I came to see you." Before I asked my question, I would dispel a myth first. "I've just seen Ivor Morgrain," I said, being as direct as possible. "He tells me you think he and I were a couple. It's not true. We weren't."

Tammara's dark brow arched. Unlike most Glancians, she had brown hair and eyes, an echo of her grandfather's Dreen heritage. She wasn't as slender as a Glancian either, and was more curvaceous in the places men liked. It meant she was rarely short of suitors, but to my knowledge, she'd encouraged very few. Ivor was fortunate. I wondered what she saw in him.

"He never outright said it," she told me. "I assumed. We all did. He was always talking about you and saying how he was going to marry you one day." A smile twisted her lips. "Not that I care anymore."

"You don't?"

"We're not together. We courted a week or so ago. It didn't last long." She tapped her chest. "I ended it with him, not the other way around." She seemed glad to be rid of him. We had that in common! "I don't doubt it," I said. "I was surprised when he told me about the two of you. He doesn't seem like your type."

"Nor yours," she said. "I don't know why I assumed you two were ever a couple."

"Does that mean he wasn't with you last night?" I asked.

"He was not. Is that what he's saying now?" She fisted her hand on her hip. "The lying little prick. Wait 'til I get my hands on him."

"Don't do that. Don't tell him I came to see you. He'll think I'm jealous and that'll only make him think he has a hope with me when he doesn't."

"Fine. I prefer not to see him anyway, but if I hear he's been spreading more lies, I'm going to have to set him straight."

"Do you think he lied just to make me jealous?" I asked.

"Probably. He's still keen on you. He's so jealous of that captain." She smiled slyly. "So he should be. The captain's far better looking than Ivor. I wouldn't mind entertaining him for an evening."

I laughed along with her despite the odd sensation in my chest that I recognized as jealousy. "Where do you think Ivor was last night then? At home? Or does he drink at one of the taverns regularly?" It had been some time since I'd enjoyed an ale with friends at a tavern. Once the newcomers began to arrive in Mull in alarming numbers, my father forbade it. He wasn't the only parent. Few of my female friends had been allowed to continue to drink in taverns these last few months, or walk in the village in the evenings.

"I think he goes to The Anchor," she said.

The Anchor was the more reputable of Mull's two taverns. It still had a village feel to it, with mostly locals frequenting it, while The Mermaid's Tail attracted the newcomers since it had accommodation upstairs and out back. It had also gained a reputation for fighting and drunkenness thanks to a few bad apples, as Mistress Swinson called them.

"He's changed, you know," she went on. "Ivor's not like he used to be."

"How do you mean?"

"I used to like him. I used to be jealous of your hold on him, Josie." She smiled wistfully. "That's why I allowed him to court me when he came to me. I suppose I still saw the man he used to be. But I quickly realized he wasn't the same. He's angry, now. He's filled with hate, and I don't like it. He scares me."

I gave her a grim smile. "He scares me too, nowadays. I saw

him at the docks and he became so angry at a migrant whose only crime was to bump me. I thought he'd attack the man. It was awful, and I couldn't get away from him fast enough. He's like a lot of people in the village though."

"Not all," she said. "Not even that many, I believe. There are certainly a few who hate all newcomers, and they've become very vocal about it. When I learned Ivor was drinking with that group at The Anchor, I wanted to distance myself from him. It's likely he was with them last night, complaining about the state Mull is in. That's all they ever do."

"Then why didn't he just tell me that?" I asked. "Why lie?"

She shrugged. "You could check with them. Start with Ned Perkin. Ivor idolizes him. He follows him around like a puppy."

I thanked her and headed home. I would indeed speak with Ned Perkin and find out if Ivor had been with him last night. If he hadn't, then Ivor was looking more and more like Ingrid's attacker.

Like Gill Swinson, Ned was a fisherman and wouldn't be in the village during the day. I'd go in search of him later at The Anchor.

First, I had a message to write to Dane. I had much to tell him, too much to put into a note. I simply wrote: "I need to speak with you. Come when you're free."

He sent a note back to tell me he would call on me later in the afternoon. I'd just finished reading it when a brisk rap on the door announced a visitor.

"Miranda!" I said, accepting her peck on my cheek. "What are you doing here?"

"Sneaking away. We both are." She indicated the carriage waiting on the street. The duchess of Gladstow waved at me through the window. "My parents and her husband don't know we're here," Miranda said. "They think we're out riding."

I spotted Meg emerging from her house opposite. She took one look at the carriage with the Gladstow ducal crest painted on the door and returned inside with a determined look on her face. It was most curious.

"Josie," the duchess called out. "Come down here and talk to me."

"Why don't you come out, Kitty?" Miranda called back with a wink for me.

The duchess screwed her nose up at the street below. "I'm not wearing the right footwear."

Miranda leaned closer to me. "She doesn't like the mud."

"It's not too muddy," I said. "Last night's rain wasn't heavy."

"Even a little mud is too much for a duchess, apparently." Miranda grinned. "This could be fun." She took my hand and led me to the carriage window. "You must come out, Kitty, or Josie will think you're snubbing her."

"Oh, no," I said, "I don't think that."

The duchess's eyes widened in alarm. "I'm not snubbing her! You're wicked for saying so, Miranda. I like Josie very much. It's just that my shoes are covered in the prettiest shade of yellow silk. Yellow, Miranda!"

"Why did you decide to wear yellow silk for a visit to the village?"

"I didn't think we were getting out of the carriage. You told me we were going for a drive, you said nothing about traipsing through mud. It's nothing against you, Josie. I would love to experience your country hospitality. You villagers are famous for hearty cakes and the like."

Not this villager, and certainly not at the moment with the larder so bare. Thank Hailia for a little mud.

"What a shame," I said in my sincerest voice. "I would be honored by your visit, Your Grace."

"Do call me Kitty since we're friends now."

"Kitty," I repeated dully, not quite sure if I wanted to be on informal terms with a duchess. It didn't seem right.

"You'll have to stay in here, Kitty," Miranda said with an elaborate sigh. "While I enjoy Josie's company inside."

Kitty pouted. "You're going to gossip, aren't you?"

"Of course."

Kitty pouted more.

I pressed my lips together to suppress my smile.

The duchess's face suddenly brightened. "I know! The coachman can carry me to the door." Before Miranda and I could say a word, she poked her head through the window. "You there! Driver! Step down and assist me."

The coachman dutifully did as ordered, leaving the well

behaved horses unattended. At Kitty's instruction, he carried her the three paces over the street and gutter and deposited her on the threshold. She smoothed her hand over the full yellow and cream silk skirt and beamed at us.

"There. Problem solved." She studied her surroundings and I was glad I'd cleaned recently. "What a charming cottage. It's so rustic and full of character. I can't wait to see the reception rooms."

She'd be disappointed when she learned the house had no reception rooms, only a kitchen. She'd be even more disappointed when I told her I could offer nothing to eat.

"Josie," Meg hissed from behind the carriage. When had she snuck up? And why was she wearing a cloak in warm weather?

"What is it?" I whispered, joining her.

She opened her cloak to reveal something wrapped in a cloth. "It's a cake," she said. "Mama baked it this morning. Take it."

"I can't take it. It's for your family."

"She'll make another, and she owes you for seeing my sister at short notice."

"That was nothing," I said. "It certainly doesn't warrant an entire cake as payment."

She pushed the bundle at me, but seeing that I wore no cloak to hide it under, lifted my skirts.

"Meg!" I swatted her hand away.

"Take it, Josie, or my mother will fret. She hates the idea of you being unable to feed those palace ladies. Who are they anyway, and what do they want?"

"Miranda was the one who was poisoned a few weeks ago. We've become friends. The other is a duchess."

"Duchess!" Her huge eyes peered past me. "So that's what a duchess looks like. She's very grand. Her gown is exquisite. Look at the luster! And it's so full. How does she fit through doorways?"

"It looks neither practical nor comfortable."

"Who cares for practicality and comfort when you can look beautiful? Here, take this." She shoved the cake up my skirt then directed my hands to hold it in place. I doubted I could fool anyone but Meg didn't seem to care. She turned me around and gave me a little push.

"Join us," I told her.

"Hailia, no. Cake with duchesses sounds horrible."

"Only one is a duchess. Miranda is lovely and funny. You two would get along."

She shook her head and shooed me away.

I sighed and gave up. I knew a lost cause when I saw one. "Thank your mother for me. I'll visit your sister later to see how she is."

I waddled awkwardly back to Kitty and Miranda, waiting just inside the door. Miranda eyed the lump under my skirt with suspicion but Kitty was too busy lifting her own skirts high off the floor to notice.

"I cleaned only yesterday," I told her as I passed. "So the mice won't disturb us."

"Mice?" Kitty squeaked. "Is she joking?" she whispered to Miranda. "She is, isn't she?"

"I don't know," Miranda whispered hoarsely back, "but if you spot a mouse, scream and run to the carriage. Don't worry about the mud. I hear mice detest mud as much as duchesses so they won't follow you."

I smiled at her over my shoulder. Kitty scowled at us both. "You two are made for one another," she said, following me into the kitchen.

"Please sit," I said, indicating the kitchen table. "I'll fetch something from the larder."

"It's all right," Kitty said. "We'll wait for you to show us through to the salon."

With my back to the kitchen, I removed the cake from beneath my skirt and placed it on a plate in the larder. "This *is* the salon," I called out. "It's also the kitchen and medicine room."

"Medicine room?"

"Where I make up the medicines, ointments, unguents and the like," I said, rejoining them.

"Delightful," she muttered through a tight smile.

"Sit down, Kitty," Miranda said as she sat. "A cake? Wonderful. I love cake."

"What kind is it?" Kitty asked.

I looked at the cake as I set plates down in front of them. I wished I'd smelled it beforehand but it was too late now. "It's an old family favorite," I said. No need to tell her it wasn't *my* family's recipe.

I cut up the cake then made the tea. Despite her initial reluctance to set foot in my house, the duchess seemed to forget where she was once the gossip began. There was no shortage of it and they delighted in passing on the details even though I didn't know the people they talked about. From what I could gather, certain noble families wouldn't talk to one another, while others couldn't even be in the same room. They told me about the baroness who was so desperate to seem more important than she was that she told everyone she was a countess, and the case where a viscount accused the daughter of a marquis of stealing.

"I must tell you the gossip about Lady Grenlee," Kitty added with a gleam in her eyes.

"That's not proven," Miranda chided. "We shouldn't repeat it."

"Oh pooh. It's only to Josie, anyway." Kitty leaned forward and lowered her voice. "It's said that Lady Grenlee's three children are not her husband's."

"Who's their father?" I asked, unable to help myself. I didn't know Lady Grenlee, but I suddenly wanted to know about her illicit affairs.

"Some say it's one of their gardeners."

"Kitty!" Miranda cried. "Who says that?"

Kitty shrugged. "People. And Josie, have you heard about Lord Juke?"

"No, what about him?" I asked, leaning forward too.

"Apparently he's more interested in his valet than his new young wife."

I gasped. "Do the authorities know?"

"Perhaps, but what does it matter? There are benefits to being a nobleman, and one of those is that a count can have liaisons with his valet and the authorities will turn a blind eye." Kitty crumbled cake between her fingers. She'd eaten half a slice and declared herself too full to eat any more but had proceeded to pick it apart instead. "Josie, perhaps you know the answer to something I've been wondering about ever since hearing that story. You are an expert on the human body and its functions. How do two men...you know?"

Miranda groaned. "Not this again."

"Well, *you* wouldn't tell me. You're such a prude. Josie isn't, though."

"I'm a prude too," I assured her. "Very much so. Speaking of scandals, has Lady Morgrave become the king's favorite?"

"She has," Miranda said, eager to move the discussion away from Lord Juke and his valet. "They spend a lot of time in one another's company. Kitty thinks they're sleeping together."

Kitty nodded wisely. "I can tell by the look on their faces when I saw them yesterday. It was quite obvious they'd been for a tumble."

"What does her husband think?" I asked.

"Lord Morgrave pretends not to notice," Miranda said. "Some people think he's going to ask for compensation from the king." She made him sound like a common whoremaster.

"Money?"

Kitty looked appalled. "Merdu, no. He'll ask for a higher title or the rights to collect taxes at a toll bridge or something like that. Perhaps even an ambassadorial role."

"How is that different to money?" I asked.

"Well..." Kitty looked to Miranda but Miranda merely shrugged. "It just is."

"And what about her mother?"

"Lady Deerhorn is prancing around the palace with her nose in the air. You'd think *she* was the king's favorite. Lord Xavier has become even more arrogant, if you can believe it."

"We try to avoid the Deerhorns," Miranda told me. "Particularly Lord Xavier. I don't want his attention."

"There is someone else paying Miranda extra attention lately, too," Kitty said with a smug smile. "A certain Vytill representative with only one arm."

"Lord Barborough?" I blurted out. When they both looked at me, I added, "I've heard about him."

"So you'll know he has *two* arms," Miranda said pointedly.

"One doesn't work," Kitty shot back. "But I suppose only one is necessary in his line of work. Anyway, he has been very attentive to our mutual friend, Josie. Very friendly indeed."

I picked up my teacup and took my time sipping. I wanted to

warn them about Lord Barborough, but it would only lead to questions I couldn't answer. I'd promised Ruth not to tell anyone what had happened to her, and I'd promised Dane and the others not to mention the memory loss and magic.

"Be careful," I simply said. "Make sure you know him thoroughly before being alone with him."

Miranda cocked her head to the side, frowning. "Why?"

I lifted a shoulder. "I am not convinced his arm is useless. It may be an affectation."

Miranda's frown deepened. She suspected there was more.

"Why would someone lie about that?" Kitty asked, rising. "Of course it doesn't work. Nobody would pretend to have only one arm."

"He has *two* arms, Kitty," Miranda said again.

"We ought to get back, Miranda. Your mother will worry."

"As will your husband," Miranda said, following her out.

"Hardly." Kitty paused at the front door and, with a deep breath, lifted her skirts. "This is a day for new adventures," she declared and stepped onto the street. Her shoes squelched in the shallow mud.

"I don't envy her maid having to clean those shoes," Miranda said, laughing.

She kissed my cheek and promised to come visit me again, alone next time. "I'll let you know if we discover Lord Barborough's arm works after all."

I bit the inside of my cheek and waved them off, wishing I hadn't given them reason to spy on the Vytill representative when I didn't know how dangerous he could be.

CHAPTER 9

*T*here was still some cake left over for Dane when he arrived late in the afternoon. He declared it delicious and was impressed with my baking skills. I stared at my second slice for the day and thanked him. Hailia would find an appropriate punishment for my small lie but it was worth it to see the satisfied look on his face as he finished his slice.

"How long can you stay?" I asked.

"The rest of the day. The king is resting now. When he awakes, he'll dress for dinner then dine with his favorites and play cards until the early hours of the morning. He doesn't need me and the men know their duties."

"Good."

He paused with the teacup halfway to his mouth. The gaze that watched me over the rim turned smoky. "You have plans for me?"

I gulped.

"Josie?" He set the cup down. The heat had left his eyes. Or perhaps I'd simply imagined it in the first place.

"Yes, I do," I said. "We have to question some friends of Ivor's."

"Morgrain? Why?"

"To find out where he was early last night. He claims he was with Tammara Lowe, but she says he wasn't. She said he's been spending a lot of time with Ned Perkin, and I want to ask Ned if he saw Ivor last night, but I don't want to approach him alone. He's a local troublemaker, and I'd feel better if you were with me."

"What happened last night?" he asked carefully.

"Ingrid Swinson was raped."

"Merdu." He dragged his hand through his hair, down his face. When he pulled it away, his eyes were closed.

I told him all I knew, including when it had happened and how. "It seems similar to Ruth's attack," I finished.

He finally opened his eyes. "Yes."

"And Ivor lied about his whereabouts to me when I asked."

His gaze held mine. "I told you not to approach him."

"I didn't seek him out. I bumped into him in the street. The question is, why did he lie? He may have lied to make me jealous of his relationship with Tammara, or he may have lied because he's Ingrid's attacker."

"It sounds like an act of a guilty man."

I tended to agree. Ivor seemed guilty, yet I couldn't imagine him raping anyone, let alone Ingrid Swinson. In Ruth's case, she was a stranger to him, and it was a little easier to believe he might attack a woman he didn't know. But not someone he greeted when they passed in the street; someone whose brother he drank with at The Anchor.

"Is she going to tell the sheriff?" Dane asked.

"I don't know. It wouldn't surprise me if she doesn't. She's a strong woman, and she wouldn't want anyone to know this happened to her. Her father is also not a believer in the sheriff's brand of justice. If he does find her attacker, he'll enforce his own punishment."

He nodded slowly.

"There's something else, Dane." I'd debated with myself all day about what to tell him and how much. In the end, I decided to go with part of the truth. Telling him Brant had been waiting for me here would not achieve anything except a deeper fracture in their relationship. Brant hadn't hurt me, and I doubted now that he would. Whether he would harm other women or not, I wasn't yet convinced either way. "I saw Sergeant Brant late yesterday afternoon here in the village."

Except for the deep rise and fall of his chest, Dane went very still. "Go on."

"Since the rape occurred just after that time, it's possible he was still in the village. He was supposed to be on duty, wasn't he?"

He gave a single nod. Despite his silence and steady gaze, he was simmering with anger. I could see it in the rigidity of his body and sense it in the thick air that enveloped us.

I forged on. I had to tell him the rest. "He also admitted to sneaking away from his duties to search the palace for the cabinet."

His palms flattened on the table but he remained silent.

"Brant's partner is covering for his absences and lied to you about his whereabouts the night of Ruth's rape."

His fingers curled slowly into fists, the light scratch of his nails on the wood the only sound in the silence. I wished he'd say something to break it—anything. But he simply sat there like a cold, forbidding statue.

"Dane," I said quietly, hardly daring to speak at all. I hoped hearing his real name would reach through the dark cloud shrouding him.

He blinked, and a moment later, said, "Thank you for informing me. Where did you see him?"

"I... That is..."

His gaze sharpened. "He came here, didn't he?"

I folded my arms over my chest to ward off the chill in my blood.

He pushed his chair back, scraping the feet on the floor. "I have to go."

"No, you can't." I sprang up and blocked the exit. It was pathetic and futile—Dane could easily move me—but I did it anyway. "We have to pay Ned Perkin a visit."

"It can wait." He reached for his sword, leaning against the wall by the door, but I snatched it away.

"We have to do it now, tonight." I didn't know why I wanted to protect Brant from the worst of Dane's temper. He didn't deserve it. All I knew was that Dane couldn't return like this, with fury so fierce it vibrated through him. If they fought, it would divide the guard ranks. Brant had said some men believed Dane was hiding something from them. This could force them to take sides, and I didn't want anyone taking his side over Dane's. Besides, there was a very good chance that Dane would get hurt as much or more than Brant.

"Josie, give me the sword." He didn't sound as angry but fury still swirled in the depths of his eyes.

"Not until you agree to come with me. If you don't, I'll go on my own."

"You don't need to go at all. I will speak to him alone."

"You don't know where Ned Perkin lives. I do."

He sucked in a deep breath and let it out slowly. He must have released some of the anger too because his features didn't look quite so hard. "Very well, but only on the condition that he doesn't see you. Point him out to me then leave."

"Agreed."

Dane's mood didn't invite conversation so we walked to Ned Perkin's house in silence. He wasn't at home, however, and his neighbor suggested we try The Anchor since he went there every night.

The Anchor was sandwiched between a half-built warehouse and the rope maker's workshop. Unlike the larger Mermaid's Tail tavern, The Anchor was a single level wooden structure, a relic among the new multi-level buildings near the harbor. Like the rope maker's workshop, it clung to its prominent position but would most likely one day concede to the wealthy shipping companies muscling into Mull.

"It's quite safe," I said to Dane when he hesitated outside the tavern. "Besides, you'll have me to protect you." It was a pathetic attempt to lighten his mood, and deserved to fail.

He watched two men enter the tavern and his gaze moved further along the street. He suddenly turned around, forcing me to do the same. "It's Barborough," he said.

"What's he doing here?" I asked.

"Good question." He checked over his shoulder. "He went in. You go home, I can manage on my own."

"But you won't know Ned Perkin when you see him."

"I'll ask one of the staff."

"I've come all this way. I'm not leaving."

"Your house is a mere few streets away."

"Unless you've forgotten, there's a rapist on the loose."

He swore under his breath. "Come with me then, but do as I say and stay out of sight."

"That won't be easy. We're walking into a tavern where most people know me."

"No we're not."

"But—"

"Stop talking and follow me," he said, scanning the vicinity.

I sighed. "You're very demanding."

"And you talk too much."

"Only when I'm nervous."

He took my hand in his. The soft leather of his riding glove was warm against my bare skin. The move left me utterly speechless, which was perhaps his intention. "Better?" he asked.

I nodded. My nerves still twitched, but from his touch, not anxiety.

"Is there another entrance?" he asked

"There's a lane off the street that runs along the back of those properties. You don't want to go through the front door?"

"I'm too conspicuous. I want to know why Barborough is here, and I doubt I'll learn the truth by asking. Let's go, while there's no one about."

He led me to the lane where dusk had already given way to darkness. The silhouettes of the buildings guided us to the tavern's courtyard. The Anchor had only one stable, permanently occupied by the old nag that pulled the tavern keeper's dray. We paused near the rear door, listening. I could just make out the hum of voices, the odd raucous laugh, the clank of tankards. Light filtered into the courtyard from a window beside the door. The voices seemed to be coming from there. The glass was grimy but I could make out the room and people well enough. It was a private room, used by small groups. My father used to play cards in there years ago, and the market stall holders used it for the occasional meeting.

One of the men inside stood up and the light caught his pale face, his golden hair. Ivor. I swallowed my gasp even though I doubted any of them could hear it.

The door suddenly opened and Dane pushed me back against

the wall. He shielded me with his body, blocking my view of the courtyard. The gold braid at the shoulder of his uniform filled my vision. I lifted my gaze to his throat where a vein pulsed. If I stood on my toes, I could press my lips to it and feel the blood pumping through him, feel his warmth, his life. I could reassure myself that he was real.

But I didn't dare move. The person who'd come to the door mustn't have seen us, thanks to Dane's dark clothing and hair. He whistled a tune as a steady stream of water splashed against the fence. Only it probably wasn't water.

I settled my hands lightly on Dane's hips. I had to put them somewhere, after all. I felt rather than saw his head shift to peer down at me.

A moment later the man returned inside. Neither Dane nor I moved. For my part, I didn't want to. I was perfectly content where I was. Despite the sounds of the tavern, I felt like we were completely alone. With Dane so close, it was easy to forget where I was and why. So easy, in fact, that I threw caution away and gave in to my desires.

I reached up and cradled his head in my hands, drawing him down to me. It was a gentle tug that he could have resisted if he'd wanted to.

He did not. He lowered his head and skimmed his lips against mine. The touch was light, fleeting, a mere whisper of a kiss. Yet it promised so much more.

My lips parted with my sigh and I relaxed into him. It must have been the signal he needed. He circled his arms around me, splaying his hands at my back, and deepened the kiss.

It was as passionate as I'd hoped it would be. Despite his position of authority and strong willpower, I'd guessed at the emotions he tried to suppress. It was a relief to know his willpower wasn't strong enough to fight this.

I stroked his hair, raking my fingers through it. I lost sense of time and place, yet every other sense responded to him—the smell of leather and spice, his firm hold on my waist, the sound of his breath and the taste of cake and tea on his lips.

Then, suddenly, he let me go. He turned away and stood by the window, his back to me. I joined him and tried to pretend that I was concentrating on the task at hand when all I was doing was trying not to look at him, not to think about that kiss, and about what it meant.

I drew in a slow, measured breath and forced myself to take in the scene before me. Dane signaled for me to stay out of sight but I ignored him. I needed to see if Ned Perkin was inside. Besides, the window was so dirty, and the courtyard so dark, it was unlikely we'd be spotted.

None of the men seemed interested in the window anyway. All the attention was on Ned, standing at the front. Now that I was closer, I could make out what he was saying.

"This ain't right," Ned said with a shake of his fist. "Mull is *our* village, *our* home, and we got a right to say who can live here."

The other men nodded or spoke their agreement. I counted twenty-eight crammed into the small room, and I recognized all of them, including Ivor Morgrain and Lord Barborough. The latter sat quietly by the door, looking inconspicuous in ordinary working man's clothing. What was he doing at a village meeting?

"We need a law to protect us," Ned went on.

"We need more lawmakers to enforce the ones we have," said another man. "The sheriff can't cope."

"Aye," several voices chimed.

"What's the new king doing about it?" Ned asked. "That's what I want to know. It's his responsibility to make sure Glancia isn't taken over by Vytill scum. It's his responsibility to protect his people!"

"Aye!"

Ivor got to his feet and pointed in a westerly direction. "He's sitting on his arse in that big fancy palace, dancing with pretty ladies and eating Mull's best crays and drinking our best wines, but what's he giving back? What's he doing for us? Nothing. I've seen the palace from the inside. It's filled with gold. The *walls* are made of gold."

Hailia and Merdu, he was a liar, but a convincing one. All the villagers believed him. Lord Barborough merely smirked.

Ned continued with his speech in a loud voice, receiving nods of agreement from the others, but Barborough never gave an indication of his thoughts. None of the men gave an opposing view, and when Ned finished, he was applauded. He accepted a tankard and drank deeply, spilling some of the ale down his beard.

There were no more speeches and several quieter conversations mingled together; I could no longer hear what was said. Lord Barborough slipped out of the room.

Dane tapped my arm and jerked his head, indicating we should leave. I followed him out of the courtyard and lane. He didn't hold my hand. He didn't even look at me.

"I still don't know why Barborough was there," I said when we reached the street. "No one seemed to mind his presence, which is odd."

Dane led the way back toward the street opposite the docks, not in the direction of home.

"You don't think it's odd that a Vytill lord would be at a meeting about Glancia business?" I pressed.

"No."

"Why not?"

"They were voicing their discontent."

I thought about it for a moment but still couldn't fathom what it meant. "Barborough is interested in magic," I said, thinking it through as I spoke. "He wants to prove the palace was created by magic. What does that have to do with those men?"

"I don't think it has anything to do with magic. Barborough is here as the Vytill representative. He's spying on us, on Glancia."

I gasped. "He can't do that!"

"He can if he doesn't get caught. My guess is he's either fueling the discontent of a few Mullians or merely observing it. Perhaps both."

"But he's from Vytill and those men hate Vytill. They want the Glancia borders closed against them. Why accept Barborough?"

"They might not know who he is or where he's from. He might have said he's from another Glancian village. Not everyone is as honest as you, Josie."

It sounded like a barb but I couldn't be sure. The light was poor and I could only see his profile in silhouette. "So you think he's going to report back on that meeting to his king?"

"That meeting and others. He'll report on the general mood here in Mull and the rest of Glancia. He'll tell King Phillip how the

Glancians are unhappy with their new king, how their laws can't keep up with the extra people flooding into Mull. Phillip will use that to his advantage."

"To what end?"

"I don't know," he said darkly. "But by all accounts, he wanted to take over Glancia before Leon took the throne. Now that Vytill has lost The Thumb, and its treasury isn't being refilled as quickly, it's possible he wants Glancia even more."

It was a chilling thought. What did it mean for me and my friends if Vytill took over Glancia? I couldn't answer that, but I did suspect the attempted takeover would lead to an inevitable conclusion—war. And that was the most chilling thought of all.

"What will you do about Barborough?" I asked as the tired façade of the tavern once again came into view.

"Curtail his spying." He stopped me with a hand to my arm. "Will you be all right to go in alone?"

"Of course."

"You won't be in long. Avoid that back room but you don't need to hide yourself. You have every reason to be in there, whereas I'll attract suspicion."

"You want me to ask one of the staff if Ivor was there last night?"

He nodded. "Do you know them?"

"I know all the serving girls. I'll make it look like I'm jealous of Ivor spending time away from me and—"

"Don't do that. Just ask the question and come straight out again."

I didn't see how I could couch it in a way that would sound convincing but didn't say so.

A few minutes later, I joined him where he waited at the end of the street in the shadowy doorway of a warehouse. "He was there," I told him as we walked. "He, Ned and a few others drank together until midnight. They were quiet and kept to themselves, but Deena said they were discussing what they'd say at tonight's meeting. He couldn't have raped Ingrid. But why not just tell me he was here?" It seemed Ivor really had wanted to make me jealous by claiming he was with Tammara.

"He was worried you might tell me about the meeting," Dane said, bursting my bubble.

"That does seem more likely."

"He knows you and I are...friends."

"You hesitated."

"No, I didn't."

"You did. Are we not friends?"

Dane huffed out a breath. "I suppose."

I waited for him to say more, to talk about the kiss, but he did not. We kept up a steady pace to my street in complete and excruciating silence. I hazarded a glance at him out of the corner of my eye but it was impossible to gauge his mood in the poor light. I hoped he was at least thinking about the kiss, if not worrying about what to do next, like I was.

"Dane," I began, without knowing where I would finish. "I—"

"Who's that?" he asked, stopping me with a hand to my elbow.

I peered into the darkness at a shadowy figure knocking on my door. When he received no answer, the visitor looked at Dane's tethered horse, then glanced up at the sign of the cupped hands above the door as if checking he had the right house. Moonlight fell across his face.

"Lord Xavier," I said on a rush of breath.

"The Deerhorn heir? What's he doing here?"

"I don't know, but I'm going to find out. Wait here. He might not speak if he sees you." I pulled away, not waiting for Dane's response. "My lord," I called out. "Did you wish to see me?"

Lord Xavier clasped his hands behind him and regarded me down his nose. "You kept me waiting."

"As far as I'm aware, we didn't have an appointment."

He stretched his neck out of his collar. "I'm here to make you an offer, Miss."

"Cully. It's Miss Cully. Go on, what is your offer?"

"I will control my mother, if you'll do something for me."

I waited but he did not go on. "You'll need to be more specific. What do you mean 'control your mother?'"

"She's running a campaign against you, whispering in the king's ear, informing him every time she sees you at the palace, distracting the staff."

I laughed. "Good luck to her."

He bristled. "I wouldn't treat it so lightly, if I were you. The king is annoyed that someone like you seems to think she can go wherever she wants without permission or consequence."

"My lord, I am nothing to the king." I patted Dane's horse's neck. It quivered at my touch. "I am beneath his notice."

"You would think so, but apparently not. He seems quite keen to be informed."

My laughter caught in my throat. "Why?"

He smiled at my concern and took a swaggering step closer. "Who is to say what should and should not concern a king? Not I, and certainly not you. So my proposal is this. I will convince my mother to cease her troublemaking, and in return you will find out what you can about the duke of Gladstow's plans."

It was not what I'd expected him to say. His sliminess had led me to think he would want one thing from me, so I was rendered speechless to hear otherwise. The blast of the temple's horns announcing evening prayers for the priests echoed around the village. I waited for each blast to finish before speaking.

"Why do you think I'd have access to the duke of Gladstow or his plans?"

"You're friends with his wife," he said defensively.

"Kitty wouldn't know what her husband is up to. Even if she did, she probably wouldn't understand what she hears." I felt a little cruel for making her seem unintelligent, so added, "He wouldn't confide in her."

He tugged on his cuffs. "Use your common sense, Miss Cully. Invite yourself to tea in their apartments when he's not there and search the rooms."

A bubble of laughter rose up my throat and burst out. "I'm sorry, my lord, but no. I won't spy on the Gladstows for you."

He stepped toward me and bared his teeth. "Then I cannot control my mother."

"I never doubted it."

He growled and took another step closer. "Little *bitch*."

I pressed my palm to his chest but was under no illusion I could stop him if he chose to use force. "There is a very big man with a sword standing in the shadows, watching us," I said. "He won't like it if you touch me."

His gaze darted around, searching the darkness at my back. Dane must have hidden himself well because it wasn't until he cleared his throat that Lord Xavier's face dropped. He hurried off without so much as a good evening.

Once he was completely out of sight, Dane emerged from the shadows. "*Very* big?" he asked.

"Bigger than most," I said, unlocking the door. "Be content I didn't describe you as big and angry."

He merely grunted and pushed open the door.

"Do you know if it's true what he said about his mother informing the king every time I go to the palace?" I asked.

"She has been in his ear lately, but you're mostly right in that the king has other things to worry about. She also doesn't know how much he owes you."

I felt the ledge beside the door for the flint box and candle. "For saving Miranda's life? That was mostly my father's doing." I struck the flint and lit the candle.

"You saved the king's life too, or so he thinks."

I chuckled. The king had been constipated, not poisoned, but had not fully accepted my diagnosis. I'd given him a tisane to make him comfortable but that was all. His gratitude might not last too long if Lady Deerhorn continued to disparage me though.

That was a sobering thought.

"Do you want me to check each of the rooms before I go?" Dane asked.

I was about to tell him there was no need then I remembered Brant had somehow got in. I fetched another candlestick from my father's room and handed it to him. "A quick check will suffice. Thank you."

The downstairs level took him only a few moments. As he headed up the stairs I remembered my messy room, the layer of dust everywhere. I rarely cleaned up there. What was the point since I was the only one to see it?

I thought about following him but hesitated. Did he want me to follow? Would seeing the bed make things more awkward? That kiss hung between us like a blade teetering on the edge. I wasn't sure what to say to make things right again. Mentioning the kiss might cause him to deny it meant anything, and that would be worse than not knowing his feelings.

The more I thought about it, however, the more convinced I was that it had meant nothing to him. He showed no signs of awkwardness and no desire to kiss me again.

He trotted down the steps and announced the all clear. "I have to go," he said, handing the candlestick to me. "Sleep well."

Sleep well? That was all he was going to say? It was too formal considering the heat of that kiss. Desire had threatened to overrule all common sense when he'd been kissing me, and I was sure he'd felt the same way. Yet he'd managed to break it off when I had not. Clearly it hadn't been as intense for him as it had for me.

"Goodnight," I said at the door.

With his back to me, he said, "It's best if we both forget what happened."

"Of course. For the best." I didn't sound convincing but he seemed satisfied with my response.

I watched him ride off with a hundred different responses running through my head and a thousand regrets piercing my heart.

CHAPTER 10

J tried to stay away from the palace the following day. I spent most of the morning foraging for plants on the slopes of Lookout Hill then steeping leaves, crushing roots, and hanging flowers up to dry. Unfortunately those tasks were ones I did often and required little concentration, allowing my mind to wander to the previous evening's events. As much as I tried to focus on what we'd learned at the tavern, I kept thinking about Dane and the kiss. The more I thought about him, the more I wanted to see him again. Not even a visit from Meg could sway me once the decision had been made.

"Why not come with me to the palace?" I said from where I stood at the table grinding seeds with the mortar and pestle.

"You're mad." She lifted the lid on the pot hanging over the hot coals and breathed in the smell. "I can't just turn up at the palace. Neither should you."

"The guards on the gate know me, and the captain will vouch for me." Even as I said it, I hoped Lady Deerhorn wouldn't see me. I'd have to be careful.

She replaced the lid and joined me at the table. "What will you tell him when he asks why you're there?" The gleam in her eyes told me she knew exactly why I wanted to go, even though I'd not told her about the kiss.

"I'll think of something." I pushed a bunch of cavassa roots at her. "Bind those together for hanging."

She screwed up her nose and held them at arm's length. "They stink. What are they used for?"

"Skin conditions. Once they're dry, I'll boil them with a few other ingredients to make an ointment for rashes, warts— Warts! Yes, of course!" I wiped my hands down my apron and checked the larder shelves until I found the jar of ointment. There was just enough left.

"Josie, what have warts got to do with anything?"

"I almost forgot about a patient at the palace." I held up the jar. "He needs some of this."

"Now you have your excuse."

"I do. Will you come with me?"

She climbed the ladder in the larder and tied the bunch of cavassa roots to the beam. "You don't need me to deliver a jar of ointment."

"You'll see the palace finally," I said, untying my apron.

"I don't care to see it."

I knew it was a lie but didn't say so. "You'll probably see Sergeant Max too."

"Why? Does he have the warts?"

"No, but we'll go to the garrison." I waited for her to return to the kitchen so I could see her face. She was pretty, with kind eyes and full, sensual lips, yet she didn't see those features. When she saw her reflection, she only saw the birthmark.

"I have no wish to see the sergeant or the palace," she said, brushing past me. "Unlike you, I don't have the captain's confidence. His men will throw me off the estate if they catch me."

"They'll do no such thing." I caught her hand as she brushed past me. "Come with me, Meg. What else have you got to do today?"

"Quite a bit, as it happens. I'm very busy. I should be getting back. Mama will be wondering what kept me."

"Your mother can do without you for an afternoon. You do so much for her already."

"I said no, Josie, and that's final."

I sighed. There'd be no convincing her today. The problem was,

I couldn't be sure there'd ever be a day when she would overcome her reluctance to be seen by strangers.

* * *

I TOLD the guards at the gate I was delivering an ointment for Erik and that he was expecting me. They let me through, failing in their attempts to control their grins. It would seem Erik and his wart were infamous.

"Josie, you did not forget!" Erik bellowed upon seeing me in the garrison.

"Of course not." I checked to see who else occupied the room. Aside from Erik, there were only four other guards. Brant wasn't among them. "Your...predicament is impossible to forget."

"So the maids tell me."

The other men broke into raucous laughter. "Predicament doesn't mean what you think it means," one said, still chuckling. "She's talking about the lump not the, er..." He glanced at me.

"Stem?" I offered.

"Trunk," Erik said with a swell of his chest. He joined in with the laughter, and I found I couldn't help myself either.

Sergeant Max entered with Quentin, both pausing just inside the door, assessing the situation. Or perhaps, like me, they'd wanted to see if Brant was among the guards before coming in.

"What's so funny?" Quentin asked, smiling.

"Erik's lump." One of the guards pointed at Erik's crotch.

"It's a wart." I fished out the small jar of ointment from my skirt pocket and handed it to Erik. "Rub this on it twice a day until the wart disappears. It should be gone in ten days."

Erik removed the cork and sniffed the mixture. "Is wart dangerous?"

"No."

"Will his cock fall off?" asked a guard with a hopeful grin.

Max smacked the man's shoulder as he passed. "Don't say that word in front of Josie."

"She's a doctor!"

"Cock ain't a medical word," Quentin told the guard in all seriousness.

The guard threw a wedge of cheese at him. "No? Then why's cockhead the proper word for scrawny pimple-faced guards who can't hold a sword or stay on a horse?"

Max smacked him again, this time on the side of the head. The others laughed, including Quentin.

"Erik." I indicated he should come with me to the corner of the room, away from the others. I stood on my toes to whisper in his ear but he still had to lean down. "No intercourse until the wart has cleared up," I instructed him.

He looked horrified. "Ten days?"

"Ten days. Possibly more."

"More!" He muttered something in another language. "It will kill me. The maids too. Some will cry." He walked off, jar in hand, shaking his head.

With my task complete, I should have left, but I joined the men at the table and fell into conversation with Quentin. He asked me about the ointment and skin conditions, but I eventually managed to steer the discussion to Brant.

"Have you avoided him?" I said.

"Aye, and easily." He glanced at Max, sitting at the end of the table, polishing a sword blade with a cloth. "He's doing extra duty guarding the prisoners."

"Do you know why?"

"He ain't fit to be seen by the lords and ladies on account of his bruises."

"Bruises?"

"You ain't heard?"

I shook my head.

He glanced at Max again and lowered his voice. "Captain came back last night from the village all riled up. He dragged Brant outside and ordered us to remain here. They came back some time later. Brant was covered in dirt, bleeding from the nose."

I gasped. "The captain punched him?"

"Seems so. The thing is, he didn't say why, and Brant ain't saying nothing either. I think Zeke knows something though."

The door opened and the captain entered. He paused upon seeing me, and his chest rose with his deep breath. "Josie," he said with a curt nod. It was better than a demand to leave, I supposed, but a little more friendliness would have been nice. It was impossible to believe that any passion had lain between us only yesterday.

"I brought Erik some ointment." I almost added that I'd forgotten to give it to him the night before to pass on. He might not want the men to know he'd been with me.

"And stayed for the illustrious company?" he asked.

"Are you calling yourself illustrious or your men? Because I ought to tell you, the conversations up until now have centered around warts, skin conditions, and disappointed maids."

This time his smile was unmistakable. It would seem he hadn't completely lost his sense of humor overnight. Perhaps he'd spent all his frustration on Brant. My own sense of humor suddenly vanished at the thought.

"May we talk?" I asked.

He held the door open for me and we stepped into the corridor. "Balthazar's office?"

"Here will suffice." I waited for the door to close behind him and kept my voice low. "You confronted Brant over his dishonesty."

He crossed his arms. "I did."

"You hit him."

He waited.

"Was it necessary to hit him?"

I thought he wouldn't answer me again, but he eventually said, "If I am to earn the respect of a man like Brant, I have to speak his language. His language is violence."

I felt a little off kilter and pressed my palms to the wall at my back for balance. "Do you have his respect now or his resentment? Men like Brant do not like being humiliated, and he would see a defeat in a fight as a humiliation."

"That's why I made sure no one was watching."

"The men saw him afterward."

He shifted his stance. "Is that why you came today? To learn how Brant fared?"

"You know it isn't. Why are you being so contrary?"

He unfolded his arms and some of the iciness in his eyes thawed. "You want to know if he confessed to the rapes?"

I nodded. "What did he tell you?"

"That he abandoned his duties to go searching for the cabinet the night Ruth was attacked."

"You believe him?"

"I do. He didn't seem to know who Ruth was, and he pointed out that he doesn't need to rape women to…get what he wants."

I pulled a face. Brant was revolting, and I couldn't imagine any woman desiring him. "The one doesn't necessarily equate to the other. I don't think we can discount him yet."

"I know my men, Josie."

I bristled at his cool tone. I almost reminded him that he'd only known Brant for a few months, but that would be cruel and I wasn't that angry with him. Indeed, I wasn't angry with Dane at all, but I was acutely aware that my disappointment over his disinterest in the kiss was making me quarrelsome.

"I shouldn't have come. I'm sorry." I turned away to re-enter the garrison.

He caught my hand, only to let it go again. "I'm sorry too. I'm not good company today." It would seem we were both in quarrelsome moods. "There's one other thing."

"Yes?" I said on a rush of breath.

He stepped back, as if he expected me to attack him—or kiss him. I felt like one of the maids I'd seen looking at him longingly, as if a desperate look could compel him to notice them. Hailia, I was pathetic.

I cleared my throat. "What is it?" I asked, sounding quarrelsome again.

"The footman, Seb, couldn't have raped Ingrid. There is a witness who states he saw Seb here at the palace that evening."

"The witness might be a false one, just like Zeke falsely claimed Brant was with him on patrol."

"The witness is the duke of Buxton."

"Oh."

"Don't be disappointed," he said, more gently. "Our list is shrinking."

Our list. I liked that he still included me. Liked it very much. I gave him a flat smile that he returned.

"Captain Hammer, sir," said a guard striding toward us along the corridor. As he stepped into the light cast by a torch, I saw that it was Zeke. He bowed his head, not meeting Dane's gaze, and held out a note. "A message came for you, Captain."

Dane read the note then tucked it into his doublet pocket. "I have to attend to this. I can't escort you to the gate, Josie."

"I'll escort her, sir," Zeke said. "It'll be an honor." He still did not raise his gaze to meet Dane's. He must feel very sheepish about lying for Brant. At least he didn't sport signs of physical punishment.

"You've been assigned other tasks," Dane said. "I suggest you return to them."

"Yes, sir. Thank you, Captain." Zeke bobbed his head and returned the way he'd come.

"Are his other tasks arduous ones?" I asked, watching him go.

"Very," Dane said. "Quentin will escort you."

"I don't need an escort. Let me say goodbye and I'll see myself out."

He opened the door and indicated I should walk ahead of him into the garrison. "Every time you see yourself out, you find trouble."

"I can't help it if trouble finds me." At his grunt, I added, "I'll be fine. I'll avoid the Deerhorns if I see them."

"I'm sure you will, but it's the Deerhorns I don't trust."

He did not enter the garrison with me but left. I said my farewells and departed through the external door that led directly outside. On a whim, I didn't head in the direction of the forecourts and gate but instead toward the prison next door. Dane was wrong to trust me. I was more than capable of doing the opposite of what I was told, although I didn't plan on finding trouble. I simply planned to speak to Brant, and I would do so in the open where he wouldn't dare harm me.

I called out to him from the prison entrance. He rose from the chair by the far door in the outer guard's chamber and joined me. He looked around, his one good eye squinting in the sunlight. The other was swollen shut. The skin around it was various shades of black and purple, and his nose was swollen too.

"Come to inspect his handiwork?" he sneered.

"Yes, as it happens." I remained at arm's length, not the ideal way to inspect a patient's injuries, but I could see everything that I needed to know. He was lucid, his good eye focused, his speech not slurred. He moved easily enough so he sported no broken bones.

"Why do you care?" he asked.

I didn't, but I wouldn't tell him I'd wanted to see how much punishment Dane could mete out on his own men. "I'm a healer by nature. Do you have a headache?"

"No."

"Blurred vision?"

"No. It's just some bruises. I expected worse." He glanced over his shoulder toward the prison. "I've seen him do worse."

"To the prisoners?"

"When he gets real angry, he snaps." He clicked his fingers near my face. I blinked but remained where I was. He chuckled. "Hammer's a violent man, Josie. You best remember that. One of the men in there ain't never going to be the same after the captain almost killed him."

The swallowed the bile rising up my throat. "What did the man do to incur his wrath?"

"Raped one of the maids."

Balthazar and Theodore had implied it, but why hadn't Dane told me there'd been another? Perhaps it didn't matter since the prisoner couldn't have done these latest crimes, yet I couldn't help wishing he'd told me everything. I was disappointed that he still kept secrets from me. How many others did he keep?

"Why did you let him think I hurt you that night?" Brant asked.

"What?" I said, trying to focus. "I didn't say that, just that I saw you and you admitted to lying about being on patrol."

"He didn't do this because I lied." He indicated his eye.

I shook my head, frowning. "I don't follow."

"He fought me because he don't like that I got into your house. Guard duty out here is my punishment for lying about patrol." He bared his teeth. "*You* told on me. You told him you saw me at your house. Don't deny it."

"H—he guessed," I stuttered.

He wiped the sweat from above his top lip with the back of his

THE ECHO OF BROKEN DREAMS

hand. "That so?" He returned to the guard chamber and slammed the door shut.

I walked quickly away, checking over my shoulder every few paces to see if he followed. My nerves didn't settle until I'd left the main gate far behind. Despite the heat, I decided to walk home. It didn't feel right to ask for a carriage.

The long, straight Grand Avenue took me past the coach house and stables then cut through the forest like a gash. It was some distance to the intersection with the village road, but the dense trees offered shade from the burning sun. I was soon sweating, however, and considered resting when I heard hooves to my left. Bright pink and deep blue flashed between the trees and a woman called out to her companion, begging him or her to slow down.

The hooves faded and I thought them gone when they suddenly emerged from the forest up ahead. The riders were both women, their cloaks billowing behind them like sails as they approached at a gallop.

"Miranda!" cried the woman in pink. "You're going too fast!"

It was Miranda and Kitty. I stepped aside and waved so they'd see me. Miranda slowed down as she passed then came to a stop.

"Josie! What a surprise." She wheeled her horse around just as Kitty stopped beside me. "Where are you going?"

"Home," I said.

"On foot?" Kitty asked. "But the village is miles away. It must be fifty, at least."

"Five."

"It feels like fifty in this heat." She pressed the back of her gloved hand to her forehead and cheeks. "I'm so hot, I'd jump into a fountain if one were nearby."

"Oh yes, let's return to the palace and do just that." Miranda winked at me. "The one on the main forecourt is closest, although not the biggest."

Kitty lowered her hand. "You cannot be serious. I'm a duchess."

Miranda sighed theatrically. "I forgot. Duchesses can't be seen enjoying themselves."

"I enjoy myself." Kitty sniffed. "I just don't think getting wet is much fun unless one is taking a bath."

"You don't like riding fast, either."

"My husband will scold me if he finds out. He thinks ladies should walk their horses. Anything faster is undignified."

Miranda opened her mouth but shut it again and drew in a fortifying breath.

"Where have you been riding?" I asked them.

"Through the forest," Kitty said, tugging her horse's reins to keep it from turning. "Do you ride, Josie?"

"No. I haven't got a horse."

"Poor you. Riding is an excellent activity."

"But only at walking pace," Miranda chimed in.

Kitty beamed at me. "Next time you come to the palace, perhaps I can teach you."

I thanked her but declined the offer. "I can't just borrow one of the king's horses."

"Nonsense. Of course you can, if you're with me. I think it's an excellent idea. I'm in need of a project." She cast a glance toward the palace. "The days do stretch on if one is not a candidate for the king's affections. Oh." She nibbled on her lower lip. "Miranda, I am sorry. I didn't mean to be cruel."

Miranda laughed. "It's all right, Kitty. I forgive you since I am quite recovered from his disinterest. Are you going to return to the palace now?"

"Yes, why?"

Miranda dismounted and handed the reins to the duchess. "Take her back to the stables for me. I'm going to walk with Josie for a while."

"Walk? In this heat?"

"There's a pond through there." She pointed at the trees to our right. "We'll paddle in it to cool down."

Kitty blinked at her. "You're not serious." She looked at the trees then looked at Miranda again. "No, you can't be. Paddling in a pond, and dressed in your riding blues too." She smiled. "You are amusing, Miranda." She tugged on the reins and clicked her tongue for the horses to walk on. "Don't forget, Josie," she said as she headed off. "Wear a riding outfit next time."

I didn't bother telling her I didn't own a riding outfit.

"She truly isn't aware how ridiculous she is," Miranda said, linking her arm with mine.

"That's part of her charm," I said. "She isn't being cruel, she simply isn't aware of how the real world works."

"She is the most cosseted woman I've met, and believe me, there are many here. She's quite good company, though. We laugh a lot."

"Does she laugh too?"

Miranda chuckled and hugged my arm. "Usually, although it's possible she doesn't always understand why."

We veered off the avenue as a wagon passed by and headed into the trees. I'd been through this forest before, to collect sap and bark from the pomfrey trees, but not since the palace was built. The king had declared the lands surrounding the palace for his exclusive use only, and villagers were banned from foraging and poaching. Since there were other copses of pomfrey trees, I hadn't been too concerned, but the decree galled some of the villagers.

The forest soon opened up to reveal a pond. I was certain it hadn't been here before the palace was built.

I stared at the water glistening in the beam of sunshine. "I thought you'd made it up to tease Kitty."

"I found this place only yesterday." Miranda removed her riding cloak and placed it over a log. "Help me undress, please, Josie."

"You're going in?"

She flashed me a wicked grin. "Aren't you?"

I glanced around at the trees. They were utterly still. There wasn't a breath of wind in this part of the forest. The air was hot, I was hot, and the clear water looked inviting.

"We'll be able to hear riders coming in advance of seeing them," she assured me.

"Is it deep? I can't swim."

"Nor can I. We'll stay near the edge."

I unlaced her bodice and placed it next to the cloak on the log then helped her with the skirt. She hung it over a low branch and kicked off her boots. She stood in her chemise, stays and underskirt. "Don't have second thoughts now."

"I'm not," I said, removing my own clothing. Unlike hers, mine didn't need another's assistance. "I can't believe I'm doing this." Standing in my underthings in the middle of the day, outside, seemed far too daring. My father would be shocked. Meg would be shocked. I didn't care. I wasn't naked, after all. "I can't believe *you're* doing this, Miranda. You always seem so regal and composed, not wild."

She laughed. "Don't tell anyone or my reputation will be ruined."

The cool water felt wonderful lapping at my ankles. I took another step and mud squelched between my toes. I almost got out but Miranda caught my hand and together we waded to our knees. The mud gave way to sand and pebbles. The water was as clear as glass. I could see the bottom and a school of tiny fish darting by.

Miranda promptly sat and laughed at my shocked gasp. "You can't get the full benefit of the refreshing water unless you immerse yourself in it. Come on."

I plunged down beside her then decided to go further. I pulled my hair loose of its pins, shook it out, and lay back until only my face was above the water. Miranda followed suit and together we lay there, staring up at the blue sky in silence. It was relaxing, perhaps a little too much as I felt myself beginning to nod off.

"If I stay here any longer, I'll drown," I said, standing. "I'm going to dry off then I'd better go."

She followed me to the bank where we squeezed the water out of our hair and plucked wet underclothes away from our skin. "So have you shown that to the captain yet?" she asked.

"Shown him what?"

Her wicked smile lit up her face. "The body beneath the clothes."

"Miranda!" I grabbed my boot and threw it at her.

She dodged the boot, laughing. "He'll like it."

"I'm not listening to you."

She picked up the boot and tossed it back to me. "You're right not to show him yet. Secure a promise from him first *then* show him."

"Miranda, there is nothing between—"

She clapped a hand over my mouth and put a finger to her lips for silence. "Someone comes," she whispered. "Quickly."

We gathered our clothes and ducked into the forest. We separated and slipped behind a tree trunk each. I didn't dare peek but I recognized the king's voice, clear across the pond. Merdu, why did it have to be him? The other voice belonged to a woman but I couldn't hear what she said.

Miranda had more courage than I did and she watched them. I dared to follow her gaze and caught sight of the king removing his clothing with the help of the woman. Stripped down to his underthings, he then assisted her out of her clothes. She turned and— Lady Morgrave! So her efforts had been rewarded after all. She seemed to have won his affections.

I turned away when it became clear they weren't going to stop at their underthings. I didn't want to see either of them naked. Miranda turned away too and pulled a face.

"Shall we go?" she mouthed.

"They'll see," I mouthed back.

Splashes and giggles came from the pond, and I dared another peek. The king was in the middle of the pond, the water up to his waist, and Lady Morgrave was submerged to her knees. He beckoned her to join him where it was deeper but she refused. He splashed her and she squealed.

"Now," Miranda hissed.

We raced off, clutching our clothes and boots, heading further into the forest instead of toward the road. When we came across another smaller clearing, we stopped, panting and laughing. Miranda couldn't contain her giggles and made the most unladylike snort.

"Did you see it?" she asked through her tears. "Did you see his small—?"

"Miranda! Merdu, if someone hears you, you'll be in trouble for talking about the king's...appendage like that."

She pressed a hand to her chest and drew in several deep breaths. "You're right. It's time to be a lady again. It was fun being wild with you, Josie, but I must think of my parents and how horrified they'd be if I were found like this. Help me dress, will you? It's impossible to do on my own."

I glanced around, suddenly feeling self-conscious in my undergarments. Neither of us was entirely dry but we dressed anyway and I fixed her hair into the most elegant arrangement I could manage. I left mine down to dry completely.

We walked through the forest in what we hoped was the right direction until we came to a path. A sign indicated the palace was one way and the village the other so we parted with a promise to meet again.

I hadn't got far when a group of riders forced me to the side, and I almost fell into the ditch. It was immediately obvious they weren't Glancians from their shorter stature and darker hair, and a quick scan of their faces confirmed it. My stomach dropped when I recognized Lord Barborough. It was too late for me to run into the forest; he'd seen me.

He told his men to go on without him then ordered me to remain. "I wish to speak to you, Miss Cully." He didn't dismount but sat rigidly in the saddle, his useless arm resting across his lap. His good hand clutched the reins tightly. His apparent anxiety was the best proof that his arm didn't work.

"My lord?" I asked. "If you please, I must get home. I am expected."

"But you live alone."

Despite the heat, cold tingles crept down my spine. How did he know? Had he just come from the village where he'd been asking about me? Dread wrapped its fingers around my insides and squeezed. I was in a forest, far from the palace, with a man I didn't trust. A man who wanted me to spy for him or suffer the consequences.

I tried to step past him but he moved his horse to block my path. "No, Miss Cully. You're not going anywhere until I have information."

The problem was, I had no information to give.

CHAPTER 11

"This won't take long," Lord Barborough said. "I simply wanted to know how you've fared with the servants."

I wished I'd spoken to Balthazar more. If anyone had suggestions for what I should tell Barborough, it would be him. "It's been difficult, my lord. The servants are busy and unwilling to talk to me."

"Did you search your patient's room?"

"Yes," I lied. "I found nothing to indicate where she lived before working for the palace."

He shifted in the saddle and stared over my head into the forest. "What about the captain of the guards?"

"What about him?"

"Don't be coy, Miss Cully." He shifted his weight again and his useless arm slipped. He nudged it with his other hand, not loosening his grip on the reins. "You two are…friends."

"Yes, though not the sort of friend you're implying."

His eyes widened at my brazenness.

"I haven't seen his chambers," I went on. "I don't even know where he sleeps at night."

"In the room next to the king," he said.

"If you know where it is, perhaps you should search it."

"Perhaps I will. He might be the sorcerer. After all, he has access to the entire palace and is close to the king. And if I were a sorcerer and needed to disguise myself as a man, that's the form I'd choose. Don't you agree, Miss Cully?" His voice was oily, his smile slippery. "Yes, I believe you do." He eyed me closely then chuckled.

I walked off. To my surprise and relief, he didn't try to stop me.

"You must question the servants more thoroughly," he called out. "I want to hear of your progress next time we speak. Otherwise, you know what will happen."

I heard him leave in the opposite direction. I followed the path through the forest until it met the village road, only to be stopped again by another rider. This one was a much more welcome sight.

"I see you're taking the long, slow way home," Dane said, dismounting.

"Not that long or slow," I said.

"We parted hours ago." He frowned. "Your hair's damp."

"I stopped for a dip in a pond."

His gaze raked my length and back up again. "Your clothes are dry."

"Not all of them."

His brows rose and his gaze roamed over me again. It felt warm enough to dry me completely. "Did anyone see you?"

"Only Lady Miranda Claypool."

His brows shot up higher. "How did you convince her to go into a pond?"

"I didn't have to. She convinced me. She's more wicked than she lets on."

He smiled—a good sign considering the dark mood I'd left him in. He also didn't seem in a hurry to leave. Whatever had taken him from the palace must have been dealt with.

"Have you been to Mull?" I asked.

"Yes."

"Why?"

"That's confidential," he said.

"Ah, so I will assume it was very important work to keep everyone safe," I teased.

"Just everyone at the palace. The village is out of my jurisdiction." His horse tossed its head and stomped its hoof, eager to be off again. "If I tell you to be careful, will you become angry with me again?"

"Again? Dane, I wasn't angry with you ever. Frustrated, perhaps, but not angry."

He didn't ask me why I was frustrated. Part of me wished he would so we could bring the situation to a head, but mostly I was glad he didn't. It was better for my heart if I didn't hear the reasons for his rejection.

"Good," was all he said.

"I'm glad to see you here," I told him. "It saves me a journey back to the palace to report on my meeting with Lord Barborough. I saw him just now, on my way out of the forest." He didn't seem surprised so must have known the Vytill representative was nearby. Perhaps that was why he was heading back to the palace from the village—he'd followed Barborough. "He pressed upon me the need to question the servants."

"Pressed?" he echoed.

"He reminded me of the consequences if I fail."

"Damn it." His horse shifted and he stroked its neck to calm it. "Next time, tell him one of the maids told you she was born in Freedland and came to Glancia for a better life. She applied for a job as maid, when she heard the palace was being built, and was accepted. A week later, she started here. The palace had just been completed."

"Where did she apply?"

He thought for a moment. "Tilting."

"I mean, at an office? How did she hear the new palace needed staff?"

"A friend told her, and she had heard it from another friend. Be vague so he can't verify your statements, but give him enough to make it believable."

"I'll try to sound convincing."

"Hopefully his threat to tell the king about your visits was an idle one, but I don't want to test him."

"Have you been following him?"

"That's also confidential."

"Fine, I won't ask again, although I will assume you've been following him to learn his movements and who his friends are."

"People like Barborough don't have friends," he said. "They have associates, people they use to get what they want." He must

C.J. ARCHER

have thought me troubled because he added, "Don't worry about him, Josie. You feed him your false information and I'll feed him mine."

"All right." I stroked his horse's neck too, my hand close to Dane's. His fingers stilled. I felt his gaze on me, but when I looked up, I realized *he* was the troubled one. Despite his attempts at a lighter mood, something worried him. "What is it, Dane? What's wrong?"

He hesitated then said, "I found out that Barborough has been stirring up the locals, whispering in certain ears to fuel the dissent that's been simmering for some time. If we're not careful, it'll boil over and Mull's sheriff won't be able to contain it. That'll play nicely into Vytill's hands."

"What can we do?"

"*You* can stay safe in your house, especially at night. *I'll* find a way to curtail Barborough's influence. Understood?"

"Understood. I have no intention of leaving the house at night anyway."

He eyed me carefully. "That was surprisingly easy. Are you sure you're Josie Cully and not a sorceress?"

"Ha! If I were, I'd choose to be a princess and look like Miranda."

His eyes brightened with his smile. "If you're fishing for compliments, I'm not giving any out today."

Perhaps I had been. He could have obliged by giving me just a small one. Once again, we were back to being awkward when everything had begun to return to normal. I could have kicked myself.

"Speaking of the king," I said, very aware that we had not been. "I saw him with Lady Morgrave. They came to the pond as we were leaving. They didn't see us."

One side of his mouth lifted in a smirk. "Let me guess. They were swimming naked too."

"I was *not* naked. Nor was Miranda."

He pressed his lips together but couldn't quite dampen the smile.

"Yes, they removed their clothes to go swimming," I said with a lift of my chin. "Miranda and I crept away before we saw much.

But it does prove that they are now enjoying one another's company in private. You suspected, didn't you?"

"I knew. Theo discovered them together last night. He was annoyed that he had to find somewhere else to sleep."

"Poor Theo."

"Don't feel sorry for him. He slept in the room vacated by the Claypools. It's a very nice suite and he had it all to himself."

"What do you think will happen now that the king has a mistress?"

"Difficult to say. I'm not familiar with the protocol, nor am I sure how attached he is to Lady Morgrave. The relationship might be fleeting, or it might be serious enough that she chooses his wife for him."

Imagine his poor wife having to contend with her husband's mistress. I felt sorry for the future queen. At least Miranda was safely relegated to a small room with the other lesser nobles, although she must be careful not to attract his attention again. She was beautiful, kind, and witty enough that she could do it without really trying.

"I'd better go," he said, gazing over my head in the direction of the palace. "I'd give you a ride home but—"

"I know, it would be awkward."

"Actually I was going to say I have to get back for a meeting with my men."

"Oh. Right. That'll teach me to open my mouth."

He laughed softly. "I know it's a little strained between us right now, but I don't want it to be."

"Nor do I."

"Can we still be friends?"

"Of course," I said. "Nothing need change."

"I agree."

The thing was, I wanted it to change. I wanted to take our relationship from friendship to something more. Clearly, Dane did not.

* * *

THE PROBLEM with living alone was that an entire day could pass without speaking to anyone. I could have spent hours making medicines in the kitchen, if only I hadn't run out of spices. There were enough locally grown plants in the larder from my foraging expeditions, but the more exotic required a trip to the market.

I checked my purse and counted out enough ells to cover the expense—no more. I then added another five ells for food. It left my purse precariously low.

The day had begun hot and promised to grow hotter without a cloud in the sky or a breath of wind. Another dip in the palace's pond would be nice, or a paddle in the shallows at Half Moon Cove. Thinking of that beach only brought back memories of meeting Dane there and seeing the scars crossing his broad back. That pleasurable time would forever be tainted with the sickening sight and the pain of discovering my father's body afterward.

Some of the food stalls were beginning to close before the heat ruined what little produce they had left. I should have come earlier before the best fruit and vegetables were sold. What remained were the bruised, the wilted, and yesterday's leftovers. I picked the freshest and paid the exorbitant asking prices. The grocer couldn't even look me in the eye as I handed over the ells. I'd known him all my life and he must be aware that my livelihood had diminished after Father's death, yet he still charged full price for a handful of nuts and a collection of vegetables beginning to turn brown.

"Ridiculous, ain't it?" rasped a voice in my ear; the voice of someone I didn't want to meet today.

"What's ridiculous, Ivor?" I asked, moving away.

"The cost of this filth." He picked up a limp leek from the cart and waved it in the air.

The grocer glared at him. "Put that down, Morgrain."

"You should be ashamed of yourself, charging Josie those prices."

"She pays the same as everyone else. I don't discriminate."

"You're greedy."

"Get going, Morgrain. Stop stirring up trouble."

I walked away, not wanting to witness an argument between them and not wanting to be anywhere near Ivor. He followed me to Mika Tao's spice stall, however, hovering like an annoying fly as I made my purchases.

"What do you want, Ivor?" I finally asked as I placed the parcels in my basket.

He removed his hat and wiped his forehead with the back of his hand. "Can't I just have a friendly chat with a friend?"

"Shouldn't you be at work?"

"I'm on my break, and if my employer doesn't like it, he can shove it. A man's allowed to have a break on a hot day and not lose his job."

True, but I doubted his break was long enough that he could wander around the market. I wasn't interested in hearing Ivor whine about the problems Mull faced, but I was interested in hearing more about the meeting he attended with Ned Perkin in The Anchor. Perhaps I'd encourage conversation, after all.

"I agree," I told him as we walked slowly together through the market. "I hope your employer is a reasonable man."

He snorted.

"Speaking of which, there's someone new that I've seen lately in Mull who seems to be important." I stopped beneath a large tree at the edge of the market. Its shade offered welcome respite from the heat. "You know everybody and everybody knows you, so I thought you could tell me his name."

Ivor's chest swelled. "What's he look like?"

"Mid-thirties, brown, windswept hair. His right arm doesn't seem to work very well."

"Aye, I know him. He's a lord, advisor to the king."

"King Leon?"

He chuckled. "Well it ain't King Alain, is it? Course, he might have advised him at the old castle in Tilting before he died. I don't know the lord's name. He wouldn't say." He glanced around then leaned in. "He says he wants to be anonymous on account of his position."

"How did you meet him?" I asked.

"He came to The Anchor and started asking around about the palace and servants, where they're from, that sort of thing."

"But if he's an advisor to the king, shouldn't he already have that information?"

"Because he's a lord and one of the king's men, most won't tell him their problems. He says he wants to help them by getting to know their struggles—and ours too—and he can't do that unless he knows more about them and us villagers. He seems like he wants to help, like he really wants to understand the working man and woman and improve our lot. Everything he learns, he passes onto the king and the other advisers in their policy meetings."

"What have you told him?"

"About the servants? Nothing. I don't know anything about them. Me, Ned and others have told him about our own troubles, and the problems Mull is facing right now since The Rift cut off The Thumb. He seemed real interested, so we invited him to sit in on a village meeting. Why do you want to speak to him?"

I considered telling him who Barborough was really working for, but decided to leave it to Dane. It might not be a good idea to let Ivor know that I was in Dane's confidence.

"I want to petition him about allowing women into the colleges, specifically the medical college," I said. "Since he's an advisor to the king, perhaps he can suggest it in a meeting with the king."

Ivor laughed and shook his head. "That ain't never going to happen. You should worry about what can be changed, not what can't."

"A stroke of a pen on a piece of paper can change it," I said hotly.

He held up his hands. "Don't get mad with me. It ain't my fault. Besides, what's wrong with being a midwife? Why do you have to be a doctor too?

I opened my mouth, to tell him everything that was wrong with his statements, only to close it again. Debating with Ivor Morgrain about a woman's right to study at college was like trying to make water flow upstream. It was a wasted effort.

Ivor squinted into the sky. "I have to get back to work. Meet me for a drink later at The Anchor."

"I can't."

"Why? It ain't like you got anything better to do."

"There's an expectant mother I have to look in on."

"Come after."

I sighed. "Ivor, I'm not meeting you for a drink. Not tonight or any other night. I'm sorry but—"

His hand whipped out and grabbed my wrist. I gasped as pain shot up my arm. "You owe me for telling you about that lord."

I tried to pull free but his grip was too tight. With my blood circulation strangled, my hand began to throb. "I owe you nothing. You gave me that information willingly."

"Nothing's free, Josie," he snarled, teeth bared. "Not around here. Merdu, you're such a naive fool."

"You're the fool, Ivor," I snapped. "If you wanted payment, you should have negotiated beforehand. Oh, and by the way, the lord with the limp arm is Lord Barborough and he's not an advisor to King Leon, he advises King Philip of Vytill."

The shocked look on his face was worth the cost of revealing what I knew. Dane had wanted to tell Ivor, Ned and the other Mullians that Barborough wasn't on their side anyway. I no longer cared if Ivor knew I was in Dane's confidence. I no longer cared what Ivor thought about anything.

"Now let me go," I snarled. "You're hurting me." This time when I pulled, he released me. I shook out my hand to re-invigorate the circulation and hurried back through the market, where people still milled about, hoping the prices would drop on the older produce.

A glance over my shoulder proved Ivor had left. I slowed and let out a shuddery breath. That was twice he'd become angry with me and lashed out, hurting me. There would not be a third time.

* * *

I WAS STILL SHAKING with fury and indignation when I received a visitor soon after arriving home. Remy, the child from The Row, blinked up at me on the doorstep. He looked healthy yet very thin, like most children from Mull's slum.

I invited him in for tea and a bite to eat, hoping the flat oat cakes in the tin were still edible. I kept them for visitors, but I'd had so few callers lately that they were probably stale.

"Thank you, Miss, but I can't. I got to bring you back with me." He took my hand and tugged.

"What's wrong? Is it your mother?"

"No, Miss, it's our neighbor. She's having a baby but it got stuck. My Ma says you can get it out."

"I'll fetch my pack."

The women of The Row usually delivered their own babies with the help of neighbors, or sometimes with no help at all. My father had attended a difficult birth there on at least one occasion in my stead. He'd not liked me going anywhere near the lawless neighborhood. I had not told him about the time I'd been chased into it, when I'd met Remy's mother. It had been better for his peace of mind that he remained ignorant.

Despite the bright sunny day, the light was duller in The Row, and the thick air smelled fouler than usual, as if a blanket smothered the houses—if the lean-tos and derelict buildings could be called that. Remy led me along the main thoroughfare, the original row, where the whores eyed me with barely disguised animosity. Last time, they'd driven me deeper into the complex web of lanes, but this time they didn't threaten me. Remy's determined step seemed to reassure them that I wasn't going to steal their trade.

We passed few men, but those we did see watched me like they either wanted to have their way with me or steal my pack. Two followed us. They were big men, built like they were hewn from rock, certainly not starving like the others.

"I'm a midwife," I told them, clutching my pack to my chest. "There are only forceps in here and other tools of my trade. I deliver babies," I added, because they showed not a flicker of understanding.

I followed Remy into a familiar lane. It was the one in which I'd lost my money and a crayfish that I'd intended to cook for dinner. Remy climbed through a hole in the wall of a building that looked as if a strong breeze would shatter it. I squeezed through and continued on through another hole to a small room where the air was so putrid I gagged.

I covered my nose and mouth and allowed my eyes to adjust to the darkness. What I saw made me want to immediately leave again. Going by the two mattresses and a trunk, the room was a home, but there was no other furniture. Two children, younger than Remy, sat beside a heavily pregnant woman lying on one of the thin mattresses. Their clothing hung off their thin frames and their hands, feet and faces were filthy, their hair matted. Some of the smell probably came from them. They watched me through frightened eyes until Remy spoke to them in soothing tones.

Remy's mother, Dora, sat with the woman, holding her hand. She was about to speak when the woman screamed and writhed on the mattress.

"Remy, take the children outside," I told him, kneeling near the pregnant woman.

Once they were gone, I lifted her skirts and felt her protruding belly. The baby was in the correct position, thank the goddess. With such poor light, I couldn't see if it was crowning, but I could feel.

"My name is Josie Cully," I said when her pain subsided.

"I'm Marnie," she said between pants.

I smiled to reassure her. "You haven't dilated much, Marnie. How close are the contractions?"

"Not very, but they're painful." She spoke well, as if she'd had a good upbringing with some education, unlike many in the slums. "My back and hips are sore."

"She can hardly move," Dora said. "She's been bed-bound since she came here two weeks ago."

"You're not from Mull?" I asked.

Marnie shook her head. "Vytill. Port Haven on The Thumb. My husband had a good job there, operating a crane on the docks. We had to leave after The Rift."

It was an all-too common tale these days. "He doesn't have work here?"

"Not yet, but he's hopeful." From the tone of her voice, she'd lost all hope.

"That's where he is today," Dora said. "Looking for work. Any kind of work. The crane companies aren't hiring right now."

"No one's hiring," Marnie bit off. "Not Vytill folk, anyway. I wish we'd never come here. I wish we'd stayed in Vytill. He might not have work but at least we'd have a better roof over our heads than this, and we'd still have our savings."

"Did you spend it all to come here?" I asked.

"We had to give it up at the border. We had to pay the Glancia authorities to live in this country, and what was left was confiscated by the Vytill authorities. They say it was Vytill money, earned in Vytill and should stay in Vytill. It'll just go to the king's coffers. All we had left was that trunk with some clothes, brought here on a cart. We sold the cart, but the money's almost all gone now."

I sat back on my haunches. "You can't even keep your own money?" It hardly seemed worthwhile to come here at all, yet so many of them poured across the border.

"My husband wants work, Miss. He only knows how to be a crane operator, and docks are the only places that have cranes. He didn't want to stay in Vytill and learn a new trade. There aren't many jobs there anyway, except mine work and that's a fast way to an early grave. So we came here. He thought he'd get hired straight away, on account of his experience, but it's too late. All the jobs are gone."

"There's plenty of construction down by the docks," I said. "Could he find work as a laborer there?"

"He's trying but the men of Mull got the best jobs and the first wave of immigrants from The Thumb got the rest. Now, there's nothing left, only scraps for beggars." Her face crumpled and a silent sob wracked her. "We have nothing here," she said through her tears. "What hope is there for our children?"

Her tears turned to those of pain as another contraction ripped through her. It lasted several excruciating moments. By the end of it, she was sweating and panting and crying again.

Dora handed her a cup but I took it from her. I smelled it then tasted a drop. It was clean and I gave Dora nod. She had heeded my earlier advice about the need for fresh water.

"Can you do something for her pain?" she asked in her soft, fragile voice. It was easy to forget how young she was, since Remy was eight, but she couldn't have been much older than me.

"You say it hurts your hips and back?" I asked Marnie as she drank deeply.

She nodded. "We walked here."

"All that way? In your condition? Merdu, no wonder you can hardly move."

"When they got here, her husband had to carry her inside," Dora said.

"If it weren't for Dora," Marnie said, taking Dora's hand again, "I don't know where we would have slept these last nights. She saved us."

I felt Marnie's hips and found the dislocation. It was surprising the pain hadn't caused her to pass out. The birth would be excruciating.

I pulled out a bottle of Mother's Milk from my pack and measured two drops onto a spoon. I didn't like using the strong pain reliever on pregnant women, as it was important they knew when to push, but Marnie's condition left me no choice. I couldn't let her go through childbirth if there was an alternative. I measured out precisely the number of drops and no more. Too much would make her throw up as the effects wore off, but more importantly, it was my last bottle. The liquid was complicated to make, the ingredient list long, and some of those ingredients were rare and expensive. I couldn't afford to make another batch.

"This will take effect very quickly," I told her as I spooned it into her mouth. "Your body will feel numb and you may feel drowsy, but try not to succumb to sleep. I want you awake so you can push when I tell you."

Slowly Marnie's body began to relax. I knew the moment the full effects of the Mother's Milk had taken hold because she released Dora's hand and sank into the mattress. With the mother calm, I was able to place my ear trumpet to her swollen belly and listen to the baby's heartbeat. It was strong and steady.

"Were your other children born quickly?" I asked.

"They took their time." She even managed a smile. "They're still like that. Still dawdlers." She glanced at the hole in the wall.

"I'll fetch them," Dora said, rising.

She returned a moment later with the children and Remy. Marnie reassured them and told them to be good until their father returned.

"Can I send them on an errand with Remy?" I asked. "It'll give them something to do."

Marnie hesitated. "They're young."

"Remy will take care of them," Dora said. "He's very responsible."

"It's not far," I reassured her.

Marnie nodded.

"Remy, take the children to the house directly opposite where I live," I told the boy. "Tell the woman who answers that I sent you, and that I'd like her to give you something to eat."

"No, no," Marnie protested, trying to sit up and failing. "Your neighbors shouldn't be bothered with our troubles."

"They won't mind. Besides, the family owes me dozens of favors. They've never paid for my father's medical services."

Dora encouraged the children to go. Marnie protested but it was unconvincing, something I'd counted on. No mother would put pride before her own children's welfare. Meg and her family would see that all three were well fed and probably washed too. Meg's mother would give the clothes off her own back for a child.

My own stomach growled. It had been some time since I'd eaten, but at least my last meal had come that same day. Marnie and Dora probably hadn't eaten decent food for some time. Either they didn't hear my stomach or they politely ignored it.

"It's not healthful for you or the children to stay in here all day and night," I said, taking a proper look around the room. A little light filtered through the cracks in the roof, but those cracks would not be a blessing when it rained. "You need light and fresh air."

"It's safer in here," Marnie said.

Both women cast anxious glances toward the hole in the wall, no doubt worrying that their children had left The Row without incident. While it was a dangerous place for outsiders, The Row tended to leave their own alone, so Dora once assured me. Seeing their anxiety, I wasn't entirely sure if that was true now.

With the Mother's Milk taking effect, I talked to Marnie about life on The Thumb between contractions to keep her awake and pass the time. The conversation naturally progressed to the stark differences to her life in Mull. It wasn't just the poverty they faced here, and her husband's frustration at the lack of work, there was also the animosity from the Mullians.

"He's been spat on, shouted at, sworn at, and had to run from an angry mob once," she said, almost in tears again. "Every day he goes out, I worry he won't come home, or if he does, he'll be battered and bruised. The Row might look like a nasty place, but he feels safer walking the streets in here than out there in the so-called respectable parts of Mull."

"The Row is filled with migrants from The Thumb," Dora said. "And those who were here before The Rift know what it's like to have nothing, and be despised for it. We're all the same in The Row, and The Row protects us, in a way."

"The locals are afraid of losing their jobs." Even as I said, I heard how hollow the argument sounded. "But you're right, there's no excuse for how you're being treated."

"Why don't your lawmen do something about it?" Marnie asked, rubbing her belly. "Why don't they stop it before it gets out of control?"

"There aren't enough lawmen to stop them," Dora said.

"Then employ more. That way you give jobs to those in need and keep everyone safe."

"This village spend more than it has to?" Dora snorted. "There are a lot of things the governor could have done to feed and house the needy but he hasn't lifted a finger."

"Doesn't your king live nearby? Wouldn't he want peace in the village? I would think he'd worry about an uprising."

She was right but I wasn't sure if King Leon was aware of the situation in Mull. Dane certainly was, and I had to assume he informed the king and his advisers.

The children returned, sporting clothes that had probably once belonged to Meg and her brother before they grew out of them. It was just like Mrs. Diver to hold onto them for sentimental reasons or for future grandchildren. The children's faces and hair were also clean, and each carried a pack of provisions that they eagerly showed to their mothers. I finally sent them out again as Marnie's contractions came closer together.

Her husband arrived shortly after the birth of his son. Despite his exhaustion, he cradled the newborn gently and quietly sang him a song from his homeland. I left soon after, with a promise to return to check on mother and baby.

I was speaking to Dora outside when Marnie's husband squeezed through the hole in the wall. He was tall and had probably once been well built but his clothes now hung loosely from his wiry frame.

"Take this as payment," he said, pushing one of the packs at me.

I shook my head. "You can pay me when you find work."

He looked relieved. "I will. Thank you."

"In the meantime, if you need any medical assistance, come to the house with the sign of two cupped hands. Dora and Remy know the way. I'll give you credit until you can afford to pay me. Unless it's a midwifery issue, don't tell the authorities."

It didn't matter if he paid or not. I couldn't let children go without medical help. Besides, it would give me something to do and give me a reason to brush up on my doctoring skills.

He walked with me out of The Row, his presence acting as security. From there, I headed home alone. Clouds blocked the moonlight and darkness blanketed the village. The air was dense with the promise of rain, and I was soon sweaty from my brisk pace. It would be a warm night, not conducive to sleep, particularly for those of us who didn't dare leave a window open.

It wasn't late, and I expected to see others out on such a warm night. But no couples strolled hand-in-hand, no one hurried home after working late or drinking at the taverns. The hushed silence felt as thick as the air and just as expectant.

Then I heard it. A shout, followed by several in response. Another shout, louder, then a crowd's roar. Drums pounded in a rhythmic marching beat while others clanged in random, tuneless *thwacks*.

The drums and shouts drew nearer, rising and falling like the tide. I paused, unsure whether to continue home or see what was happening. My curiosity warred with common sense and common sense won.

Or would have, if I hadn't met Ingrid Swinson.

CHAPTER 12

*I*ngrid, her father and brother headed toward me. Her brother gripped a piece of wood like a club.

"You coming to the protest march, Josie?" he asked.

"What march?"

"Some folk have organized a protest against the Vytill scum coming here and taking our jobs."

"Hurting our families," Gill added, placing an arm around his daughter's shoulders.

"Taking over," Ingrid chimed in. "Come on, Josie, come with us."

"It doesn't sound safe," I said. "And there's no proof that a Vytill man hurt you. It could have been a Mullian."

"You know it ain't." Her brother smacked his club against his palm. "Come on, you need to get your voice heard or nothing will change. It'll get a whole lot worse if we don't."

"The governor needs to know how we feel," Gill said. "He needs to know how angry we are that Vytill folk are allowed to come here and turn everything to shit."

"Forget the governor," Ingrid said, linking her arm with mine and marching me off. "I want the king to hear us. I want his golden walls to shake from our shouts!"

I allowed her to sweep me with them. We marched along the street, joining others emerging from their houses, drawing ever closer to the song of protest. "Who organized this march?" I asked Ingrid.

"Don't know," she said. "Doesn't matter. Everyone in Mull will be there."

When we merged with the main group of protesters in the central village square, I could see that she was wrong. Not even half of Mull's original population had turned up. There were no shopkeepers or craftsmen and few construction workers. It was mostly dockers and fishermen, and men at that. I recognized Ivor and Ned Perkin near the front, punching their fists in the air, inciting the crowd with chants that blamed the Vytill migrants for every ill befalling the villagers.

"They take our jobs!" Ned shouted.

The crowd roared in agreement. Those with clubs smashed them into bollards or walls or simply against the ground at their feet.

"They drive the prices up!" Ned cried. "They rape our women!"

I felt Ingrid tense, but she shouted her agreement along with the rest of the crowd. Perhaps word had spread of the attack on her, despite her wish to keep it private, or perhaps Ned had simply made it up to incite the crowd.

I was contemplating slipping away when Sheriff Neerim arrived with both of his men on horseback. He called for calm, urging the crowd to disperse and go home.

Ned refused. "We will *not*! Not until you take action, Sheriff! We want them gone from Mull! Every last one of the scum should be forced out. This is *our* home! Our village!"

"You know I can't do that," Sheriff Neerim bellowed in a deep, sonorous voice that commanded attention. "You can make as much noise as you want, Ned, but it won't make a lick of difference. Legally, they're allowed to stay."

"Then the law must change!"

"Aye!" the crowd shouted.

"Go home, Ned," the sheriff said. "Don't give us trouble now or there'll be consequences."

"Get out of our way!"

"So you can go where?"

"To The Row where that scum are living! We're going to clean out that neighborhood since you're too scared to do it."

Merdu, no. Marnie was in no condition to flee a mob. I had to warn her, warn them all. But if I did, there might be a riot *and* a brawl. The sheriff might look assured, sitting atop his horse, but his men couldn't stop them. The crowd might not be large, but three against fifty wasn't nearly enough.

"Get out of our way, Sheriff!" Ned shouted. "Or we'll make you!"

The sheriff's only move was to put his fingers to his lips and whistle. A dozen horsemen emerged from the nearby lanes and streets and spread out until they'd hemmed the crowd in. I didn't need to see their crimson doublets to know they were palace guards. I recognized them all, including the one wearing black with the gold braid at his shoulder.

Dane claimed he had no jurisdiction in the village, but perhaps an angry mob gathered a mere five miles from the palace was considered enough of a danger to the king to involve his guards. The numbers were still stacked in favor of the crowd, but the sight of the armed men on horseback was enough to see it dwindle more and more with each passing moment.

Ned continued to rant at the sheriff, but his tone was edged with uncertainty, and the protestors at his back drifted away. It was time for me to leave too, but I couldn't do so without being seen by at least one of the guards.

I bowed my head and made my way between the two nearest. Unfortunately, one of them was Erik.

"Josie?" His booming voice seemed to echo around the square, bouncing off walls, directly to Dane's ears.

The captain's head jerked toward us and his eyes narrowed upon seeing me. Thankfully he didn't approach.

"What are you doing here?" Erik asked, sounding angry enough for the both of them. "This is no place for you."

"It's a peaceful protest," I shot back.

"Because we are here now. Otherwise, it could be bad."

"I wouldn't have stayed if it got bad." I glanced at Dane again, now facing forward, his back rigid. "In fact, I ended up here by accident."

One of the riders at the end approached. I could tell from his stocky silhouette that it was Max but I couldn't see his face until he drew closer. "Josie, what are you doing here?"

"Getting a lecture, it seems. I'm on my way home."

"Not alone, you're not. There are too many men about. Angry men. Captain!"

Dane joined us, but his gaze did not settle on me. He scanned the square, keeping an eye on the mob to insure it didn't gather again. Only Ned, Ivor and a handful of others remained, talking in a group.

"I don't need an escort home," I said. "I don't live far and I know all of these people. They wouldn't harm me."

Finally Dane's gaze met mine. I wasn't sure what I expected, but I didn't expect it to be devoid of emotion. It was as if the man I knew was nowhere in sight. Was that how he always looked in charged situations that required his attention?

"Erik, inform the others to disperse among the streets in pairs," Dane said. "Make sure the peace is kept. I'll remain here. Max, you'll disperse in the direction of Josie's house."

I marched off, not waiting for my escort, which, despite Dane's words, was precisely what Max was. He walked his horse behind me all the way, only stopping at the end of my street when Meg ran toward me from the opposite direction. Her brother trailed behind, not in quite as much of a hurry as his sister.

"Josie, where have you been?" Meg cried, pulling me into a hug. "We were so worried. We knew you were seeing to your patient, but didn't think much of it until Lyle came home from work and said a protest march had been organized."

"I didn't hear about it 'til late," Lyle said, joining her. "When Meg said you were out, we got worried. The Mull folk won't hurt you, but who knows about the others."

"Not you too," I said on a groan. "I've just come from helping a woman from Vytill give birth to her third child. The entire family lives in squalor, afraid for their lives in The Row, and afraid for the husband's safety when he goes out looking for work. He came here to find a way to feed his family and give them a better future than what they faced on The Thumb after The Rift destroyed their livelihood. Why can't you see that, Lyle?"

At least he had the decency to look embarrassed. Many Mullians wouldn't, but Lyle was a good man, albeit a little slow. He bristled, however, as Max drew up alongside us.

"Evening, Miss Meg," Max said.

Meg turned her head to the side, hiding the birthmark from him. "Evening, Sergeant Max," she muttered into her chin.

"Just Max," he told her.

"And I'm just Meg." She sounded like she was smiling.

Lyle frowned at her then glared at Max. "Who're you?"

"Sergeant Max of the royal guards," Max said, straightening. "And you are?"

"Lyle Diver."

"Meg's brother," I added, and was gratified to see Max relax.

"Pleased to meet you, Mr. Diver," he said.

Lyle crossed his arms and his frown deepened. He looked as if he was about to interrogate the sergeant, which was my cue to steer him away and leave Max and Meg alone. Lyle complied willingly enough, but unfortunately Meg followed us after a hasty goodbye to Max.

I sighed. If she didn't start believing she was worthy, he would think her uninterested when I knew her to be the opposite.

"Why was he escorting you home?" Meg asked when Lyle left us outside my door.

"I got swept up into the march. Don't look so worried. It was peaceful."

"For now. Next time, it might be different. Next time, their numbers could be more, or they might be more inclined to violence."

"I can't imagine they'll become violent. These are people we've known all our lives, Meg. A handful of them should be avoided, but most of the protestors I saw tonight are just ordinary men, not bad people."

"I hope you're right. I really do, but I'm not so sure."

* * *

I WANTED to visit Marnie the following morning, to check on her and the baby, but was reluctant to head into The Row alone. I walked to the market instead, dodging puddles and the worst of the mud. The previous night's rain had brought an end to the oppressive heat and today was clear and a little cooler. I wasn't buying anything at the market. I merely wanted to gauge the temperature of the village. It seemed I wasn't the only one with that idea. Two guards watched on from horseback.

I was about to head home when Dane joined them. He spotted me and approached. Dark shadows smudged the skin beneath his eyes and bristles shadowed his jaw.

"You haven't been back to the palace all night, have you?" I said.

"Good morning to you too." He checked the vicinity then dismounted.

"But it rained last night."

"Very observant of you."

I gave him a withering glare.

"Speaking of last night," he went on, "why were you in the march?"

I sighed. "Straight to the lecture, I see."

"It's a question, not a lecture."

I sighed again. "I was on my way home when I met Ingrid Swinson and her family coming to join the protestors. Ingrid sort of swept me along with them."

He cocked his head to the side as if he hadn't heard me properly. "You were on your way home? At night? Josie, you promised you'd be careful." His voice was surprisingly gentle.

"I am being careful, but babies don't keep regular hours."

He huffed out a breath. "Next time, go straight home. Don't get inquisitive and allow yourself to be swept into a crowd like that one."

He knew me too well already. I *had* been perfectly capable of leaving Ingrid's side, but my curiosity got the better of me. "You think there'll be a next time?"

"I'm almost certain of it, but hopefully not for a while. Most of the crowd didn't seem interested once we showed up, but we can't always be here, and they might be angrier next time."

"The sheriff needs to put on more men," I said.

"He's been told as much."

I waited for him to tell me more, perhaps that the sheriff was hiring, but he said nothing. "You could always send for the warrior priests in Tilting," I said.

His gaze sharpened. "Warrior priests? There are such a thing?"

"A collection of about fifty or so, all elite fighters, all dedicated to the god, Merdu. They're known as Merdu's Guards and live at a fortified temple in Tilting. They'll fight for the king if called upon, but they'll put the god before the king if it came to a choice."

"Good to know."

"Hopefully the instigators will calm down now. I told Ivor Morgrain that Barborough works for Vytill not Glancia. I doubt they'll listen to him anymore. And before you lecture me," I cut in when he opened his mouth to speak, "I didn't approach Ivor with the intention of informing him. He approached me and I merely saw the opportunity to pass on the knowledge."

"I'm not going to lecture you. I'm going to thank you."

"Oh. Good." I stroked the horse's neck, my hand close to Dane's. His gaze tracked it. "Will you remain in the village long?"

He touched my wrist where the bruise Ivor had caused the day before darkened the skin. "What happened?" he asked.

"It's nothing." I lowered my arm and clasped my hands in front of me. "I knocked it on the table when I was making some medicines."

He gently took my hand and turned it over, palm up, revealing the bruise on the underside of my wrist. He caressed it with his thumb, lightly stroking the blue-black patch, and then lifted it. I thought he was going to kiss it but he suddenly let go.

"You should be more careful," was all he said.

I folded my arms and willed my nerves to calm. "Are you returning to the palace?" I asked. "Because you should get some sleep. You look tired."

"Now who's lecturing?" he said with a crooked smile.

"It's a question, not a lecture," I said, echoing his earlier words.

"I suppose I deserved that. I will return to the palace when Max brings men for the next shift."

"Can you spare a man for a while? I want an escort into The Row to check on a newborn and his mother."

"You went into The Row last night?"

I arched my brows.

"Fine, no lectures," he muttered, "but I wish to express my unease at you entering The Row alone."

"I had an escort. He's well known there and is quite fearless." I didn't tell him my escort had been an eight year-old.

"I'll take you." He put out his hand then quickly withdrew it, balling it into a fist at his side. It wasn't until we walked off, leading his horse, that I realized he'd been about to help me up into the saddle but had thought better of it. I was relieved. It would have been excruciating on my nerves to be that close to him again. I did not want him to know how he affected me.

Dane spoke to one of his men then we walked to The Row. It quickly became obvious that Dane was a novelty in the slum. Whores emerged from behind frayed curtains that shielded their beds from passersby, and their whoremasters stepped forward with threatening glares, prepared to protect their territory if necessary. The children playing in the gutters were far more interested in Dane's horse than us. A cluster followed us all the way to Dora's street.

Remy greeted me but he also only had eyes for the horse. Marnie's two children weren't quite as awestruck, probably because they'd seen horses on their journey to Mull.

"Where does your patient live?" Dane asked, looking around at the hovels.

"Through there." I pointed at the hole in the wall.

"That's a hole, not a door."

"Actually it's a *doorway*."

"I don't think it's wise for you to go in. I can't follow you."

It was true, I realized. He was too big. "The families of these children live inside. No one else. I'll be quite safe."

I'd probably be safer in there than outside. A small crowd had followed us, many of them children, but there were several men and not all of them looked half-starved like Marnie's husband. These were the so-called protectors of The Row, the whoremasters and gang members who made sure the sheriff's men felt unwelcome. They were the law in this neighborhood, and they would not like a palace guard on their territory. I shouldn't have brought Dane. He was in more danger here than me.

"Perhaps we should go," I said.

"Check on your patient first. I'll wait here."

I climbed through the hole and glanced back from the other side. Dane stood facing the lane, his hand resting on his sword hilt. He spoke quietly to the children, encouraging them to pat the horse's nose, but he did not take his gaze off the mouth of the lane and the small, mean crowd gathered there. I resolved to be quick.

Marnie and her baby were fine. She assured me she had eaten because Dora made her. Their water was fresh and the air didn't seem quite so oppressive today. With the baby born, Marnie's hips and back had dramatically improved and she was able to stand and walk, although she was weak. She promised to walk a little outside for sunlight and exercise as soon as she was strong enough.

I returned through the hole to see Dane talking to Marnie's husband while several children patted his horse. One of Marnie's children even sat on the saddle while her father held her. He chatted quietly to Dane. Upon seeing me, he lifted the child off and greeted me with a smile.

"I told him the sheriff was looking for new recruits to train," Dane said as we left.

"You think the sheriff will employ someone from outside of Mull?" I asked. "Someone not even from Glancia?"

"He has been encouraged to do so, since a lot of the trouble is coming from Vytill men who've come here without their families. Having Vytillians in a position of authority might settle them, make them feel accepted. Whether the sheriff heeds that advice is up to him."

"Sheriff Neerim is a sensible man."

"So I've been told, but I hear the governor is not."

"True, and the governor has the power to overrule the sheriff," I said, in case he wasn't aware.

He seemed to already know, however. He must have researched the local administrative structure of the kingdom.

By the time we returned to the market, Max and the new guards had arrived to relieve the others, including Dane. They exchanged some words then Dane walked me home. He did not insist on the escort but I didn't ask him to leave either. I was hopeful for another quiet moment together, perhaps even another kiss.

My hopes were soon dashed. He gave no sign that he thought of me as anything other than a friend, and I was too cowardly to grasp his face with both hands and plant a kiss on his lips.

He made sure I was safely inside before leaving. I watched him go then went to shut the door but opened it wide again as Meg emerged from her house opposite. She also watched Dane ride off and waited until he was out of sight before joining me.

"What was he doing here?" she asked with a mischievous smile.

"Nothing at all," I said on a sigh.

"You like him, don't you?"

I just looked at her.

"Then you should let him know how you feel," she said.

"How?"

"Kiss him."

"We have kissed. It didn't end well."

She stared at me, her jaw slack. "When?"

"Three days ago."

"And you didn't tell me?"

"Sorry," I said wryly. "I've been trying to forget about it. He made it clear he's not interested in me in that way."

She gazed up the street again in the direction he'd gone. "Are you quite sure? I consider myself an expert at matchmaking, and I think he does like you in *that* way."

I gripped her shoulders and made sure she looked me in the eyes. "If you're an expert matchmaker, you'd go to the market right now," I said, eager to change the topic.

"Why?"

"Max is there."

"I have no need to go," she said, pulling free.

"You could invent a reason."

She clicked her tongue. "You're being childish, Josie."

I grinned.

"Wipe that foolish smile off your face. You look ridiculous." She marched back to her side of the street and slammed the door.

* * *

I took a small bottle of cough medicine over to Meg's house in the early afternoon as a peace offering. She accepted it on the condition I never mention Max's name to her again. I promised and returned home to find a note had been slipped under my door. It was from Lord Barborough, demanding my presence at the palace.

A meeting with him was inevitable, and I was glad the time had finally arrived. Ever since discussing the false information to feed him with Dane, I'd wanted to bring the situation to a head. I wanted to learn what he knew about the sorcerer.

I immediately left for the palace, hitching a ride on the back of a wagon taking freshly caught crayfish and oysters to the palace kitchens. I stank when I arrived and asked one of the kitchen servants waiting for the delivery where I could wash. He directed me to the central fountain in the commons' courtyard.

Other palace servants washed there too, some lingering to chat. I expected them to stop when I approached, but they didn't seem to mind if I overheard them. Some of the maids even nodded at me in greeting and another loaned me a small bottle of rosewater to scent my hands.

With the stink of seafood reduced, I went in search of a footman to pass on a message to Lord Barborough that I had arrived. But the first footman I found heading to the palace along the breezeway between the commons and the pavilion was Seb.

As with the other times I'd seen him, he eyed me thoroughly, as if inspecting a vegetable in the market. The tip of his tongue poked through his pressed lips like a pink, slimy creature emerging from a burrow. The skin on the back of my neck prickled, even after he'd disappeared into the palace.

"Stay away from that one," said a maid heading in the opposite direction, a yellow silk gown over her arm. "He's taken a liking to you, I can tell, and that ain't a good thing."

"Why do you say that?" It was possible the maids knew something and hadn't gone to Dane with the information. Sometimes women who'd been violated didn't want to talk to a man about it.

"It's just a feeling I get," she said. "But it ain't me who has to be careful around him."

"Why not? Who should be careful?"

171

"You pretty ones."

"Has he done something to one of the maids? Hurt any of them?"

"He's pinched more than one arse, but I think he won't stop at that. One day, a fiddle won't be enough for him. He'll want more, and no one's willing to give it to him because he's slime. But like I said, I'm too old and fat for Seb. It's you young ones who should watch out."

"I think everyone should be careful of him," I said. "Men like Seb will take the opportunity if it arises."

She nodded at my warning and continued on toward the commons. I hailed a passing footman and asked him to find Lord Barborough. It was a long time before he returned and informed me that Barborough would meet me in the same enclosed garden as our first meeting.

I felt conspicuous as I followed the northern wing's walls past the garrison and prison entrance. Two guards greeted me as they exited the garrison, and I asked them to inform Dane of my visit when they saw him. I rounded the practice yard at the very end of the palace, where another two guards sparred with swords, and made my way along the path between the garden sections. It was a quiet part of the formal gardens, with most nobles preferring to wander in the center between the palace entrance and Lake Grand where they could be seen. Those I did pass eyed me with suspicion, no doubt wondering why a woman dressed like a villager was in their domain.

Would any of them inform Lady Deerhorn of my presence? Would she inform the king? Despite telling her I didn't care if she did, I no longer felt indifferent. Lady Deerhorn and her family would make powerful enemies, and I feared I'd already set Lord Xavier against me by refusing to spy on the duke of Gladstow for him.

Lord Barborough sat on the stone bench in the enclosed garden, his legs crossed and his right arm lying limply in his lap. He neither rose nor smiled upon seeing me, merely inviting me to sit beside him. I did, ensuring there was space between us.

"I don't know why you're afraid of me, Josie. I can't do anything to you with this pathetic arm." He nudged it with his good hand. "You're more likely to overpower me." It was said too smugly for it to be entirely true. Either he was stronger than he looked, and knew it, or he'd stashed a weapon somewhere on his person.

"I'm naturally cautious," I said. "Particularly these days. Just last night there was trouble in the village."

"So I heard. I'm sure a careful girl like you kept away."

"No, sir, I did not," I said, all innocence. "But the palace guards intervened so nothing came of the march, thank Hailia. I don't know how they knew about it."

"Spies in the enemy camp?"

"I suppose, but I don't know about these things."

"Of course you wouldn't." He seemed to have bought my simple village girl act. This was one man I didn't want knowing that I was aware of his spying activities. The Deerhorns were not nearly as dangerous as a Vytill lord, a man almost beyond the reach of Glancian laws.

"You know why I've asked you here, don't you?" he said.

"I do."

"And do you have something for me?"

"Yes, my lord." I told him the story Dane and I concocted about a palace maid I'd befriended who claimed she came from Freedland originally and had heard about employment at the palace from a friend in Tilting. "She came here immediately and started straight away," I finished.

He gave no indication whether he believed me or not. He simply sat there, his thumb stroking the dead hand in his lap. "How did her friend learn of the position?" he finally asked.

"I don't know."

"When she arrived here, how many other staff were already working?"

"I don't know."

"Did you ask her if she has spoken to any other servants about their pasts?"

"No, sir."

He huffed out a breath. "Why not?"

I shrugged. "I didn't think to ask, sir."

"Merdu, I thought you cleverer than that." He continued

stroking his thumb along the back of his limp hand. "Why did she leave Freedland in the first place?"

That was an innocent enough question for me to give an innocent answer to. "Freedland is poor, my lord."

"I know that," he snapped.

"The mine where her father worked let some workers go so her family came to Glancia for a better life."

"Glancia has been far too lax with its borders, although I'm sure that will change, given the recent problems."

I wasn't sure if he expected me to offer an opinion, but I chose not to, since it might ruin my innocent act.

He stood and addressed me down his nose. "I want you to ask her some more questions and try to enlist her assistance."

"I don't understand," I said, knowing what he was going to ask, yet not wanting to hear it.

"Ask her to spy for you. Tell her you'll pay her."

"I have no money to pay her."

With a shake of his head and a muttered "Merdu," he pulled two coins from his doublet pocket. "I expect answers for this, Josie, better ones than you've given me so far." He pressed the coins into my palm.

"And what about me?" I asked. "You owe me for telling you what the maid said."

"I'm giving you my silence. I won't tell anyone of your interest in the king's use of magic."

I shot to my feet. "You promised me information about the sorcerer."

"The information you gave me isn't worth much."

"Then don't expect anything more." I held out the coins between thumb and forefinger.

He grabbed my hand, his long fingers enclosing mine like a cage. "Keep the money. I'll tell you something about the sorcerer." He released me only to stroke my arm. I tried to pull away but he wrapped his fingers around my wrist, right over the bruise. He was stronger than he looked, and I hissed in pain. He only smiled. "It gives three wishes to the one who frees it."

It was more information than I'd hoped for and it took me a

moment to digest and think what it meant. "What kind of wishes?" I asked.

"Anything the heart desires."

"Why only three?"

"I don't know. Perhaps it likes clichés. If I ever meet the sorcerer, I'll ask."

"Where does it need to be freed from?"

"Nobody knows. If they did, the sorcerer would have been found and freed many times throughout history, but it has not been seen for a thousand years. Until now."

"Perhaps," I said.

He frowned. "You don't think it has been found? Isn't that why you came to me, because you think the palace is a result of magic, the servants too?"

"I used to, but after speaking to that maid, I'm no longer sure," I said. "I think she told the truth. She and the others seem very real to me, and this place too."

He loosened his grip and I pulled free. "Surely you don't believe that?" he said.

"Why not? The palace's construction is improbable, I grant you that, but not impossible. And how could magic account for all the staff? That maid had a life before coming here, and I suspect the others do too."

He grunted. "You seem to have thought this through." It sounded like he no longer believed my innocent village girl act.

I was about to make my excuses to leave but he got in first. "I want more information in two days' time, Miss Cully. Or I will tell the king about your visits and this kind of talk. Is that clear?"

I swallowed and watched him leave through the garden arch. I promptly sat on the stone bench and lowered my head into my hands. What story should I make up to satisfy him next?

The sound of his voice had me sitting up again, even though it wasn't close by. Other voices, men's voices, joined his and I caught snippets of their conversation on the breeze.

"...told you were here." I didn't recognize the speaker, but he spoke to Lord Barborough as an equal. "...talk to you about...progress."

Progress? Was the man referring to Barborough's efforts at infiltrating Ned Perkin's group? I crouched beside the bushes edging the garden and parted the leaves and twigs. I couldn't see anyone but their voices were clearer.

"He has become more accepting of the idea," Barborough said. "Thank you for all your efforts at convincing him of the benefits."

"Our pleasure," one said.

"We do it for Glancia's benefit, not Vytill's," said a gruff voice. "Of course we'll advocate for the Princess Illiriya. Marrying her is the sensible option."

"There's a problem, however," Barborough went on. "He has taken a keen interest in Lady Morgrave, and my sources tell me she's a manipulative bitch. I don't care who he fucks, as long as she doesn't sway him against the princess."

"Let us take care of her," said one of the others.

"I was planning to." Barborough's voice sounded further away, as if he'd walked off.

"I know her father," said the man. "And her husband."

"It's the mother you need to speak to," his companion said with a bitter sneer. "She wields the power."

Their voices drifted off as they walked away. I left the garden behind and returned to the palace, even more relieved that I'd told Lord Barborough I didn't believe the palace was created by magic. Hopefully it would sway his own opinion, because if he started a rumor that the king had used magic to inherit the throne, the entire kingdom could fall apart. Leon may not be a great king, but he was the best option when the alternative was infighting at best, or, at worst, war.

CHAPTER 13

J hesitated in the doorway to the garrison. Brant sat on a chair, his booted feet on the table. Erik and Quentin were there too, which meant a truce had been called. That might be the reason for Brant's sullenness.

"Your eye looks better," I said, closing the door.

He merely glared at me.

"Is the captain around?" I asked.

"He's in a meeting with the king," Quentin said. He offered me a cup of ale that I gratefully took. I drank the lot in one gulp.

Erik laughed and slapped my shoulder. "You drink like a man."

"She was thirsty," Quentin said in my defense. He offered to pour me another but I refused. "What brings you to the palace today, Josie?"

"I have something to discuss with the captain."

"Oh? What?"

"It's a private matter."

Brant snorted. "You're a fool if you believe her. It ain't a private matter, they just don't want us to know why she's here meeting Barborough, the Vytill lord."

So the footman had talked. I doubted it would be kept secret for long, but I wasn't expecting Brant to use the information as a weapon in his argument.

"Enough," Erik growled. "The captain would not keep a secret from us if it was about our memories."

"How do you know? How do any of us know what *he's* like, or what *any* of us are like? We don't know ourselves, let alone each other."

"I know you're an arsehole," Quentin muttered. He was far enough away that Brant couldn't hear him, thankfully. Even so, it was reckless. He must be very sure Brant had learned from his punishment and wouldn't attack.

"He's keeping something from us," Brant said, stamping his feet on the floor. "He, Bal, Theo and the king. They know something about our pasts, about why we're here, and it's got to do with that cabinet and what's in it."

If Max had been present, he would have denied it. He would have defended Dane's need for secrecy or claimed the cabinet was just an ordinary cabinet. But he wasn't present, and the others were either too afraid of Brant to defend the captain's actions—or they agreed with him.

From the nods of at least two other guards, I suspected more fell into the latter category than the former.

I, for one, could not let Brant disparage Dane, however. "The captain has your best interests at heart. He would never withhold information if it helps solve the mystery of your missing memories."

"*We* should decide if it might help, not him," Brant said. "It's our business too, our *lives*. No one should keep something important from us."

"Not even the king," one of the other guards said. He gave me an apologetic shrug but couldn't quite meet my gaze. He wasn't a supporter of Brant, but he supported Brant's logic.

The sergeant stood and snatched his sword belt from the hook where it hung by the door. "You know where to find me if the captain changes his mind and wants to tell us what's in that cabinet."

I was more relieved than I liked to admit to see him go. If he continued to accuse Dane of withholding information, I might end up saying the wrong thing to defend him—or I might blurt out the truth. Dane thought it safer to keep the gemstone a secret from all but a few, until we knew more about it, but part of me agreed with Brant. The servants deserved to know. What if one of them could shed light on it?

"He is troublemaker," Erik said to the other men. "Do not listen to him."

"He has a point," one said. "If the captain has evidence of something that affects us, we need to know. We need to decide for ourselves if it's relevant."

"Maybe it doesn't affect us," Quentin chimed in. "Maybe what the captain found in that cabinet is just a personal item of the king's, like he said. Why would he lie to us?"

The guard shrugged. "All I know is Brant says he felt the cabinet pulse in his hands, like it was alive or something in it was alive. That's not something Brant would make up. He ain't got the imagination for storytelling."

"That doesn't mean Hammer felt it too," Quentin said. "If he had, he would say so. Wouldn't he, Josie?"

"I don't pretend to know what goes through the captain's mind," I said. "Or why he does or does not do something." It was a cowardly answer, but I could give no other without lying, and I wasn't a very good liar. "Erik, how is the wart?"

My change of topic was met with a frustrated sigh from the guard, but Erik seemed to welcome it. "Smaller," he said, sounding pleased.

"And the heartbroken maids?"

"Their tears are like waterfalls."

Quentin faked a gagging sound. "Enough or I'll throw up."

"You should take advice from Erik," Erik said, tapping his chest. "I sleep with many maids, make them happy. You, little Quentin? How many do you make happy?"

Quentin flushed to the roots of his hair and cast a sideways glance at me. "Plenty."

Erik laughed that deep, rolling laugh of his, and slapped Quentin so hard on the back that Quentin spilled some of his ale. "Ask me if you want advice with maids," Erik said. "Or if you want to share one of mine."

"Erik!" I cried.

He blinked innocently. "What?"

"Be sure to ask the maid first if she would like to be shared with Quentin. Or with anyone. I suspect you might find she prefers exclusivity. Indeed, she probably would prefer it if you were exclusive to her too."

"This is true, but they know I have many maids, and that if they want me they must share."

Dane entered through the internal door and, as I suspected, wasn't surprised to see me. He looked worried, and that worried expression was directed at me. "Come with me, Josie."

I followed him, expecting to be taken to Balthazar's office where we'd talk privately about my meeting with Barborough, but it quickly became apparent we were heading in the wrong direction. When we climbed a flight of stairs, I had a suspicion where we were going but didn't want to ask. There were too many servants within earshot.

"The king wishes to see you," Dane said quietly when we found ourselves alone in a corridor.

"Why?"

He checked behind us, then said, "He wants to discuss the situation in Mull with a local he trusts."

"And you suggested me?"

"I didn't have to. He suggested you himself. When Balthazar told him you were already here at the palace, the king decided it was fortuitous and asked me to fetch you."

"You told Balthazar I was here?"

"He knew. He knows everything that happens within this estate. A rat can't sneeze in the stables without him finding out."

My step slowed and I fell behind.

When Dane realized, he waited for me. "You look worried. There's no need to be. Just answer him truthfully."

"Then why are *you* worried?" When he didn't answer, and merely set off again at a brisk pace, I caught his arm, halting him. "Tell me, D— Captain."

His gaze met mine. "He says it's your payment for being allowed to come to the palace. He's not happy that you come and go as you please. I had to tell him one of the maids needed medical attention. He wanted specifics so I was forced to tell him about the rape. I can't lie to the king."

"Was he satisfied with that explanation?"

"He was, in a way."

"What does that mean?"

He dismissed my question with a shake of his head. "The point is, he knows you've been here lately. Someone is informing him, most likely Lady Morgrave."

My heart sank. "Lady Morgrave is becoming influential."

"The more time he spends with her, the deeper he falls under her spell. For now, we've managed to explain your presence and undermine the Deerhorns' campaign against you."

"I don't understand why they care what I do."

"In the past, it probably wasn't specific to you, but what you represent—a village girl allowed into their domain. By going to the ball, Lady Deerhorn assumed you had pretensions above your station."

I scoffed. "That's ridiculous."

"Not to her and people like her. They think they were born special, and you fitting into their world undetected goes against those beliefs. But like I said, that was before. Lady Deerhorn's dislike of you specifically probably intensified after you refused to spy for Lord Xavier."

That made sense but it was also more troubling. Given time, she would have forgotten her campaign against me, as Dane called it, if it were just a matter of being annoyed by a village girl with pretensions. Now she must worry that I would tattle on her son to the duke of Gladstow himself.

We exited the servants' corridor through a hidden door in the wall of an antechamber, one of the many rooms that made up the complex of the king's apartments. The room contained a throne covered in crimson velvet, the king's personal insignia of two entwined Ls embroidered onto the backrest in gold thread. There was nowhere else to sit, just a vast expanse of blue and white tiled floor with the Lockhart coat of arms in the middle. It must be a room for the king to receive his closest confidants in a formal setting, rather than the council chamber or the informal sitting room beyond.

We passed through the sitting room to a games room, set out with round tables, then into a long dining room with a table set for at least thirty, followed by a smaller chamber whose function I couldn't discern, and finally a library then an office. All rooms were opulently furnished and guarded by Dane's men.

The office's proportions were intimate compared to the others we'd just passed through. The king must work on his most private tasks here, and perhaps meet with his closest, most trusted advisors. It was strange to think that I was one of them.

The king sat behind a large desk that made him look small. It was mostly bare except for a few papers laid out before him, a gilded inkstand and writing implements, candlesticks and an hourglass dripping sand. He did not look up as he dipped the pen in the ink then set it to the paper. His moment's hesitation caused a small blob of ink to bloom before he neatly signed his name.

Theodore accepted the document and placed it with the others at the edge of the desk. "Captain Hammer and Joselyn Cully are here, sire," he announced, as if the king hadn't seen us.

I curtseyed and Dane offered a small bow. A movement beyond the corner of my eye caught my attention. Balthazar sat on a chair by the door, both hands clasped over the head of his walking stick. I nodded at him and he nodded back.

"Do you know why you've been summoned, Miss Cully?" the king asked with a regal thrust of his chin in my direction.

"The captain informed me that I am to answer any questions you have about Mull, sire. Thank you for the trust you put in me. I am at your service."

"Good. What do you know of the dissenters?"

The abrupt question caught me off guard. Dane had said I shouldn't be worried about answering truthfully, but the king was clearly annoyed, and if he knew I had been friends with Ivor Morgrain for all my life, he might think me on their side. On the other hand, I didn't want to see Ivor and the others get in serious trouble. Not even Ned.

"They're just ordinary village men," I said. "Ned Perkin appears to be the leader, and I'll admit that he has a certain reputation for drinking and causing headaches for the sheriff." I held my breath, hoping he wouldn't ask about anyone else. It was one thing to cause Ned problems, and quite another to bring the king's wrath down on families like the Swinsons.

"I've been informed that the rioters are upset over Mull's population increase," the king said. "Is that what you believe too?"

"They weren't rioters." At the sudden flare in his eyes, I swallowed and added, "Your advisers are right, and the villagers are worried they'll lose their jobs to the newcomers from Vytill. Food has become expensive, and rents are rising. Some will be forced out of their homes and many already struggle to feed their families."

"That is a shame, but it's the way of the world. What do they expect me to do about it?"

Theodore exchanged a glance with Dane.

"They expect you to intervene, sire," Balthazar said without rising from his chair.

"Do they expect me to conjure up food? Housing?" The reference to magic cut close to the bone, and I suspected the king realized too late. He shifted in the chair, slumping into the corner, and nibbled on his thumb nail.

"This is perhaps a matter for your advisers," Theodore said quickly. "Shall I organize a meeting?"

"My advisers are hopeless and selfish." The king flicked his hand in a dismissive wave. "They fight amongst themselves and make decisions to benefit them, not the kingdom."

"That's not entirely true," Balthazar said.

I held my breath as the king glared at him. Balthazar met the glare with his own steady one, and it was the king who looked away first.

"Some of your advisers are good men," Dane said. "It's a matter of knowing which ones and listening to them."

"And weighing up their suggestions," Theodore added.

The king rubbed his temples. "I want to hear *your* suggestions. I know you have some. You three always do." I couldn't tell if he spoke sarcastically or not.

"You have a few options." Balthazar paused as if expecting the king to tell him to keep his opinions to himself, but the king remained quiet. It seemed he hadn't been sarcastic at all, and he did indeed put more stock in the suggestions made by these three than his own ministers. "You could close the border to outsiders," Balthazar said.

The king shook his head. "Vytill has been a rich country because it had a lot of people. Now those people want to move here, which will make Glancia rich."

Balthazar shook his head and Theodore and Dane exchanged another glance. "That's not why Vytill is rich," Balthazar said. "It became rich because its port was important to the entire peninsula. All trade routes on The Fist led to Port Haven, so traders had to pass through Vytill to reach it. With Port Haven's influence ended, Vytill must now rely on its mines for income. I don't know how profitable those mines are, but it's a surety that the kingdom will grow poorer by the day."

"If I may, sire," I said.

"Yes, Miss Cully."

"I spoke to a Vytill family yesterday. They told me they came here to find a better life but, so far, have found only worse. It's not just Mull villagers who are suffering but the Vytill migrants. They can't get jobs and they have no money."

"And I say again, what do they expect me to do?" the king asked. "I can't create the jobs for them, and I can't pay them to do nothing. They're not my people. I shouldn't have to feed them."

"They are your people now," Dane said.

The king sighed heavily and rubbed his temples again. "This is giving me a headache."

"It's clear there needs to be a short term solution to prevent starvation," Balthazar said, "and a long term plan to provide employment."

"Oh, really?" the king said with a roll of his eyes. This time there was no doubt he spoke sarcastically. "So far I am not hearing solutions, only a restatement of the problems. And no, closing the border isn't a solution. The people of The Fist should be allowed to move between countries if they wish, if they pay a nominal fee."

"There are better solutions," Dane said, "but they'll require sacrifice."

"Who by?"

"You, and the other nobles."

The king pushed to his feet and strode to the window. He rested his hands on the sill and stared down at the gardens below.

"It's a beautiful day. I should be out there with my friends, not stuck in here doing paperwork."

"You're not doing paperwork," Dane said. "You're discussing ways to save your people from starvation."

The king shot Dane a flinty glare over his shoulder. "You'll speak to me without that tone, thank you, Hammer. You've already angered me once today, by neglecting your duty, don't add to the tally."

Neglecting his duty?

"Sire," Dane said icily.

"You want to be a good king, don't you, sire?" Theodore asked quickly. "Isn't that how you'd like to be remembered?"

The king sat back in the chair again and clasped his hands over his stomach. "Let me hear your suggestions."

"Offer food from your own gardens and allow villagers to hunt in your forests in low numbers," Balthazar said. He spoke smoothly, and neither Dane nor Theodore seemed surprised by his suggestion. I suspected they'd already discussed it. "The grand huntsman can monitor wildlife numbers and stop the hunts if the animal populations dwindle too much. We see this as a temporary measure only, sire."

The king glanced between all three, as if he too suddenly real- ized they'd already discussed this among themselves. His lips pressed together. "No. Absolutely not. A king must have his own land. He must have food aplenty to feed everyone at the palace."

"You don't need to have all the nobles here," Dane said. "Send them home. Let them feed themselves from their own lands."

"But I like having them here," the king whined. He chewed on his nail again. "What else do you suggest?"

Dane's shoulders tensed and Theodore's gaze drifted to the ceiling. The knuckles gripping the head of Balthazar's walking stick turned white.

"In the longer term," Balthazar went on in an even tone, "you could generate employment through capital works."

"What's that?"

"Building roads, municipal buildings, that sort of thing. If Mull becomes the administrative center of Glancia, then it will need better paved roads, good bridges, bigger buildings, a proper market."

The king's fingers tapped lightly on the desk as he thought, and his lips twisted this way and that. "I do see merit in your suggestions, but what if I need to raise an army only to find I've spent all my money on buildings and roads that may never be needed? Glancia doesn't have a proper army and it should, as it becomes more important. King Phillip has an army."

"You won't need to fight Vytill if you marry the Princess Illiriyia," Theodore said.

"Don't, Theo," the king barked. "I'm tired of hearing her name."

Theodore bowed his head. "Apologies, sire."

"Hammer, tell me, does Dreen have an army?"

"A small one," Dane said. "A Glancian army could be formed if the need arose, but there's no evidence that one is needed, sire. Besides, most of the nobles have well-trained retainers and arms that we can call on in the event of trouble. There are also fifty warrior priests in Tilting at your disposal."

"That isn't enough. Besides, they're dedicated to Merdu, not me. The king of what will become The Fist's most important kingdom should have his own dedicated army." He heaved a sigh and looked longingly at the window. "What do the people want me to do, Miss Cully? I'd like to hear your suggestions."

"Me?" I'd felt like a fly on the wall for most of the meeting as the men discussed matters that had nothing to do with me. I thought the king had forgotten about me.

"Yes, you. You're my window to the world of Mull and the common people." He must have liked how that sounded because he smiled. "So tell me, what do the people think should be done?"

"It depends on who you talk to," I said carefully. "First and foremost, they want better law enforcement. If the sheriff employs more men, and arrests are made, the Vytill migrants who are getting drunk and starting fights will know there are consequences to their actions, and the Glancian dissenters won't be so eager to get rid of them if they see justice is served."

"That's already being implemented." He looked pleased. "Good. Then it's settled."

"There's more," I said quickly, lest Dane, Theodore and Balt-hazar think I didn't like their suggestions.

"That will do for now. Better law enforcement is vital, not just for Mull but for the entire kingdom. An army can be used in domestic situations too, like in last night's riot. Thank you, Miss Cully, you've been very helpful."

"But—"

"Speaking of the sheriff, what do you know about him?"

I swallowed what I was going to say with great difficulty. It galled me that he thought I'd been suggesting law enforcement as the only necessary solution, but he didn't want to hear the truth from me. I doubted he wanted to hear it from his men either, but at least they were paid to speak honestly. My presence at the palace was too precarious to push too hard.

"He's a good man," I said.

"And the governor?"

I hesitated.

"Go on, Miss Cully."

"He's your man, sire."

"I know that, but I asked what you think of him. Does he do a good job, in your opinion and that of other Mullians?"

I glanced at Dane, and he gave a barely perceptible nod of encouragement. "The governor isn't well liked or respected by the villagers," I said.

The king frowned. "Really? That's not what I heard."

No doubt Lady Morgrave had whispered something in his ear to the opposite effect. The governor was, after all, firmly in her family's pocket. "You asked me what the *villagers* thought of him, sire," I said. "I can only speak on their behalf."

His fingers tapped on the desk to an erratic beat. "He's in a difficult position. I can't imagine he has easy decisions to make. Much like a king, only on a smaller scale. You understand, Miss Cully?"

"I do, sire, but there are stories of his corruption, of him making decisions to benefit a few, rather than the many."

"Perhaps those were the best decisions for the village. Thank you, Miss Cully, that will be all. The rest of you may leave too. I have a headache and wish to lie down. Theo, come back later and help me dress for a stroll in the garden. Inform Lady Morgrave that I wish to walk with her."

I curtseyed and the men bowed themselves out of the room. Dane shut the door and jerked his head for us to follow him.

In deference to Balthazar's limp, we made our way slowly down to his office near the garrison. No one spoke except to greet the palace servants we passed in the corridors. It was as if a bubble enveloped us, growing ever larger with each step until it was so big it must burst.

The bubble lasted until we made it to Balthazar's office. Dane was the one to wield the pin that popped it. "He thinks the treasury is his personal coffer," he muttered, closing the door.

Balthazar stamped the end of his walking stick into the floor with each step. "And that the role of king requires nothing more than dressing well and attending balls."

"That's not true, Bal, and you know it," Theodore said, holding a chair out for me. "He's trying to be a good king. You've heard him say he wants to be a good king."

"That was months ago. And he's not trying hard enough."

"Shhh. Lower your voice."

Balthazar huffed out a breath. "I'm old. I don't know why I bother trying to make him a better king and Glancia a better place. I'll be dead before any plans are fully implemented, even if he starts a major capital works programs tomorrow."

"Perhaps it's something in your past that drives you to care about the kingdom," I said.

The Master of the Palace narrowed his gaze at me. "Is that your professional opinion or do you just like stating the obvious?"

"Bal!" Dane snapped. "Don't take your frustration out on her, or anyone."

"I blame your age, Balthazar," I shot back. "And that is both my professional opinion *and* a statement of the obvious."

The wrinkles in Balthazar's brow flattened and the ones around his eyes deepened. My retort had almost earned me a smile.

"Give the king time," Theodore said as he lowered himself onto the other chair, "he just needs to think about what we said today, to weigh up his options."

"For how long?" Balthazar asked. "And what if he makes a foolish decision?"

Dane was the only one with an answer to that question, and it came in the form of a cup of strong wine from a jug on the sideboard. He handed it to Balthazar and rested his hand on the old man's shoulder. "We can only do so much. Trust that he'll make the right decision."

Balthazar grunted as he accepted the cup. "You have more faith than I do, Hammer."

"He's a good man, deep down. He's just overwhelmed. Like Theo said, he needs to think about it for a while, then present the options to the advisors as if they were his own."

"Everything's black and white for you."

Dane poured more wine and handed a cup to me and another to Theodore. "I sense an insult coming, but go on."

"You see people as either good or bad, but I think people can be both. Indeed, I think everyone has capacity for both good and bad, right and wrong."

"I agree," I said. "Take Ivor and Ned, for example, and the Swinsons. They're essentially good people who've been driven to make trouble. Fear is powerful. It can change people."

Dane shook his head. "If they're essentially good, they'll stop themselves from going too far. So time will tell if that's the case or not."

"I know my friends, Captain."

"She does," Theodore cut in before Dane could respond again. "She also knows more about human character than we do. What do we know about our own characters, let alone those of others we've never met?" It was so similar to what Brant had said in the garrison that I wondered if Theo had been listening in.

"I'm willing to concede I might be wrong," Dane said, lifting his cup in salute.

"Gracious of you," Balthazar said. Theodore, ever the peacemaker, seemed pleased with Dane's concession, however.

"Josie, how did your meeting with Lord Barborough go?" Balthazar asked.

Before I could answer, Dane cut in, "You should have waited for me. I wanted to be nearby if you needed me."

"Barborough is not a danger," I told him. "At least not a phys-ical one. He is certainly dangerous in other ways—if he talks to the king about our discussions."

"If he does, the king will believe the three of us over him. You won't have to worry about that."

Theodore nodded. Balthazar merely looked annoyed at the interruption. "The meeting, Josie. What did he say?"

"I fed him the false information we made up, but it wasn't enough to satisfy him," I said. "He wanted more. He did, however, give me a piece of information about the sorcerer in exchange."

They all leaned forward.

"The sorcerer gives three wishes to the one who frees him. Before you ask, he did not tell me what the sorcerer is freed from. Whatever it is, must be difficult to find. There's been no evidence of magic performed anywhere on The Fist or Zemaya in a thou-sand years."

"Until now," Dane said to the ceiling where, one level above, the king was resting.

The other two men did not attempt to defend the king. It would seem they were all in agreement and suspected the king was involved in the palace's creation.

Theodore wagged his finger. "It may not have been difficult to find the sorcerer's prison. It could be quite ordinary so no one real-ized it contained a sorcerer, like a simple cottage."

"Blending in is a good way to disguise oneself," Dane agreed.

"Or the door could have a complicated lock," Theodore added.

Balthazar grunted. "Not if Leon could open it."

Theodore hushed him with a finger to his lips and a glance at the door.

"He could have stumbled upon the key," Dane said.

"Do you think the gemstone is the housing for the sorcerer?" Balthazar asked. "The so-called prison?"

The breath left my body in a rush. I hadn't thought of that, and by the stunned look on Theodore's face, he hadn't either. Either Dane was better at schooling his features or he had considered it already.

"If it is, all the more reason to keep it from the king," he said.

"We have to assume he hasn't used all his wishes yet. He could be biding his time until the need arises."

Balthazar's theory about the gem made sense. The king had reacted with irrational anger when the cabinet containing it was touched. "If the sorcerer is inside the gemstone, wouldn't the king want to keep it close?" I asked.

"He asked for the cabinet to be put somewhere safe," Dane said. "He knows I could hide it better than him, with his every step scrutinized by the visiting nobles."

"Where is it?" Balthazar asked. "Are you going to tell us?"

Dane shifted his weight from foot to foot then finally nodded. "In the cottage at the north western corner of the estate. The cottage is empty and is too far away from the palace for the nobles to bother going there. I buried it in the garden."

"Good. Keep it there until he asks for it."

"Thank you," Theodore said with a flat smile for Dane. "We'll keep the knowledge of its whereabouts safe."

"That was never my concern," Dane said. "It was *your* safety I was trying to protect, not the cabinet itself."

"What will you do if the king asks for it back?" I said. "What if he wants to see the gemstone?"

Balthazar's wrinkles folded into a smug smile. "Hopefully, by then, the jeweler in Tilting I commissioned to make a replica will have completed his task. He's due to bring it soon."

I couldn't help my own smug smile from spreading. "Very clever."

"I'm sure I don't need to impress upon you how important it is to keep this information private, Josie," Balthazar said.

"You know you don't," Dane said.

"Bal," Theodore chided. "She's one of us, in a way. She won't tattle."

"I won't," I promised. "But I do think you need to tell the servants something. Brant can't keep his mouth shut. He and several others are angry that you're not sharing information about the cabinet with them. You have dissenters in the village, but I don't think you want them in the palace too."

"I disagree," Balthazar bit off, as if it were my fault that Brant couldn't keep his mouth shut. "We don't have proper answers yet, and talk of magic will only cause fear and panic among the staff."

Dane shook his head. "Josie's right. Let me address a few of my men."

Balthazar threw his hands in the air. "Then *you'll* be responsible for them and their actions, Hammer, not me."

"You underestimate them, Bal," Theodore said. "They're smart enough to know when to keep quiet."

I rather thought Balthazar was underestimating Dane. *He* was smart enough to know how much of the truth to feed Brant and which lies to weave through it.

CHAPTER 14

*D*ane decided it was best if he talk to his men without Theodore and Balthazar present. Balthazar didn't like it, but Dane convinced him an informal meeting would invite less confrontation.

He was wrong. Sergeant Brant was determined to stoke the embers beneath the simmering pot.

"Where is it?" he asked when Dane said he'd removed the cabinet to a safe place.

Dane stood at the end of the long table in the garrison, his arms crossed, while his guards all sat. I stood by the door, trying to look inconspicuous. "Buried in the north west of the estate," Dane said.

The quick response momentarily rendered Brant speechless, though not for long enough. "You're lying," he said.

"No."

The guards muttered among themselves, and Brant said, "Why not keep it in the garrison where there's always someone to watch over it?"

"Because there are too many people coming and going, and not just guards."

Brant's gaze slid to me. "That can be easily stopped."

I wished I'd left Dane to meet with his men alone, but he'd insisted I be there to prove I was one of them, that they could trust me. I wasn't so sure if we were accurately conveying that message.

"What's in the cabinet?" one of the other guards asked.

"It contains a gemstone that pulses when touched," Dane said.

I tried very hard not to show surprise that he told the truth about the gem. I hadn't expected him to be this honest.

"Or goes near it," Brant corrected him. "I only touched the cabinet, but I felt the thing inside throb, like it were alive."

Magic.

The word rippled around the room, passed from guard to guard in whispered wonder. Only Brant seemed unsurprised. He'd felt the pulse and suspected all along that magic caused it. Perhaps the others hadn't fully believed him and expected Dane to give them a different explanation, something more reasonable and tangible. But he had not, and now the notion that magic had been used to clear their memories seemed very real. And very troubling.

"Do *you* think that's what's in the gemstone, Captain?" one asked. "Magic?"

"I don't know," was all Dane said. "I don't know what magic should feel like."

"Course it was magic," Brant said. "What else could explain it? What did the king say, Hammer?"

"*Captain* Hammer," Erik snapped. Brant ignored him.

"I haven't asked the king, and nor will I," Dane said. "Not yet."

"Why not?" Brant exploded.

"Aye," several others chimed in, including Erik. Quentin, however, didn't protest. The youth trusted Dane implicitly.

"The king must know what the stone's for," Brant said. "He must have used it to make the palace."

"Probably," Dane agreed.

Brant slapped both palms on the table, making his tankard and my nerves jump. "Then why not ask him about it? You a coward, Hammer?"

"*Captain!*" Erik snapped again.

"He's not a coward," Quentin added. "He's smart, and he's thinking about all of us. All of *you.*"

Brant stabbed a finger at Quentin. "Shut your hole, Pest."

Quentin folded his arms. "Pest? That the best you can do?" He was cocky when Dane stood beside him.

"I haven't asked the king about it because I doubt he'll give me the truth," Dane told them. "If he used the magic gemstone on us, on himself, or this palace, then why would he admit it? He'd be a fool to do so. Not only will he lie, but confronting him will make him aware of our suspicions. If he sees that as a threat, he might take steps to remove us."

"Not if you threaten to slit his throat if he don't talk," Brant snarled. "A blade to the throat loosens tongues."

"And then what will I do if he refuses to talk? Kill the one person who can give us answers?"

"See?" Quentin said. "Told you the captain is smart. He does things for a reason."

Brant shot out of his chair and lunged at Quentin. Quentin yelped and fell off his chair in an attempt to scurry away. Brant sat back down with a harsh chuckle, but no one laughed with him.

"So how are you going to get answers?" one of the guards asked Dane.

"Investigate and research," Dane said. "Balthazar and Theodore are reading books from the palace library. Josie is speaking to an expert on magic to find out what he knows."

"And? What have they learned?"

"Nothing yet." It was the only lie he'd told so far. "We'll keep looking, keep asking."

"And if you fail?" Brant said. "What then?"

"We won't fail."

Brant snorted and wiped his nose on his sleeve. Some of the others looked skeptical but none disagreed with Dane, not even Brant.

Dane leaned forward, palms on the table. "This cannot be spoken about outside servant circles. Is that understood?" He met the gazes of each of his men, lingering longest on Brant. "If anyone outside the palace staff hears that the king may have gained his position through magic, there will be repercussions. I don't think I need to remind everyone that our lives are linked to his. If he loses the crown—"

"Or his head," one of the guards cut in.

"—then we could disappear from here just as quickly as we apparently arrived. No one yet knows what will happen to us. We should never suppose or assume anything. I won't risk a single life. If one of you gets impatient for answers, and takes matters into your own hands, there's a prison cell waiting for you." A hushed silence blanketed the room. Dane straightened and folded his arms again, a commanding presence that had recaptured his men's respect, even Brant's. "If you do discuss what I've said with the other servants, you must impress this fact on them too. Is that clear?"

Quentin nodded eagerly. "Yes, sir."

"Aye, Captain," Erik added.

The other guards agreed, including Brant. I'd never seen the sergeant so amenable. The fear of what might happen to them, of not knowing what would happen if the king was suddenly no longer the king, was a powerful motivator for obedience.

Dane studied a slate board hanging from a hook on the wall above the sideboard. He glanced at the names written on it in chalk. "Erik, you'll lead the next group of men on the roster into the village and relieve Sergeant Max's shift. We'll maintain a presence in Mull until the danger of a riot has passed. That means a skeleton shift will patrol here."

"There ain't much happening here anyway," Quentin said, gathering up his sword belt.

He didn't know about Ruth, but even so, he was right. Ruth had been the rapist's only victim at the palace. It wasn't even clear if the rapist was based here.

"And me?" Brant asked.

"Patrol duty," Dane said.

Brant didn't argue, perhaps relieved he wasn't assigned to the prison anymore.

Dane and I left the men as they strapped on their weapons and organized themselves for duty.

"I don't think telling them so much was a good idea," Dane said as we headed through the warren of service corridors. "If one of the Glancian dukes gets wind of it, or one of the Vytill or Dreen representatives, then the king will be in danger, and so will we."

"I admit I wasn't expecting you to tell them the entire truth," I said.

He stopped and his narrowed gaze slid to me. We stepped aside to allow two footmen carrying a small table between them to pass by. I watched them rather than the captain of the guards, although I felt the sharpness of his glare.

"However, your judgment proved better than mine in this instance," I added in a whisper.

"Are you buttering me up so I don't lecture you about being more specific with your suggestions?"

"Is it working?"

"You should have told me you didn't mean for such honesty, Josie."

"I didn't think you required direction from me, Captain."

"I didn't think so either." He set off, his long strides making it difficult for me to keep up. "But it turns out I appreciate your opinion."

"Why?"

"To confirm that my instincts are correct."

I couldn't decide if he was being arrogant or sweet. Perhaps a little of both.

"You were right to trust your instincts," I said. "Brant is a different man after that meeting. He trusts you again."

"For now."

It took us some time but we eventually left the palace through the servants' entrance opposite the commons building. By taking the service corridors, from the northern garrison to the exit in the south wing, we'd avoided the forecourts where the nobles preferred the vicinity be unsullied by the likes of me. I was equally glad to avoid them, in case Lady Deerhorn or one of her offspring was near. I'd walked those corridors so many times now, I could probably even find my own way out, but I didn't tell Dane. I liked that he escorted me.

Our place slowed to an amble. I wasn't in a hurry to leave, even though the shadows grew long and dusk would soon settle. It would be light long enough yet for me to walk home.

"Do you think Brant or any of the others will tattle to the wrong person?" I asked.

"They'll inform the other servants they've befriended but they won't tell outsiders. Of that, I'm sure. It's the other servants I can't be certain about. I don't know them as well as I know my men."

"I'm still digesting what it all means," I said, not wanting to elaborate as a stream of servants passed, hurrying toward the palace. Some carried trays of clean glasses or covered platters, while others held fine clothes or shoes that had most likely come from the laundry. It was a pleasant time of day for a walk in the gardens, now that the sun had lost some of its heat. The liveried footmen were probably on their way to setting up food and drinks around the fountains and in the secluded gardens where lovers conducted their trysts.

I would've liked to have my own lovers' rendezvous behind one of the garden fountains, but that was unlikely to happen now that Dane had made his disinterest clear. Besides, the more I thought about it, the more I couldn't help being reminded of poor Lady Claypool, accosted by the duke of Gladstow behind a hedge. Kitty's husband was a revolting man, and she didn't even know it.

"The implications of what we suspect to be true about the gemstone are troubling," I added.

"It's important to remember they are only suspicions," he said.

"Suspicions that must be correct. There are no other explanations."

We had reached the commons where more servants accumulated, some lounging against a wall during a quiet moment, others waiting for food or linen to be brought out by the servants tasked with those duties. The palace was a complex mechanism with each maid, footman, guard, gardener or groom acting as a cog. If one failed, the entire system failed until a working replacement stepped in. It never ceased to amaze me that they each knew what to do on the first day they woke up without their memories. Knowing only their names and their function at the palace was key to solving the mystery of their memory loss, yet a vital piece of the puzzle was still missing—perhaps several pieces. We might have learned about the sorcerer and his three wishes, and we might be certain the king freed the sorcerer and was the one to be granted those wishes, yet we were no closer to getting the palace staff's memories back. No wonder they were all frustrated, their nerves and tempers stretched to breaking point.

"Come with me," Dane said, continuing past the commons.

"Where are we going?"

"For a ride."

"I can't ride."

"I'll see that you're given a quiet mare. All you have to do is hold the reins."

His strides lengthened, and I raced to keep up. "Why are you determined to torture me? A lecture would suffice."

He shot me a smirk and slowed down. "Riding isn't torture."

"It is for someone who doesn't ride."

"You'll learn to enjoy it, given enough practice."

He sounded like he planned more rides for me. That, at least, was something to look forward to. "You sound like Kitty."

"The duchess of Gladstow does enjoy riding, particularly with Lady Miranda. Are they trying to avoid someone, by any chance?"

"Several someones, most likely. In Kitty's instance, it's probably her husband." I kept my voice low as we rounded the pavilion and made our way to the main gate where sedan chairs waited to ferry nobles to the front steps of the palace. They lay idle, with few nobles in sight. They must all be inside preparing for the entertainments before dinner.

It was a short walk to the stables, where Dane asked for his horse and a calm one for me. "Very calm," I told the groom. "Something that considers a plod too fast."

"You want an old nag ready for the knackery then, miss," the cheeky youth said with a grin.

"You understand perfectly."

Dane led me to the edges of the practice yard, which was as long as my entire street. Grooms put horses through their paces and several strong ones were being fitted with armor to protect their faces, necks and flanks.

"Why do the horses look as though they're about to head to war?" I asked.

"They need protection if we're called to break up a riot in the village." He leaned against the wall and crossed his ankles and arms. It was a relaxed stance, but his eyes betrayed him. His gaze darted around, ever watchful, taking in each of the faces nearby. Once or twice it even flitted to me, though it did not settle.

"They'll be ready if war arises too," I said heavily. I still couldn't fathom it. There hadn't been a war in Glancia for nearly two centuries. Most of The Fist Peninsula had been trouble-free for that

.J. ARCHER

time too, except for Freedland, where a revolution had overthrown the last king some forty years ago.

"There won't be a war," Dane said gently.

When I didn't respond, or even look at him, he touched my chin and forced me to.

"There won't be a war, Josie. Not if I have anything to do with it."

A weak smile was all I could manage. He was kind to try to allay my fears, but although he was a capable man, stopping wars before they began was not one of his many talents.

Instead of letting me go, he gave my chin a gentle shake until I lifted my gaze again. "You don't believe me," he said.

"Given everything we've learned today, and given Barborough's own suspicions about magic and the king, it's hard to think that anything other than war is in Glancia's future. If King Phillip believes King Leon isn't the rightful heir, Vytill won't wait. They can afford to pay an army now, but they may not be able to in the future. If they wait too long, Glancia will have raised and trained her own army."

"I'm not so sure. If Barborough thinks magic is at play, Phillip would be mad to start a war if Leon has the sorcerer in his pocket."

I nodded slowly, seeing his point. "If I were King Phillip, I'd wait for our two dukes to expose Leon as a fraud, remove the sorcerer from his possession, and let them fight for the throne among themselves, and only then bring my army here, when Glancia has had enough of their nobles' squabbling."

He let me go. "Now you're thinking like a ruler."

"There are only two problems. One, the sorcerer is an unknown. Neither we nor Barborough know how many wishes Leon has left, and two, there's the danger of one of the dukes taking the sorcerer's power for themselves."

"If that's even possible."

"That's the whole problem. We don't know what's possible."

"And Barborough does."

"I'm not so sure," I said. "I think he's guessing too, and perhaps hoping to learn more while he's here. That's why we have to get rid of him. He might find out more than us and use that knowledge against Glancia."

He blinked hard. "I thought you believed in non-violent measures to solve problems."

"I meant sending him home to Vytill, not killing him!"

"Right. I meant that too." He leaned back against the wall, his arms crossed again.

The groom approached leading two horses. I recognized the one Dane usually rode, a muscular stallion with a sure step and head held high. The other looked as if she wanted to be in her stall with a feedbag strapped around her neck. The groom informed me her name was Sky.

"I understand how you feel, Sky," I said, stroking her nose. "But I promise not to go faster than a walk, if you promise not to startle at anything or think it amusing to throw me off."

"I put a sidesaddle on for you, miss," the groom said. "All the ladies use them. Let me help you."

"I'll help her," Dane said, stepping forward. He showed me where to put my hands and feet then ordered me to lift myself up. It took two attempts but the horse remained steady, even as I hooked my right leg around the pommel and secured my knee against the part Dane called the horn. "Now take the reins."

"Can't you lead me out until we're away from people?"

"You'll be fine. Nobody's been holding her this entire time." He showed me his empty hands. The groom showed me his, grinning from ear to ear. I decided I no longer liked him.

"She won't bolt," the youth said, stroking the horse's neck. "She's too agreeable for that."

"How do I make her move?" I asked. "Is there a command?"

"She'll follow Lightning."

"The perfect female," Dane said with a wink for the groom.

The youth laughed. I scowled at them both.

Dane mounted and rode out of the yard through the arch. Sky followed a few paces behind, her steps slow but steady. We headed toward the palace, but instead of going through the main gate, we turned right and followed the palace's northern wing.

"It would have been faster to walk ourselves," I said as we left the palace behind.

"Want to ride faster?"

"No!"

He chuckled. "Then stop complaining and enjoy yourself. Sometimes it's nice not to walk everywhere."

That was true, at least, but I was used to walking. I wasn't used to sitting on the back of a creature that could crush me if it fell on top of me. I'd attended patients who'd been struck by a kicking horse, fallen off a horse, or been trampled. The latter was a drunk who'd stumbled into the path of the Deerhorns' speeding carriage. The coachman hadn't stopped to see if he was all right.

The avenue met the village road outside the palace estate. A short ride to the east would see us pass the intersection, where the palace's Grand Avenue also met the village road, and then it was a further five miles to Mull. We rode west, however, in the direction of Glancia's capital city, Tilting, a journey that took three days if the roads were good.

We followed the wall of the palace until it disappeared behind dense trees. After several more minutes, Dane veered off the road and into the forest. The track was barely visible. Low hanging branches brushed my face, and Sky had to step around bushes encroaching on her path.

"How did you know this track was here?" I asked. "If I hadn't been watching, I would have missed it."

"I just knew."

"You mean it was one of the things you knew when you woke up that first day? Like your name, your job, and the names of the others?"

He nodded. "I seemed to know my way around the palace and every inch of its grounds, although I'd never been here. Not that I remembered, anyway. I came looking for the gate recently and here it was."

"The gate?"

Just as I said it, he dismounted. I waited, not feeling confident enough to dismount without assistance, and watched as he pushed aside some thick vines growing up the estate's outer wall to reveal an arched wooden door. He fished a key out of his doublet pocket and unlocked it.

"Mind your head," he said, leading Lightning through.

Beyond the gate were more trees and bushes. The path was clearer here, however, and no vines grew up the wall.

"Where are we?" I asked, following Dane along the narrow path.

"Back on the palace estate."

"Why have you brought me here?"

"You'll see."

I was about to tell him I didn't like surprises when we passed beneath a natural arch, formed by low-hanging branches, into a clearing. At the center of the clearing was a quaint stone cottage with a steeply pitched roof, bookended by chimneys. White shutters covered the two windows on the lower level and the central dormer window above, and a climbing rose rambled between them, disappearing around the corner, the blush pink flowers adding a splash of color.

A path cut through an overgrown garden of roses, honeysuckle, lavender, and a mix of wildflowers, all in full bloom. The heads of the white pompom flower and blue spears of a tall delphinium swayed in the light breeze, and a vine strangled what appeared to be a stone bench seat.

The cottage might have been on the same estate as the palace, but it felt like a world away from the orderly opulence, the bustle of organized chaos. The palace was all dazzling glory, whereas the cottage was wild yet an oasis of calm. The palace dominated its landscape, demanding attention, but the cottage blended into its surrounds, as if it were part of the forest.

"It's as if it has always been here," I murmured.

"And yet it didn't exist mere months ago?" Dane asked in quiet earnest.

"It did not. I've been in this valley before, and walked through this forest collecting plants for my medicines. I don't know every inch, but I would have heard of the existence of a cottage like this."

"I thought as much."

I accepted his help to dismount. His hands did not linger on my waist and his gaze did not meet mine. He quickly moved away once both of my feet were firmly on the ground.

"Come with me," he said.

He indicated I should walk ahead of him along the path to the front door. Up close, I could see patches of mildwood, hollyroot and catspaw growing between the larger bushes.

"Can I collect some herbs?" I asked.

"Take all you need, but let me show you inside first."

"Is this where you buried the king's cabinet?"

"Beyond that iron gate," he said, pointing to the side of the cottage. "It's under a thorny yellow rose."

"Is that why you brought me here? To show me where it's hidden?"

"No."

"Then why?" I asked, glancing at him over my shoulder.

"Has anyone ever told you that you lack patience?"

"My father, frequently." I stepped aside to allow him to unlock the cottage door. "Meg, too."

He pushed open the door and entered first. "Come in."

"I can't believe no one lives here, not even the head gardener."

"I doubt any of the gardeners ever come this far," he said. "There are no signs of their work in that garden. The only people I'm certain know the location of this cottage are Balthazar and myself, and now you."

The cottage wasn't unfurnished, as I expected it to be. The front door opened to the kitchen, similar to the one at my house, with a large fireplace and a good sized table, buttery and pantry. It even had a bread oven. A wall divided the kitchen from the parlor, a cozy space with two chairs angled toward the hearth. Dane opened the shutters, exposing the layers of dust and cobwebs. Despite that and the stale air, the cottage was in good condition. The fireplaces were clear of ash, the door hinges free of rust, yet it felt like it had stood in this spot for decades.

"There's one large bedroom upstairs," Dane said, pointing at the staircase. "It needs a clean and airing out, but otherwise, it's habitable."

"It's more than habitable, it's delightful. I know some families in The Row who would be quite happy to live here."

He just looked at me.

"I know, I know, it's not possible. It was just a passing thought."

"This is on the palace estate," he said. "I can't risk people I don't know living here."

"I understand. Forget I mentioned it. So why did you bring me here?"

He held up the iron key he'd used to unlock the front door. "It also unlocks the gate hidden behind the vines on the village road. It's now yours."

I frowned. "I don't follow."

He took my hand and pressed the key into my palm. "I want you to come here if it gets dangerous in the village."

I stared at him. Then a bubble of laughter rose up my throat. Trying to suppress it only ended in a choke. "Dane, have you gone mad? The trouble the other night was over before it began. It can hardly even be called trouble. I won't need this." I tried to give back the key but he refused.

"Keep it, just in case."

"In case of what?"

"In case you need it."

I sighed and followed him outside again, only to stop to take in the beautiful scenery spread before me like a tapestry. Beams of late afternoon sun speared through the trees surrounding the clearing and fell across the garden. Against the backdrop of the darkening forest, the flowers seemed more vibrant, and the bees and butterflies seemed to think so too as they hopped between them. Birds struck up a loud chorus in the trees circling the clearing, although I couldn't see them. They would soon be settling down for the night, and I needed to go too to make it home in daylight.

"Josie?"

"Hmmm?"

One side of Dane's mouth lifted. "So you are listening. Can you lock the door?"

I opened my palm and stared at the key. How strange to be given permission to walk into this cottage any time I wished. Well, not anytime. He'd made it clear it was for emergencies only. Since I couldn't imagine there ever being an emergency that would warrant me fleeing Mull, I would never get to use it. Still, it was very thoughtful.

I locked the door and stuffed a handful of herbs into my skirt pocket along with the key. Dane helped me onto the saddle then led Lightning back through the forest to the gate. Sky plodded along, happy enough to be in the stallion's company. Dane locked the gate after we passed through and gave the key back to me.

"Keep it safe," he said.

I slipped it into my pocket again and we rode back the way we'd come. The palace roof came into view, its golden capping dazzling in the sun, a bold reminder that it was the star of the show, not the smaller, less significant cottage.

"Perhaps the sorcerer is in the palace itself," I said. "In its very walls, I mean. In its fabric."

Dane's gaze lifted to the palace roof too. "You think that may now be its home? Or its prison, if what Barborough says is correct?"

I shrugged a shoulder. "I don't know. It seems more likely it's in that gemstone, but sometimes...I feel as though the palace has a... a presence. Not a mind of its own, exactly, just..." I trailed off before he thought me mad.

"As if it holds our memories," he murmured.

We rode in silence, turning off the village road back into the palace estate. As more of the building came into view, I was reminded of Ruth and the very real urgency to find her attacker before he struck again.

"What did the king mean when he said you'd been neglecting your duty?" I asked. "It's something to do with Ruth, isn't it?"

"He blames me for her rape. He says I should have been more vigilant, that I should keep dangerous people out."

"That's not fair. He can't blame you for what happened to her. There are so many people coming and going at all times, it's impossible for you to be aware of every single one."

He said nothing, merely stared straight ahead, his back ramrod straight.

"Don't blame yourself, Dane. It's not your fault." I wished I could get close to him and force him to look at me, but I didn't know how to steer Sky. "You couldn't have prevented what happened to her if you had a hundred guards at your command. If I were the king's adviser, I'd have told him so." I wasn't sure if Balthazar or Theodore would say as much to the king but I knew Dane would defend them if they found themselves in his position.

He remained silent the rest of the way to the stables, and I regretted souring the mood. Our visit to the cottage had been pleasant, and I'd enjoyed his company, but it had come to an abrupt end.

"You didn't fall off, miss?" asked the same groom as earlier.

"She's a lovely horse," I said. "Don't send her to the knackery."

"She's yours whenever you want to ride her."

"Thank you, but I doubt I'll be riding again." I accepted Dane's assistance to dismount. "I have no reason to come back here," I said for his benefit.

Dane turned away so I couldn't see his reaction.

The groom led the horses off and Dane headed for the exit. "It'll be dusk soon," he said. "Take a carriage back to the village."

"I will," I said, unsure if I would bother but not wanting an argument about it.

He gave me a nod, a flat smile, and a simple, "Farewell," and then he was gone, striding along Grand Avenue toward the palace. I almost chased him, to tell him again that Ruth's situation wasn't his fault, but I suspected my words wouldn't be welcome.

I headed in the opposite direction, deciding to walk after all. It took several minutes to reach the end of the stable and coach house buildings. The avenue ahead was quiet, with no deliveries this late and no nobles returning after a day out. They would all be safely ensconced inside the palace, having their hair arranged, choosing their evening outfits, sipping fine wine and eating sweetmeats.

If it hadn't been so quiet, I would not have heard the muffled cry.

I spun around, just in time to see Ruth being dragged behind the stable building, her mouth covered by her attacker's hand. His face was turned away from me but he was dressed like a gentleman in a silver and peacock blue doublet.

Merdu! I picked up my skirts and ran. It wasn't until I rounded the stables that I realized I had no weapon on me and could not fight off the gentleman alone.

CHAPTER 15

"Unhand her!" I shouted.

The gentleman looked up and we both gasped. Lord Xavier Deerhorn!

Thank the god and goddess, he let Ruth go. I wouldn't have known what to do if he had not.

She rushed to my side and we clasped one another tightly. "Are you all right?" I asked.

She nodded through her tears, but her shaking implied otherwise.

"Did he hurt you?"

She looked at Lord Xavier then shook her head.

"Go!" he ordered her. "Get going! I wish to speak with the midwife alone." He stood with his feet apart, hands clenched into fists at his sides. It wasn't until he stepped toward us that she picked up her skirts and ran off.

"You have nothing to say that I want to hear," I told him. I turned to follow her, but he caught my arm. "Let me go!"

"Not yet. I need to talk to you. If I let you go, will you stay?"

"That depends on what it is you want from me."

My answer must have satisfied him because he loosened his grip enough for me to jerk free. "Stand there and talk," I said, pointing to a spot on the gravel at a safe distance.

"No," he said in a harsh voice that seemed to come from the depths of him. "*You* do not tell *me* what to do."

I inched backward to where I thought I would be safe. He watched, his dark grey eyes glittering as his gaze traveled my length. The man had an insatiable appetite for women, so I'd heard. What would he do if he found satisfaction difficult to come by of late here at the palace?

I glanced behind me to make sure Ruth had made her escape. "What were you doing with her?" I asked.

"I don't have to answer you," he sneered. "How dare you even presume such a thing!"

"Then state your business with me. I'd like to leave."

He rubbed his lips together, moistening them. "I want to urge you to reconsider my proposition."

"To spy on the duke of Gladstow for you? My decision stands. I won't spy on him or anyone else."

I went to walk off but he grabbed my arm and hauled me back. I stumbled but his bruising grip held me upright.

"Stop struggling," he hissed. "You do not get to walk away until I've dismissed you."

"Unhand me! You are not my master." I tried pulling free but he was too strong, too determined that he not be thwarted again.

"My father is your lord and I am his heir."

"I am a free woman, not a Deerhorn servant."

His chuckle held no humor, only cruelty. "You're stupid if you believe we have no influence over you. All of Mull is under our influence. Your father was allowed to work as a doctor there because my father let him. It suited us to have a healer nearby. But he's gone now, and you are nothing. It would be easy for you to become less than nothing. All it would take would be an accusation of doctoring."

"I have not done any medical work other than midwifery, and I am allowed to sell medicines."

"Who'll believe your denials when the noble Deerhorn family states otherwise?"

An icy chill seeped through to my bones. He would do it, too. He and his mother would take delight in seeing me punished. They knew I couldn't pay a fine, that I would have to sell my belongings. He was wrong in that no one from the village would believe his family over me, but he was right in that it didn't matter what the villagers believed. The Deerhorns would get their way. If they wanted to crush me, they could.

He dragged me closer, slamming my body against his, crushing my skirts. The lump in his breeches proved just how excited our conversation made him. Perhaps not the conversation but the power he held over me. Lord Xavier liked women to be vulnerable and afraid.

I wouldn't give him satisfaction by showing my fear. He might have the upper hand, but I would not let him see that I knew it. It was tempting to jerk my knee into his groin, but even if it forced him to let me go, he would catch me again when I fled.

"Spy for me, Josie," he said, "or there *will* be consequences."

His gaze suddenly shifted and he glanced over my head. He released me and I stepped away, stumbling in my haste. I regained my balance just as Lady Deerhorn rode up to us on a pristine white horse.

"What is the meaning of this?" she barked. "Why are you bothering my son?"

"*He* was bothering *me*," I said, rubbing my arm. "Before that, he was bothering one of the maids."

Lady Deerhorn's nostrils flared, but her accusatory glare remained on me. "Don't be absurd. He has better taste than to dabble with a village girl and maid."

We all knew that wasn't true, but he'd never been arrested for raping the village girl some years ago. Rumor had it the governor wouldn't even allow the sheriff to question him.

Lord Xavier snorted a laugh. His mother finally turned that steely glare onto him.

He swallowed. "I thought I'd ask her again if she'd spy for us, Mother. She refused."

So Lady Deerhorn did know about the spying. Perhaps it had been her idea to enlist me, thinking me easy to manipulate. It was telling that she seemed annoyed he'd taken it upon himself to ask me again. She must have told him not to.

I picked up my skirts and walked away, not wanting to linger, but Lady Deerhorn wheeled her horse around and cut me off. The horse was jittery, tossing its head and trying to turn again. She pulled hard on the reins and the horse jerked its head in protest.

"Do not run to the captain or there will be consequences," she said.

"What does it matter what I do?" I snapped back. "I am nobody, aren't I? I'm nothing. If I accuse you or your son of asking me to spy for you, I won't be taken seriously, will I?"

Her nostrils flared again, and it was in that moment that I realized I did have some power. She was worried that I'd talk. I might not be believed by the other nobles, but Dane would believe me, and he had the king's ear. Kitty might also believe me, and if she told her husband, the Deerhorns' plotting would come to naught.

I marched back to Grand Avenue with my head high and my stomach in knots. While it was a relief to know I wasn't entirely powerless, I was very aware that the Deerhorns would want to keep a close eye on me.

Instead of heading toward the village, I slipped into the shadows of the stable's long colonnaded portico. The faint conversation between mother and son gradually grew louder as they returned to Grand Avenue too.

"You fool," Lady Deerhorn spat. "You should not have asked her again."

"I agree," he said. "I should not have *asked*, I should have *forced* her."

"Stop this! Stop this obsession with her at once before it goes too far. She should be ignored. She's beneath your notice."

"I'm not obsessed."

Lady Deerhorn said nothing.

"Besides, if she's not important, why does the king trust her?" Lord Xavier asked petulantly. "Why does she have his ear?"

How did they know the king had asked for my advice? Perhaps they'd guessed after seeing me coming or going from his apartments. Gossip in the palace spread faster than the plague and was just as deadly, so it was possible they hadn't even seen me in that part of the palace at all but had merely heard about it.

Gravel crunched beneath the horse's hooves. I moved behind one of the columns and prayed they wouldn't peer too hard into the shadows.

C.J. ARCHER

"He should be asking Father for local advice," Lord Xavier said with a pout in his voice.

I hugged the cool stone column and watched as Lord Xavier walked alongside the horse, his shoulders a little rounder than before, the sneering curl to his lip no longer in evidence.

His mother sat in the saddle with all the elegance of one born to ride magnificent white horses. Her purple riding cape spread behind her over the horse's rump without a single crease; her broad-brimmed hat sat perfectly askew at just the right angle to send the plumes shooting straight up. Every inch of her, from her haughty bearing to her pristine white boots, was carefully considered to convey authority, wealth, and privilege.

"I'm going to bury her," she said, teeth clenched so that only her lips moved.

Everything inside me recoiled. I wanted to shrink further into the shadows but didn't dare move. I wanted to gasp for air because suddenly it seemed scarce, yet I didn't dare make a sound.

I watched mother and son as they made their way to the stable entrance where a groom took the horse and Lady Deerhorn dismounted. Two sedan chairs trotted up to carry them back to the palace.

Still I did not move. I wanted them well gone before I returned to the palace. Going back was something I had to do. I had to check on Ruth and find out what Lord Xavier wanted from her.

Two grooms emerged from the stables with blazing torches in hand. One went left and the other turned right. They reached up and lit the torches fixed to the portico columns. On the other side of the Grand Avenue, servants emerged from the coach house entrance and did the same. More servants lit the torches closer to the palace and in the forecourts, and suddenly the twilit indigo sky no longer looked so forbidding.

I hurried toward the palace, eyeing the shadows in case any surprises lurked there. Only the guards at the gate stopped me, however, and they let me through without requiring an explanation. They were so used to me in Dane's company that they trusted me. Now.

I headed to the commons but didn't go inside. I had to ask several staff where Ruth could be found, and eventually someone knew where she was. Not wanting to disturb her while she was at work, I decided to wait for her at the commons' courtyard fountain.

It was a busy time of day. No one stood idly at the fountain, chatting or washing. All the servants who crossed the courtyard seemed to be in a hurry, many of them carrying trays, buckets, linen, clothing. A nod for one another was all they could spare, though some smiled at me. I recognized several faces and smiled back, but not always. I did not smile at Seb the footman, nor did he smile at me. His gaze lingered, however, as slick and putrid as the gutters in The Row.

I looked away first and shivered, although the air was still warm. There was no breeze in the internal courtyard and perhaps warmth from the vast basement kitchens had somehow risen up through the ground and surrounding walls. If I listened very carefully, I could just make out the shouted orders of the cook as he managed the massive task of feeding the hundreds of nobles and thousand-strong staff.

As twilight faded to dusk, I moved closer to the commons entrance. There were fewer torches here than near the palace, but I could see the maids' faces well enough as they came and went. Finally, Ruth appeared. She walked with another maid, both holding buckets that must have been empty, going by the ease with which they carried them.

"May I have a word?" I asked her.

She hesitated then nodded and handed the bucket to her companion. Ruth sat alongside me at the fountain edge. It was the closest we'd get to privacy, but we'd have to keep our voices low.

"Did Lord Xavier hurt you?" I asked.

"He just frightened me." She glanced toward the exit, as if she expected him to appear there.

"Did he seem...familiar?" I hazarded. I didn't want to upset her, but I had to be blunt to make myself clear. "Do you think he was the one who attacked you?"

"Lord Xavier! No, Miss Cully, I don't think so. He wouldn't go into the service corridors. That's not what he wanted from me, anyway, so he said."

"Then what did he want?"

"He asked me why you were in my room."

How had he known that? Did everyone have spies? "What did you tell him?"

"That it was a private medical matter and of no concern to him. That's when you arrived, miss. He didn't like my answer. I think..." She sniffed. "I think he might have struck me if you hadn't come."

My heart thundered in my chest. "Did you use the word medical? Or did you say midwifery?"

She lowered her head and clasped her hands in her lap, her knees together. "I...I don't remember. I'm sorry."

I placed my hand over hers. "It's all right, Ruth. It's not important."

How I wished that were so.

I released her in case she felt my hand shake. "You should inform the captain of the incident," I said.

She nodded. "I'll go in search of him now. I should have spoken to him earlier about something else, but I put it off."

"Has something happened?"

She glanced at the entrance again and dropped her voice further. "There's been another rape."

"Oh, Hailia, no. Who is it? Is she all right?"

"She's another maid. She's upset but seems to be coping, and she didn't want to summon you. She came to me because she guessed I'd been affected too after word got around that you'd been to check on me. She swore me to secrecy."

"The captain must be told."

"I know, and I'll tell him now. I'll take her with me. I'm not sure if it will help, since she didn't see his face. He attacked her from behind, like he did me."

Like he had Ingrid, too.

"Do you want me to come?" I asked, my mind reeling with questions.

"No, thank you, miss. She won't want too many to hear what he did. I just hope it ain't too late, leaving it so long, and she hasn't forgotten an important detail."

"When did the attack happen?"

"Three nights ago."

Three nights ago. I remembered that night well. It was the night Dane kissed me.

"She said she heard the village horns in the distance," Ruth said.

"The temple's horns? They carry this far?"

"Only if the wind is blowing the right way."

She gave me a flat smile then went on her way. I watched her go yet hardly saw her. My mind was too focused on recalling that night—the kiss, and witnessing the village meeting through The Anchor's rear courtyard window. Both Ivor Morgrain and Lord Barborough had been at that meeting. It would have been impossible for them to get from Mull to the palace, even with the swiftest horse. Not before the temple's horns announced evening prayers, anyway. Neither man could be the rapist.

"The temple's horns," I muttered, blinking into the empty space where Ruth had sat beside me. Lord Xavier had accosted me on my doorstep that night, and the horns had blasted through the night air during our conversation. So he couldn't be the rapist either.

That left Seb.

I shot to my feet and ran across the courtyard, only to stop when I reached the breezeway outside the commons. The footman had been with the duke of Buxton at the time of Ruth's rape. The duke had confirmed it himself.

Not a single one of our suspects could have committed all three attacks.

There must be someone else we hadn't considered, or perhaps it was Brant after all. I'd believed him when he'd claimed to be looking for the cabinet the night of Ruth's rape, however, and so did Dane. If he hadn't lied to Dane in the first place and asked Zeke to lie for him—

Zeke!

He'd been left to patrol alone while his partner sought the cabinet. There were no witnesses to his whereabouts, but because no one sensed danger in his presence, we'd not suspected him.

I hurried toward the palace but didn't enter through the service door. The dark corridors would be unsafe, and I didn't want to come across Zeke alone.

CHAPTER 16

*J*ust thinking of him as the rapist felt odd. I sensed no danger when near him. He didn't repulse me or make me want to flee. Yet who else could it be? He couldn't be accounted for.

Even as I thought it, I realized how many other servants probably couldn't be accounted for either. I'd never felt threatened by Zeke, yet he was now a suspect. Shouldn't every other male in the palace also be a suspect if they couldn't account for their whereabouts on the nights of the three rapes?

I continued north, crossing the inner forecourt near the palace's main entrance. I was focusing on the puzzle at hand rather than my way and almost barreled into a lady stepping off the stairs.

"Josie!" Kitty cried. "Be careful or you'll crush my gown, and there's nothing worse than crushed silk. It's simply *the worst*." She smoothed down her skirts, even though I'd not touched her.

"My humblest apologies, your grace," I said, curtseying.

"How many times do I have to ask you to call me Kitty?" She hooked her arm with mine, proving that she didn't care about her silk after all—or that she might be seen with me. "It's a little late for riding."

"Pardon?"

"That is why you're here, isn't it? To take me up on my offer of riding lessons?"

She'd be upset to learn my first solo ride had taken place without her a mere hour earlier, so I decided not to tell her. "I'm on my way to speak to the captain," I said, eyeing the direction I had to take. I shouldn't linger, but how to extricate myself without seeming rude?

"The captain again?" she said slyly. "Can we expect an announcement soon?"

I choked, half laughing, half protesting, earning me a scowl from Kitty. "It's not like that between us. It's... Never mind. Shouldn't you be on the other side of the palace or dining with the king?"

An ensemble of stringed instruments had struck up a gentle tune while we talked. I was reminded of the last time I'd heard music at the palace, on the night of the ball. The musicians had not been visible from any of the gardens or paths, and their music seemed to fall from the stars themselves. Balthazar had told me the musicians had simply been hidden well, but in a place such as this, it seemed magic must have played a part.

"Actually, I'm meeting Miranda here," Kitty whispered as she steered me toward the fountain on the large forecourt. There were only two guards on patrol and a handful of nobles strolling in pairs, but it was quite open and not a good place to have a secret rendezvous. A quiet chat with a friend, however, wouldn't raise attention. "I have something to tell her."

"Palace gossip?" I asked, glancing back over my shoulder in the direction I *should* be heading. Movement in the shadows at the far end of the northern pavilion caught my eye, but whoever was there wasn't close enough to hear us.

"Oh, all right, I'll tell you too," Kitty said.

I pressed my lips together to suppress both my smile and a protest that I hadn't asked her to share the gossip with me. I was beginning to think that Kitty liked company—any company, even mine. What must her life be like at home, living with an aging husband who'd been in love with another for much of his life? Kitty may have an easy life, but I didn't envy her.

"You see, it's a little dull here for ladies like us," she began.

"Ladies like you?"

"Who aren't interested in the king. We have nothing better to do than play cards or stroll around the garden. We aren't really supposed to ride off alone, but as long as the king doesn't mind, and my husband doesn't find out, we can. Of course, the parties are fun but one can't indulge too often or one will grow fat. So we've taken up a hobby."

"Do you mean riding in the forest?"

"No, silly. Magic."

I stared at her. "Magic has become your hobby?"

"Not performing it." She laughed, a girlish giggle that she hid behind her gloved hand. "We want to find out if the palace was made by magic. You know the rumors, of course."

"I do."

"We thought we'd try to find evidence of it. Isn't that fun?"

"It might be dangerous," I said carefully.

Before I could explain, she said, "Nonsense. All we do is ride around, looking for signs of magic."

"What sort of signs?"

Her brow creased in thought. "That's the problem. We don't know what we're looking for. So far we haven't found anything. Well, there was a shiny object in the bushes, but on closer inspection, it turned out to be a ring someone had lost. Anyway, we've had such fun looking. I do adore riding through the forest, although Miranda does go too fast sometimes. You must learn to ride too so you can come with us, Josie. We'll have such a laugh investigating together."

I nodded and smiled, torn between warning her and letting her go on her innocent way, thinking there was nothing dangerous in searching for the truth about the palace's origins.

She tried to draw even closer to me, but it was impossible with her broad skirts and voluminous sleeve. She was dressed in yellow tonight, with a diamond pattern embroidered in gold thread across the bodice and at the hem. With a large yellow pendant dangling from a gold chain nestled on the swell of her breasts, and gold armbands above her glove and more yellow gems dangling from her ears, she was a beacon in the night. She wasn't dressed for clandestine investigating.

She gave up trying to get closer and instead tilted her head and whispered, "I came across something quite by chance. That's why I sent a message to Miranda to meet me here. I think it might be important."

"What is it?"

"Promise not to tell. Not even your captain of the guards."

I ignored the implication that he was mine and said, "As long as it's not necessary to tell him, I won't."

Her brow momentarily creased again then I felt her shrug, even though her shoulders didn't seem to move. Despite her empty-headedness, she was graceful to her bones. "I overheard my husband and the duke of Buxton talking about the Vytill man."

"Lord Barborough?"

"The very same. And hear this, Josie, you will be amazed." She lowered her voice to a whisper. "Apparently, he's an expert on magic." She paused, nodding earnestly. "What do you think of that?"

"I think it interesting."

"It is, isn't it? He has written a book and even been to Zemaya." She made it sound as if it were a different world when it wasn't uncommon for Fist folk to travel to Zemaya. My father, for one, had visited in his youth. "That's not all—and this is the most shocking part—Buxton says the only reason Barborough's here as the official representative of Vytill is because he killed the man who was supposed to come."

"Are you sure?"

"Buxton sounded sure. I heard him myself."

"Does he know you were listening in?"

"Hailia, no. Nor does my husband. Neither were aware I was napping in the next room, and do not tell them, Josie."

"I don't intend to. How does the duke of Buxton know that Barborough killed the man who was supposed to represent King Phillip's interests?"

"He has spies in Vytill, of course. Everyone does, and Dreen and Freedland too, and all of those countries will have spies here." She hugged my arm and giggled again. "You village girls are so naive. It's rather quaint."

I was about to make a snippy retort, but she was right. Until I'd become embroiled in palace politics, I'd never given such things a second thought. I had been ignorant of the ways of kings and nobles, their plots and manipulations. For someone who prided herself on knowledge, of all kinds, I didn't wish for that ignorance again, even though my life had been simpler.

"Why is the duke of Buxton sharing the information with your husband?" I asked, all innocence. "Don't they dislike one another?"

"It's true they don't get along, but they meet from time to time, in either our apartments or his."

It would be so easy for me to ask her to eavesdrop on more of their conversations, then pass any information onto the Deerhorns. But I would not. For one thing, I wouldn't help the Deerhorns with anything, and more importantly, if Kitty was discovered, her husband might mistreat her. I'd caught him hurting Lady Claypool, and he'd claimed to love her. What would he do to his young, foolish wife?

So it was true, just as Dane, Balthazar and Theodore suspected. The dukes had joined forces to prove King Leon shouldn't be on the throne because he'd used magic to get it. It seemed the dukes also suspected that Vytill had the same aim. I wondered if they were aware that Barborough had a second task while here—stirring up trouble in Mull.

"So what do you think of that, Josie?" Kitty asked. "Isn't it a good piece of information?"

"It is," I said. "But you must be careful not to be caught listening in to conversations."

She didn't seem to be listening to me. She'd caught sight of Miranda, coming down the palace steps, and waved at her.

Miranda joined us, all smiles. "Am I missing the party?" She was dressed all in blue with her hair unbound to declare her unmarried status. Unlike Kitty, she wore very little jewelry, just one golden band on her finger and small earrings.

"The party doesn't begin until you're here, dearest Miranda," Kitty said, taking her friend's hand. "Do come and listen to what I've just told Josie. It's most interesting."

She repeated her information about Lord Barborough. Miranda was quite speechless by the end. Clearly she hadn't known about Barborough's interest in magic and was appalled at the suggestion that he'd killed another to win the position of representative. She didn't seem surprised to hear the dukes were collaborating, however. Like Kitty, she was more worldly than me, and she must have known they had joined forces. Perhaps she even discussed it with her parents.

"So what shall we do with this information?" Kitty asked.

"Nothing," both Miranda and I said together. She looked at me and I could see she had realized the danger Kitty had stumbled into.

Kitty pouted. "Why not? We could spy on Lord Barborough—"

"No!" Miranda said, slicing her hand through the air. "We do nothing, Kitty. Do you understand? We can keep looking for signs of magic around the palace, but we will not approach Barborough or anyone from Vytill. Nor will you discuss it with your husband."

"But this is such a good opportunity to learn more."

Miranda clasped Kitty's arms and met her gaze. "If he killed his rival, he is not a nice man. He's ruthless. What do you think he'd do if he learned two Glancia ladies are inquiring about magic?"

Kitty looked as if she was about to cry, so stern was Miranda. "I don't know."

"Nor do I, but I do know we can't trust him."

"He might use you to find out more," I said. Kitty blinked big, watery eyes at me, and Miranda's pinched at the corners as she studied me. "He might use you to spy on the king for him." As soon as I said it, I was quite sure it was precisely what Barborough would do.

"We wouldn't do that," Kitty said.

"You might, if he threatened to tell the king that you were investigating his link to magic."

Miranda pressed her fingers to her lips and her other hand to her stomach. "She's right," she said to Kitty. "Think about what the king would do if he heard we were looking for that link, what it would mean for his claim to the throne if we *found* a link."

Kitty gasped. "Oh! Yes, I see now. You're right. If we discovered the throne was gained with the aid of magic, he shouldn't be king." She glanced around then put her hand over her heart to swear an oath. "I promise the god and goddess not to breathe a word about this to anyone. Swear it, Miranda."

Miranda repeated the oath then both women turned grim faces to me. I swore the oath too.

"Now, I must go," I said. "I shouldn't have lingered so long."

"You're not going home?" Miranda asked, as she and Kitty fell into step with me.

"Not yet. I need to speak to the captain about something."

Kitty nudged Miranda with her elbow. "Of course you do, Josie. I'm sure it's *very* important."

Miranda smiled, but it was half-hearted. Like me, her mind was probably elsewhere, not on romantic liaisons.

We crossed the large forecourt, their heeled shoes *click clacking* on the paving stones, until we reached the end of the pavilion on the northern side where we had to part. Miranda grasped my hand before I could walk off. She had the most curious look on her face, part apologetic, part worried.

"You may think it's not my place," she said, "but I consider us friends now, and as your friend, I have to say this. Be careful, Josie. You know nothing about him."

I stared at her, searching for the right words. I wanted to tell her that Dane didn't even know himself, but I would never reveal his secret.

"Do you?" she prompted, clearly fishing for details of his past.

"We are like strangers to one another," was all I said.

"Ignore her," Kitty said with a roll of her eyes. "She's worrying over nothing. The captain seems like a good man."

"You hardly know him either," Miranda said. "Have you ever spoken directly to him, Kitty?"

"Of course not. But I can tell from his face that he's a good man."

"Kitty, you do surprise me," Miranda teased. "I thought all the servants were the same to you duchesses, as interchangeable as your jewels."

Kitty touched the pendant at her bosom. "My jewels are not interchangeable. Anyway," she added with a toss of her head, "the captain is different. One cannot fail to notice him. Besides, his uniform is black and the other guards wear red. I can't tell *them* apart, nor the footmen and maids. They should wear different caps or something identifiable. Oh! I've just had a marvelous idea! They should pin little engraved nameplates on their uniforms. I'll suggest it to the king."

"Will it help you remember them?" Miranda asked. "You'd probably take as much notice of a nameplate as you do of a face. Faces are unique yet you cannot tell the footman who brings your wine from the one who opens the door."

"Not at the palace, no. I know most of our footmen at home. Honestly, Miranda, Josie will think me a snob when I'm merely stupid."

Miranda couldn't hold her laughter in any longer. It burst out of her like a geyser and she clamped both hands over her mouth to smother the unladylike sound. Kitty laughed too, but I did not.

If the footmen all looked alike to Kitty and her ilk, then perhaps the duke of Buxton was wrong. Perhaps it hadn't been Seb with him at the time of Ruth's rape. Perhaps it had been a different footman, similar enough that the duke confused them.

It was a slim possibility but plausible, and I had to report it to Dane. Even more reason to hurry to the garrison. I'd spent far too long chatting.

Miranda and Kitty headed toward the palace steps while I rounded the northern pavilion where it almost but not quite met the palace. I'd walked between the two buildings several times, heading to and from the garrison. The space was wide enough for two small pushcarts to pass one another. There were no carts now, no passersby, either noble or servant, no guards on patrol, only the jaunty melody played by the ensemble on the other side of the palace.

And the barely audible grunt of the man who lunged out of the pavilion's shadows and grabbed me from behind.

He wrapped one arm around my waist, the other around my mouth and nose so that I couldn't breathe. I tried to scream but received a mouthful of cotton sleeve and an empty pair of lungs for my efforts.

I struggled, tried to wriggle free, to kick him, but the angle was all wrong with him behind me, and I couldn't free my arms. My blood thundered through my body, and my throat and chest burned from the lack of air. The edges of my vision blurred, as if the world were a book and the reader was closing it with me trapped in the pages.

A profound sense of dread crept through me, an insidious monster that reached every part of me and burrowed deep.

Yet a small part of my heart fought the bleakness, fought the smothering fog, and opened the book a crack.

It was, perhaps, a good thing that I had given up for a few moments. I'd gone limp in my attacker's arms and he changed his hold to drag me back further into the shadows. My booted heels scraped against the gravel, but it wouldn't do them much damage. They were excellent quality boots with a sturdy heel. They were my only weapon.

I mustered every ounce of determination I possessed and stomped down hard on my attacker's foot.

I caught the edge of his shoe, but it was enough. He grunted and his grip loosened enough for me to use my last bit of strength to break free. I ran.

Or tried to. I fell to the ground on my hands and knees, utterly spent. I gasped in as much beautiful, delicious air as I could and tried to scream. Nothing came out. My throat was on fire and my chest felt as though a giant's fist strangled it.

I tried to get up, but could only manage to crawl a short way before collapsing again. I half turned, and caught sight of my attacker's face as he lunged at me.

Seb.

It was no consolation to have my theory proved correct.

CHAPTER 17

S eb hauled me to my feet. He was wiry but strong and I
was weak, pathetic.

He wrenched my arms behind my back and shoved me into the
pavilion wall. My cheek struck stone and I cried out as pain flared.
Tears blurred my vision, choked my throat, but at least I could
breathe now. If I could breathe, I could scream.

"Get off me!" I tried to shout, but it came out as a brittle squeak.
I struggled, pushing back against him and against the pain in my
wrists as he squeezed.

"That's it," he said, chuckling in my ear. "I like it when you
fight." His tongue flicked out and licked my throat at my throbbing
pulse, leaving behind a trail of sticky, hot saliva. "Delicious."

And then he was gone. Disappeared into thin air.

No, not vanished. He was there, on the ground, ripped off me
by Dane. I had not heard him approach.

Dane's knee pressed down on Seb's chest, and his fist slammed
into footman's face, over and over. Dane hadn't drawn his sword
and it remained in its scabbard, strapped to his hip.

Seb tried to protect himself, but Dane batted his hands away as
if they were no more threat than flies, and continued to pound
him. Seb stopped struggling.

"Enough," I said, finding my voice. "Enough, Captain." I tried to
pull him off Seb, but he didn't budge. "Stop, please!"

Dane eased back. He was breathing hard, his face damp with sweat. Seb's eyes were closed and blood smeared his mouth, nose and cheek. I went to check for a heartbeat, but Dane's arm whipped out, blocking me.

"Don't go near him," he growled in a voice I didn't recognize.

"I have to make sure he lives."

He looked at me, and despite the darkness, I could see the cold hatred in his eyes, or perhaps I could *feel* it. "Why?"

"Because...because I have to."

He continued to stare at me as if he was trying to *see* me, understand me. Could he? Or did his anger block him like his arm blocked me? The hand on the end of that arm was balled into a fist, as was the other.

This was not the man I'd come to know. Dane was kind, thoughtful, intelligent. Where was he?

I don't know why I touched his jaw. Perhaps it was instinct, or simply a desire to remove the mask and see the gentle man again.

He sucked in a roughened breath and his eyes fluttered closed. He turned his face into my hand and kissed my wrist, still sore from Seb's grip. His body seemed to sigh and his fists opened. He lowered his arm and circled it around me, holding me gingerly, as if I were fragile.

I pressed my forehead to his and clung to him, scrunching his doublet in my fingers. He was solid, strong, everything I needed in that moment.

"Thank you," I whispered, unable to say more with the tears once again clogging my throat. I hoped he understood that I wasn't just thanking him for rescuing me, but also for holding me like I was precious.

Seb groaned. He wasn't dead, and I wasn't as relieved about that as I thought I'd be.

Dane stood and helped me to my feet. Two guards walked past on patrol, oblivious to us in the pavilion's shadows.

"Tom, Rylan!" Dane called out.

Both men peered into the shadows. "Captain?" asked Tom. "That you?"

"Take this man to the cells."

The two guards followed his orders without question. They

half-carried, half-dragged Seb between them. We stood side by side in silence and watched them go.

I was very aware of Dane and his presence. Very aware of everything. The evening air felt like feathers brushing my skin, cooling my hot neck. It smelled faintly of summer flowers, a far more pleasant scent than Seb's breath. I shivered, although I wasn't cold, but it seemed to be the signal Dane was waiting for.

He wrapped his arms around me and tucked my head under his chin. His fingers lightly massaged my neck as my silent tears soaked his doublet.

We stayed like that, neither of us moving, until my tears dried. I pulled back a little, and reluctantly released him. He touched my jaw, and lightly skimmed his thumb beneath my sore cheek.

"I should put something on it for the bruising," I said.

He took my hand. "I'll take you home." He glanced over his shoulder in the direction of the garrison and prison.

"You should inform your men first."

He kept hold of my hand as we followed the wall of the northern wing, as if he knew I needed the comfort still.

"It's fortunate you walked past at that moment," I said.

His hand went to the sword at his hip. "Ruth came to see me. She said you'd urged her to do so. She told me about the other rape, and about the Deerhorn lordling accosting you behind the stables. I wanted to find you before you left and see if you were all right."

The incident with Lord Xavier seemed insignificant now. "He wanted to ask me again to spy on the duke of Gladstow for him. His mother interrupted us. I think she's furious that he tried to persuade me a second time."

Dane's fingers flexed around mine. "Did he hurt you?"

I blew out a ragged breath. "No."

He squeezed my hand. "Seb will claim innocence," he said. "Not for tonight, but for the rapes. He didn't hurt Ruth, yet I'd swear all three were committed by the same person."

"It was him. I'm certain of it. A conversation with Kitty tonight got me thinking. She can't tell the palace footmen apart. They're too similar, she says. What if the duke of Buxton thinks as she does? What if it wasn't Seb with him, at the time of Ruth's rape, but another footman?"

"I'll question the duke again tomorrow. Even if Seb isn't guilty, he's not going free."

"Will he stand trial?"

He didn't respond until we reached the garrison door. "I can't risk it, not until we know more about ourselves. If he talks about his memory loss…"

There was no need to finish the sentence. He was right, and I knew it. A public trial would expose too many secrets, not only about the memory loss but also the names of the women he'd raped. Ingrid wanted secrecy, and Ruth preferred it too. While I believed in a fair trial for all, my desire to protect those women was stronger.

"It's the right thing to do," I told him.

He blinked, as if he hadn't expected me to agree with him. Then he let go of my hand and pushed open the door.

I was glad to see there were only four guards inside. The rest would be either on patrol at the palace or in the village, or perhaps sleeping before they returned to duty. I was doubly glad that Brant wasn't among them.

"Josie?" Quentin's severe frown cut a deep line across his forehead. "What happened to you?" He indicated my cheek.

"A run-in with a footman." I gently felt the bone beneath the swelling. The pain was fierce but I expected that and managed to school my reaction. Even so, Quentin and Dane both winced.

"Pour Josie a drink," Dane told Quentin. "Something strong."

"Is the bone broken?" Quentin asked.

"I don't think so," I said.

"There's blood," Dane said simply.

"It has stopped."

Quentin removed the stops from three different bottles on the sideboard and sniffed the contents of each before settling on the third. He poured a good amount into a cup and handed it to me.

The spirit smelled strong and burned my throat as it went down. I coughed and tried to pass the cup back but Dane ordered Quentin not to take it.

"It'll help," he said.

"Help me get drunk."

"And numb the pain," Quentin added. "But you should still put something on that cheek."

"Thank you, Doctor." I smiled. He tried to look nonchalant but his smile gave him away.

"There's a new prisoner in the cells," Dane said to his men. "See that he gets food and water."

"A servant?" one of the guards asked.

"The footman who attacked Josie," Dane said.

The men exchanged glances. Quentin swore under his breath. "That's four prisoners now," he muttered.

Dane told me to drink the rest of the spirit. We were about to leave when he marched to the sideboard, grabbed the bottle, and escorted me out.

He roused a groom at the stables and ordered a horse be saddled. Just the one. He did not suggest I ride Sky, but seemed to want me on his horse with him this time.

The groom brought out Lightning, and Dane tucked the bottle into the bag strapped to the saddle. He assisted me up then settled in front of me and steered Lightning out of the stable yard to Grand Avenue.

He rode stiffly, both hands on the reins, and didn't speak. After the intimacy of earlier, I wanted more. I leaned into his back and wrapped both arms around his waist. His body relaxed.

We didn't speak all the way to Mull, but the silence didn't feel strained. It was peaceful in the dark, with only the stars and a crescent moon lighting our way. By the time we reached the edge of the village, Dane had relaxed enough to hold the reins with only one hand. His other rested on his thigh. It felt like an invitation for me to hold it, but I refrained. I liked having him circled in both my arms.

Once home, I dipped a clean cloth into a jar of salve and dabbed it on my cheek. Dane ordered me to sit and poured me a cup of the strong spirit. He didn't pour one for himself but he joined me at the kitchen table.

"Drink it all," he said when I merely sipped.

"It's very strong."

"It'll help you sleep."

He was right. It would help. Without it, I'd replay the events over and over in my mind. When I closed my eyes, I'd see Seb's face in the darkness, smell his stinking breath, feel his wet tongue on my neck.

I drank the entire contents in a single gulp and held the cup out for more. "Just one," I said as he poured. "And just for tonight. I can't block it out forever."

He eyed the bottle.

"I won't drink to forget, Dane. Not after tonight. I've seen what happens to those who do."

"I wish I could make you forget."

The irony of his words wasn't lost on either of us. We exchanged small smiles. It helped a little. The spirit helped a lot.

After the next cup, I could no longer keep my eyes open. I could feel myself slumping in the chair, my head nodding.

"Come on," came Dane's voice, very close. Next thing I knew, I was being scooped up and carried up the stairs.

"You can't come into my room." My voice slurred, and sounded distant.

"I'm just putting you to bed."

"My room...it's a mess. You can't see it." I struggled but it was pathetic and his step didn't even falter. I gave up and snuggled into him. I didn't care if it was wrong or that my father wouldn't have approved.

"I've already seen your room and you're right, it is a mess. Even Quentin's tidier than you." His rich, melodic voice vibrated through me. I tightened my grip on him, wanting to capture that voice and hold it.

"That's because he's scared of you," I said.

"Quentin? I doubt it."

We must have reached the landing because we no longer climbed. I cracked open an eye then closed it again as he carried me into my bedchamber.

"You need a maid to free your time for making medicines," he said. "Why not ask your friend from The Row, the one with the boy?"

"Can't," I said around a yawn. "No money." I was vaguely

aware that I hadn't wanted to tell him that, then I promptly forgot as he placed me on the bed.

I ought to pose seductively, but I didn't know how, and in truth, I didn't want to be seductive tonight. I sighed deeply.

I felt my shoes being removed and the blanket settle over me. "Josie?" he murmured.

"Hmmm?"

"Sleep well."

"And you."

I was so tired I couldn't even open my eyes when he kissed my forehead, couldn't even cherish the kiss. Couldn't ask him to stay.

I HAD to face the palace sooner or later. It wasn't the memory of the attack that worried me but the questions and the looks on everyone's faces when they saw my cheek. It was bad enough that Quentin and the other guards who'd been in the garrison last night knew, but for some reason, I didn't want to explain to Miranda and Kitty. And I certainly didn't want to see Brant or any of the Deerhorns. Dealing with them would only shatter my still fragile nerves. I did, however, want to deliver some of the salve to Seb. I didn't think it would be enough for his wounds, but it was something.

Dane came to see me, however, saving me the journey.

"I can't stay long," he said, following me into the kitchen.

"Long enough for tea?"

"Tea will be nice." He unstrapped his sword and leaned it by the door. "How do you feel?"

"Like I drank too much of that awful spirit. How do your men do it?"

"They've got strong constitutions. Except Quentin. He learned early to avoid it. I meant how is your cheek?"

"Better, thanks. And your hands? I forgot to ask you last night."

He wore gloves, as he had done the night before. They would have protected his knuckles while allowing him to inflict damage to Seb. "Fine." He didn't remove the gloves and I didn't ask to see his hands.

I poured tea from the pot simmering over the hot coals and handed him a cup. "Are you here to see me or patrol the village?" I asked, sitting too.

"Both, but mostly to see you."

I sipped my tea to hide my smile of satisfaction. He sipped too and avoided my gaze.

"It's calmer in Mull," he said. "There's been no further trouble."

"For now. Ned Perkin won't stand down that easily. He'll still be scheming, drumming up support for his cause. I'm sure Lord Barborough will poke Ned if he thinks he gets too quiet."

"Are you sure you don't have spies at the palace?" he asked with a crooked smile.

"Why?"

"Barborough is sending coded messages back to Vytill stating that he's doing exactly that to Ned. I've been intercepting them. Some I let through to their destination, some I don't."

"You deciphered the code?"

"Balthazar did."

"A man of many talents."

"A man of many years. He seems to be familiar with codes."

Now that was interesting. "What do you think that means about Balthazar's past?" I asked, more to myself than Dane. "What sort of profession would require a code breaker?"

"Spy," he said, his answer quick and ready, proving they'd already discussed it among themselves.

"Perhaps," I said. "But sea captains use codes in their log books, and traders in their ledgers. Smugglers certainly use them in their messages."

"I can see him being captain of a ship, ordering sailors about." He drank the rest of his tea then got up to leave. "I have to go, but I wanted you to know that I spoke to the duke of Buxton this morning. He agrees that he might have mixed Seb up with one of the other footmen. It turns out that Seb was the one who planted the idea in his head, telling the duke that he was with him at that time. Seb must have heard I was asking all the male servants where they were at the time of Ruth's rape, and he secured himself a false witness."

"The duke of Buxton ought to face some sort of consequence

too. He needs to know how much his mistake cost. Two women would not have been raped if he'd paid more attention to the servants."

"To be fair, his eyesight is poor."

"Then he ought to wear spectacles."

"I'll give him the name of the man who made Balthazar's."

I thought he was mocking me, but he looked utterly serious.

"I've also just come from the Swinsons'," he said. "I told Ingrid her attacker has been caught and is locked in the palace cells, never to be released."

Never. He said it with such certainty and finality that I didn't question him. But to be locked away without a trial, or the possibility of one, seemed wrong. Yet Seb had raped those women and attacked me. There was no doubt of his guilt. Perhaps he was precisely where he ought to be, where he couldn't harm anyone again.

"Ingrid was pleased," he said. "Although she asked if she could visit him. I refused."

"Why does she want to visit him?"

"I can't say for sure, but she had a murderous look in her eye. Seb's lucky I refused her. If she wanted revenge, I might not be able to hold her back."

There was that dark side again, the one lurking beneath the surface, the one Brant had warned me about. Now that I'd seen Dane's anger for myself, I wasn't sure what to make of it. Was it borne from his fear of what might have happened if he hadn't come along at the right time last night? Perhaps it was a release of the built-up pressure he felt over not knowing what had happened to him and of being responsible for the servants and the palace guards in particular.

Or was it simply madness, a violent side that was a part of him? Without knowing his past, it was impossible to be sure.

I fetched a jar of salve from the larder and handed it to him. "Seb should use this on his injuries." It wouldn't be enough. He would have broken bones after such a beating but only time could heal those.

Dane simply looked at the jar in my hand. "He doesn't deserve it."

"I have to give it to him, Dane. If there's something I can do then I have to do it, or I won't forgive myself. Do you understand?"

He hesitated then nodded. "You're a better person than I am."

"A better person would *want* to give it to him. I'm doing it out of a sense of obligation to my profession."

"I'm not so sure." He took the jar and trapped my hand at the same time. Hope rose in my chest and fluttered, only to die when he lifted his gaze to mine. His eyes had that haunted look again, the one I'd seen when he worried about his past, about who he was. And the worry that he couldn't have a future until he knew the answers.

He let me go and turned away. "I can't be anything more to you than a friend," he said without facing me.

"It's not a betrayal if you don't remember a loved one," I said, my voice small.

"You can't let Seb rot in prison knowing you can help him, and I can't be with a woman until I know what and who I've left behind. It's just the way I am. It wouldn't be fair to you, either."

He was right and I knew it, although it pained me to admit it. He could never entirely relax with me, couldn't give all of himself himself to me, without knowing he was free to do so.

I stared at him and tried to suppress the ache in my chest. Last night, I'd pressed myself into that broad back and wrapped my arms around him when we'd ridden home. It had been a comfort for me, and I thought it had been a comfort for him too, that he'd needed the contact just as much. I hoped he would want to feel me close again, that he might set aside his convictions and allow himself to be intimate with me.

But this was a man with strong convictions, and I admired him greatly for upholding them. I would not make it difficult for him to keep those convictions. I couldn't do that to him.

I saw him out and watched him mount Lightning. He was about to ride off when Remy called out from the end of the street. Dane waited for him as the boy ran toward us. He slowed when he neared the horse.

"Can I pat him?" Remy asked.

"Of course." Dane fished an apple out of his saddlebag. "Hold this flat on your palm."

"I could have brought one myself, you know," Remy said proudly.

"An apple?" I asked.

The boy giggled as Lightning ate the apple off his palm. "We got some fruit, pastries, cakes, and meat today. It came on carts. Lots of 'em, one after the other. Palace men drove 'em."

That explained the pastries and cake.

"My Ma says she'll come and thank you herself later," Remy told me. "But I couldn't wait."

"It's not my doing." I looked at Dane. Last night, I'd told him I couldn't afford to pay for help. I might have told him I couldn't even afford to feed another mouth, but my memory was hazy. "This is the man you have to thank, Remy."

"Thank the ladies and their desire for small waists," Dane said. "If it weren't for them, there wouldn't be extra for the servants, and if there wasn't extra for the servants there wouldn't be extra for you, Remy."

The boy looked from Dane to me then back to Dane. "But the ladies aren't here."

Dane leaned down and ruffled the boy's hair. "Perhaps one day I'll take you to the palace and introduce you to a duchess."

"What's a duchess?"

"A pretty lady," I said.

"A lady with fine jewels," Dane shot back. "Do you want a ride home, Remy? It's the least I can do since you fed Lightning for me."

"With *your* apple," Remy said, as if Dane were stupid for forgetting.

Dane laughed and reached down, easily lifting the boy onto the saddle with one arm. Remy beamed, until the horse moved. He grabbed hold of Lightning's mane and sat as stiff as a board.

Dane waited until the boy got used to the horse beneath him before clicking his tongue for Lightning to walk on. Remy's smile returned.

"Goodbye, Josie," he called out. "I can't let go to wave or I'll fall off."

"Goodbye, Remy. Don't be afraid. The captain won't let

anything bad happen to you. He's very good at protecting people," I added, quieter.

Remy faced forward again, but Dane turned in the saddle. He gave me a small, sad smile that sent my heart into my throat. He mouthed "goodbye," then he too faced forward.

I watched them until they turned the corner before heading inside to nurse my bruised cheek and sore heart.

Look Out For:

THE WHISPER OF SILENCED VOICES
The 3rd After The Rift novel by C.J. Archer.

To be notified about new books, subscribe to C.J's newsletter on her website:
http://cjarcher.com/newsletter/

A MESSAGE FROM THE AUTHOR

I hope you enjoyed reading THE ECHO OF BROKEN DREAMS as much as I enjoyed writing it. As an independent author, getting the word out about my book is vital to its success, so if you liked this book please consider telling your friends and writing a review at the store where you purchased it. If you would like to be contacted when I release a new book, subscribe to my newsletter at http://cjarcher.com/contact-cj/newsletter/.

ALSO BY C.J. ARCHER

SERIES WITH 2 OR MORE BOOKS

After The Rift

Glass and Steele

The Ministry of Curiosities Series

The Emily Chambers Spirit Medium Trilogy

The 1st Freak House Trilogy

The 2nd Freak House Trilogy

The 3rd Freak House Trilogy

The Assassins Guild Series

Lord Hawkesbury's Players Series

The Witchblade Chronicles

SINGLE TITLES NOT IN A SERIES

Courting His Countess

Surrender

Redemption

The Mercenary's Price

ABOUT THE AUTHOR

C.J. Archer has loved history and books for as long as she can remember and feels fortunate that she found a way to combine the two. She spent her early childhood in the dramatic beauty of outback Queensland, Australia, but now lives in suburban Melbourne with her husband, two children and a mischievous black & white cat named Coco.

Subscribe to C.J.'s newsletter through her website to be notified when she releases a new book, as well as get access to exclusive content and subscriber-only giveaways. Her website also contains up to date details on all her books: http://cjarcher.com She loves to hear from readers. You can contact her through email cj@cjarcher.com or follow her on social media to get the latest updates on her books.

CPSIA information can be obtained
at www.ICGtesting.com
Printed in the USA
LVHW011057261118
598272LV00003B/194/P